THE PROTECTOR

THE PROTECTOR

A Green Ridge Series - Book Two

J.J. Marcell

ISBN: 979-8-9884260-1-1

Library of Congress Control Number: 2025927259

Interior Design: Dandelion Formatting, Charlie Ray

First Edition 2026

For those who supported me every step of the way... you know who you are.
Thank you from the bottom of my heart.

Prologue

It was back—that slow, unnerving dread that sent my heart plummeting into my stomach as I felt eyes on me. Intense. Penetrating. Watching. But no matter where I looked, I couldn't see anyone. I just knew. Someone was there. Lurking. He found me. *Again.* And I had no choice but to run.
Again.

Chapter One
JENNA
PRESENT

*I*t was the third time this week I'd received a bouquet of eleven white roses, short of a dozen, because that was how he held on to the much-needed, unfounded control he had always wanted. A dozen red roses weren't romantic to my husband, Jim; they were cliché—his words. So, he would always send me eleven white roses to be different in his disturbed mind.

Along with the bouquet came the prickling sensation at the back of my neck—a constant reminder that someone was watching my every move. Then came the calls. At first, I dismissed them as spam—just another annoyance. But they kept coming—more and more. The caller would hang up the second I answered. Other times, I heard breathing. *His* breathing.

Nervous, I looked through the blinds of my apartment window, scanning the street up and down. He wasn't there. I let out a sigh of relief, but then suddenly, a frantic knock on the door made me jump. The knock came again; this time, louder; my heart jumped out of my chest, knowing that if I peeked through the peephole, I would see his face. I grabbed the baseball bat Oliver, one of my best friends, had given me.

"Open the door, Kate. My hands can't hold these to-go bags forever."

The sound of Hannah's voice quickly calmed my nerves—well, kind of. I opened the door, and Hannah rushed past me to the kitchen, awkwardly carrying bags in her hands.

Just as I closed the door, Ol caught it with his hand and slipped inside. "Hey, kiddo," he greeted as he passed by me, heading straight for the fridge.

I shut the door and joined Hannah and Oliver in the kitchen.

"I know, I know, you said you weren't feeling good, but I thought we'd drop by and bring you food. Got Thai," Hannah announced as she unpacked, setting it out, then kissed me on the cheek. "Feeling better?"

My forehead tightened, unsure of what she was talking about.

"Migraine?" She lifted her brows. "You told me you had a migraine attack." She squinted, crossed her arms, and tapped her foot on the floor. "I knew you were lying." Hannah said, chuckling as she gathered the trash, threw it in the bin, then froze, staring at the contents inside. "Kate, what's going on?"

Oliver flicked the bottle cap into the bin just as Hannah was about to close it. "Hey—white roses. Got a new admirer?" he asked as he tipped the bottle to his mouth. "Though I'm guessing you're not interested, seeing as they're in the trash," he said, then walked back to the living room and sat on the couch.

I smiled. "Something like that." I glanced at Hannah, staring at me with questions in her eyes.

"I know this guy, Kate?" Oliver asked further. "You know, I'd have to vet him, right?" he chuckled, leaning back.

Hannah grabbed my hand, led me to the bedroom, and shut the door behind us. "The flowers—were they the ones from the clinic or are they new?" she asked, her eyes sharp with panic and brows tightly knitted together with concern.

"They were outside my door when I got home last night," I confessed as I flopped on the foot of the bed. "Please don't tell Ol. I need to get all of this figured out first."

Hannah sat beside me. "Kate, we need to do something different. You can't keep running."

"I know, I know. Please let's just go out there and enjoy some food, okay? I promise we'll figure something out."

"I'm hungry," Oliver called out from the living room.

"Coming," I yelled back, gave Hannah a faint smile, and hugged her. "Let's go."

✳✳✳

Although my new friends in Sacramento had made it easier to forget that I was hiding, it was time to run again, and the thought of it broke my heart into pieces.

At seven o'clock the following night, usually, Dr. Rossi (Hannah) and I would close the clinic together, but she had left early to spend time with her kids. I pulled the clip off, let down my box-dyed red hair that barely touched my shoulders, adjusted the glasses on my face, and picked up my purse before looking out the window of Sacramento Animal Clinic, where I worked. I had to make sure he wasn't out there waiting for me. The street was empty except for a woman getting into a car across the street and a young couple walking into another establishment. Feeling somewhat safe, I headed to my car, a few feet from our building. Suddenly, the eerie feeling returned, and I felt my blood run cold. My phone rang. Caller *unknown. This can't be happening again.* I rechecked my surroundings, and he was nowhere to be found, but that didn't mean he wasn't around, lurking, watching my every move.

I saw Jim last in Moreno Valley when I first ran away. One day, out of nowhere, he was right in front of me as I walked down the street.

"Jenna, please. I just want to talk." He stared at me with those lying eyes, blocking my way.

I was shocked, speechless for a few seconds, then I regained my composure. "What are you doing here, Jim?" I asked, trying to hide the shakiness in my voice as I looked around. There were people. Surely, he wouldn't do anything to hurt me in front of them. I felt a little safer.

"Sweetheart, please come home. Let's start over. I promise I've changed." He reached for my hand, but I pulled away before he could touch me. His face twisted in surprise, but it didn't last long. He masked it quickly and kept pleading. I didn't listen. I'd heard it all before. Jim couldn't have changed. Men like him don't. It was in his blood.

"You think you can run away from me? We're still married. You're still my wife," he snipped.

There it was. The real Jim.

I turned to walk past him, and that's when he grabbed my arm. Hard. So hard I nearly lost my balance. "You think you can run from me?" His voice dropped, low and burning. "We're still married. You're still my wife," he repeated, as if it had actually meant something to him.

"Then sign the divorce papers, Jim," I snapped, struggling against his grip. "Let go. You're hurting me."

His eyes flared—the kind that scorches. His fingers tightened. "I will always be around. When you think I'm not, *I am.* When you think you're alone, *you're not.* Jenna, I will always be your husband. And I. Will. Always. Be...*Around.*"

"Let go of me, Jim. Let go!" I gritted my teeth, trying to avoid a scene.

"Are you alright, ma'am?" a voice called out. A tall guy, probably in his twenties, wearing jeans and a Kings jersey, had just stepped out of a deli nearby.

I nodded, forcing a smile. "Yes, I'm okay, thank you."

Jim froze. Then, like someone flipping a switch, he let go. He smiled, a smile that I knew so well—fake. "So, I'll see you at home, sweetheart," he said casually, as if nothing had happened, and then turned away.

The stranger looked at me, eyebrows drawn. "You sure you're okay, ma'am? He had a pretty tight grip on you," he said as his eyes followed Jim.

I smiled. "Yes. He's my husband. Just helping me. I lost my balance," I lied.

He didn't look convinced, but he gave me a polite nod. "Alright... take care." Then he walked off.

I had waited a while before heading back to my apartment. When I finally made it home, I checked twice before going inside. The street was empty. Later that night, a knock at the door jolted me upright. I crept to the peephole. No one. Heart racing, I cracked the door open. A bouquet of eleven white roses sat on the doormat. I picked it up, and a small card fell to the floor: **"If I can't have you, no one will."** I shut the door behind me, slid the lock into place, and tossed the bouquet into the trash can. Then I ran to the window to close the blinds. Across the street, half-shrouded in darkness and soaked in rain, Jim stood motionless, staring straight at me.

That night, I packed everything I owned and drove away, not knowing where I would go. The next thing I knew, I ended up in Sacramento.

Chapter Two

JENNA

PRESENT

"Where would you even go?" Hannah asked as I paced around my bedroom, which looked like a bomb had exploded. Hannah was the only person who knew. After a few weeks of working at Sacramento Animal Clinic, I felt compelled to tell her the truth. I'm glad I did. It felt good. It had been gnawing at me, unable to share what I was going through with anyone. I was not only scared for my life—I also felt alone. There was something about Hannah; I knew I could trust her. I needed a job outside of what I was doing back home—photography and art. I stumbled upon a veterinary clinic on one of my walks, and Hannah Presten-Rossi was the veterinarian. We'd hit it off right away and became friends, but I couldn't go on with our friendship without telling her the truth. It wouldn't have been fair.

Though she knew me as Kate, I had told her my real name: Jenna Miller. I was born and raised in San Diego and moved to Temecula when I got married to my emotionally abusive husband, Jim Miller, a well-known psychiatrist.

"I'm not sure. Maybe somewhere south," I told her.

"Kate, this is the third place you've moved to, and your husband still found you. What makes you think he won't find you again? Please let me tell Ol so that he can help us. You can't keep running. If you stay here, we can help you. If you move somewhere else and your husband finds you, I wouldn't forgive myself," she said, her eyes welling up with tears as she held my hand.

I knew there was something about Hannah that made me trust her. Perhaps she was right.

"Do you really think he can help me?"

"Yes, I know he can, but we must come clean. Plus, I don't like keeping secrets from my husband. I felt bad not telling Ethan when he was alive," she said, gently pulling her hand away from mine before tucking a few hair strands behind her ear. There was sadness in her tone.

Ethan Presten was Hannah's late husband, who tragically passed a few years back. I had never lost a loved one, but I was there when she did, and I could just imagine the pain she suffered inside.

"I know, and I'm sorry for putting you in that situation, *then* and..." I looked down. "*Now,*" I explained, as I sat on the bed, tugging on the shirt under a pile of shoes.

She sat next to me and tilted my chin up. "Stop it. You know I would do anything for you." She squeezed my hand, then smiled as if remembering something fun. "You know, before Ethan and I went to Green Ridge, he stopped by at the clinic and asked me why you wear those gigantic, God-forsaken glasses you wear all the time?" She snickered.

"He did?" I chuckled, remembering Ethan. He had been a great guy—very much in love with Hannah.

"Yeah, he asked questions about you. You know how Ethan was; he always knew when something was off. I came close to telling him one day that you were an undercover cop, just to shut him up, but I just changed the subject like I always did."

"I *really* am sorry, Han." I felt the knot in my stomach, not liking the fact that I had made Hannah lie to the people she loved.

Hannah scooted closer and placed a hand on my cold and shaky hand. "Hey, there's no need for apologies. I made that decision, and I'll do it again if I have to, but for now, we need to think of your safety, starting with telling Ol everything. He knows bits and pieces, but not the whole story. I thought I'd leave that to you. He has a family who works for a security service; he can find Jim before he finds you."

She was right.

I cleaned up the room and packed what I could. It was almost six-thirty at night when Hannah came back to my apartment, and we rode together, headed for downtown. She must have told Oliver the summary of my story because he insisted on going to a hotel to meet and hear everything about it. Ol was always ahead of everything, and I couldn't blame him for not wanting to meet at their house after what Hannah went through years back. He had to make sure his family was safe, *that* I understood.

We pulled into the garage of the Grand Plaza Hotel, and as we stepped out of the car, Oliver was already walking toward us... Another guy walked beside him, probably an inch taller than Oliver. He wore light denim jeans and a blue long-sleeved shirt, sleeves rolled up to the elbows.

Oliver narrowed his eyes at me, then shook his head as if to say, 'I can't believe you kept all this a secret.' Then, he pulled me in for a hug. "Are you okay?" Oliver asked, then paused before giving his wife, who was busy texting, a quick kiss on the lips, pulling her away from the parked cars she had nearly walked into.

"I'm okay." I lied as I glanced at the strange man in front of me.

Hannah heard what I said despite being buried in her phone, and she squinted at me before continuing to tap the screen.

"Okay, I'm terrified," I confessed, rubbing my hands together.

I could see the concern in Oliver's eyes.

"I understand, Kate, but we need to know everything."

They continued to walk in front of me.

I stood frozen. "Ahem..."

They stopped across the parking lot and looked over their shoulders, including the man next to Oliver, who seemed confused as to why I didn't follow.

"Am I the only one who could see the strange man next to you guys?" I asked, my hands on my waist.

Hannah practically ran back to where I stood. "I'll call you back, Mom," she said before hanging up. "Oh my gosh, Kate. I'm so sorry. I was so busy trying to give my mom instructions for the kids that I thought Oliver had already introduced you to Michael," she explained as she gently pulled my hand. We walked across to where the guys were.

"Really?" Oliver said, shaking his head. "You didn't tell her about Mikey?"

"And you didn't introduce them to each other?" Hannah replied with a bit of feistiness, placing her hands on her waist as I did.

"Okay, kids, still waiting," I announced as I watched who, apparently, was *Mikey,* watching them in amusement.

"I'm Michael." He offered his hand for me to shake.

"I'm Kate, Kate Rivers," I replied.

He smiled.

"I'm so sorry. Mikey is my cousin." Oliver patted Mikey on the back. "I told Hannah to tell you I was bringing him along. He's the one who's going to help us," he explained.

I had so many questions, but I waited until we were settled in the hotel.

We walked toward the entrance with Hannah beside me, still apologizing.

As we entered the lobby, the hustle and bustle were unmistakable. Guests lined up at the counter to check in or out, while others milled about, busy with whatever they were doing. In the center, an older man played the piano, and the melody of *"Someone to Watch Over Me"* by Sinatra wafted through the air, mingling with the scent of bergamot and citrus.

I'd never been to this hotel, and I had my share of stays and visits in five-star hotels when I was with Jim. Everything was grand with the infamous psychiatrist in California. We wined and dined in expensive restaurants and attended charity balls almost year-round, so the elegance and extravagance of this place did not surprise me. The question was: why this hotel? I'd expected Hannah and Ol to take me to a low-key hotel somewhere. I parted with the thoughts as I admired the ginormous crystal chandelier hanging in the center of the lobby.

We were next in line, and a tall, young blonde with bright blue eyes who could pass for a model was behind the gold, button-tufted front desk. She smiled at Oliver, revealing her shiny white teeth, which contrasted with her dark red lipstick. "Welcome back, Mr. Rossi."

Oliver smiled back.

After fast-clicking on the keyboard with her long, red-painted nails, she smiled again and said, "Same room, sir."

"We will use our apps, thank you," Oliver told the lady before turning his attention to us.

I knew Oliver came from a wealthy family, but I'd never seen this side of him before. Oliver carried himself well, dressed nicely, spoke sophisticatedly when needed, but the day-to-day Oliver was simple, *elegant*, but simple; without the poise he showed, I would not have pegged him to come from a wealthy family. I liked that about him; he was humble and down-to-earth. He gestured for us to follow. Hannah knew the way too, like they'd been here before. I followed as I tugged on her arm.

We hopped into the elevator, and Mikey pressed the button for the thirty-fifth floor. He, too knew his way around the hotel.

"Top floor?" I asked with my arms crossed, smirking while we all stood inside the spacious elevator, studying my reflection in a floor-to-ceiling mirror that lined every wall. *God, I looked awful.*

"Not quite," Oliver said, a faint smile brushed across his face as he leaned back on the glass wall behind him, pulling his wife into his arms. "There are thirty-eight floors. The penthouse is reserved for special guests and, of course, Uncle Robert and his family."

"Oh, yeah, *of course, Uncle Robert,*" I replied sarcastically. "Who are you?" I joked, shaking my head as I tug on the handle of my roller bag.

Michael, who stood next to me, gave a faint laugh. I tried to read him, but he was closed off. Oliver, used to my attitude, just smiled. His phone buzzed.

"Oliver insisted you stay here; it's safer, and I agree," Michael said.

I nodded.

"It was the sitter. Mom just picked up the boys," Oliver told Hannah.

A sudden sense of guilt enveloped me for involving them in my mess. "I'm *so* sorry for involving your family in my problem." I swallowed back, trying not to be emotional. It was not fair to involve them. Jim was dangerous, no matter how much other people told me otherwise, and I wouldn't forgive myself if my friends got hurt because of me.

"Jenna, you *are* family, and we take care of family," Hannah said as she reached for my hand.

"So, it's *Jenna*, is it?" Oliver asked with a grin, still hugging his wife from behind. I glanced at *Mikey* (to me, he was Michael), who stood next to me, to see if he was getting uncomfortable with the PDA, but he seemed fine.

I stuck out my hand in front of Oliver. "Yes, Jenna Miller. Nice to meet you."

Oliver played along. "So, the chatterbox act was fake?"

I admitted. "I'm afraid so."

Oliver had been very kind to me. We became very close over the years. In fact, Hannah and her late husband, Ethan, tried to fix me up with him, but I'd always known how Oliver felt about Hannah. There was something in the way he looked at her. There was love, but there was also pain from watching her with Ethan—Oliver's best friend.

The elevator chimed to a stop on the thirty-fifth floor. Oliver exited first, then looked over his shoulder and said, "You'll always be *chatterbox Kate* to me."

Hannah and I exchanged glances and smiled. After walking the hallway, we reached a double door at the end. Oliver pressed his phone against the magnet next to the mahogany door and held the door open for Hannah and me to pass through, and the scent of lavender in the air immediately greeted us.

Though it was not the penthouse, it may as well have been because the room was ginormous, bigger than any room Jim and I had stayed in, and he was always grand. Have I already said that? Yeah, he was always grand, but only behind closed doors. In front of other people, he was the humble, down-to-earth, generous doctor. Ha! If they only knew the real man behind the façade.

Well, I confided in one of our friends once, and her reply was, *"Oh my gosh, you must be mad! You are very lucky to be wed to Dr. Miller. He's quite a catch,"* she'd blabbered in her fakest English accent. That was a mistake I never made again. After discovering the real man I married, I quickly realized I couldn't trust anyone. He had fooled all of them.

I stepped down into what I considered the living room of the hotel suite, where a white leather sofa with yellow and blue throw pillows faced a pair of blue accent chairs. To my right was a white marble bar counter with crystal glasses hanging overhead. On the counter sat a couple of wine bottles—one already chilling in an ice bucket next to four spotless wine glasses. On the white wall hung an abstract painting of red, yellow, and black swirls, making my heart tighten a little. I missed my gallery.

"Are we having a party?" Joking, I placed my luggage in the corner.

"I thought we'd have a drink or two while you tell us your story. I have a feeling it will be *very* interesting. By the way, that's your room; I'll bring your luggage in for you." Oliver pointed at one of the white double doors.

"Why don't you settle in first, and then we can go to the patio and have some drinks?" Hannah said.

Doubt suddenly filled me as I walked to my room. I sat down on the queen-sized bed, neatly made with white linen and a fluffy duvet. What had I dragged my friends into? Maybe after I told Oliver my story, he'd back out. I would understand, of course, but then what? *What would I do? Where would I go?*

I thought about the South—a small town in South Carolina that Jim would never dream of visiting, even to find me. *I heard Greenville was nice. That's it. That would be my Plan B.* I hadn't decided whether to divulge that information to Hannah and Ol, but that was the plan. *Later tonight, I will Google a small town in South Carolina.* I wondered what I'd find.

I parted with my thoughts and joined Oliver, Mikey, and Hannah on the patio. Spring had just started, so the weather was pleasant—neither too hot nor too cold, bouncing between the fifties and seventies. The aluminum-framed, white-padded furniture, accented with blue rectangular lumbar pillows, was inviting, especially with the three votive candles of varying sizes in the center of the glass table. The view of the downtown skyline was magnificent, even in daylight.

Hannah handed me a glass of Rosé wine while she set the glass of her favorite Chardonnay on the table.

"Okay, start from the beginning," Michael said as he tilted the glass of bourbon to his lips and took a sip before sitting down next to me. I was a little surprised by his sudden take-charge attitude, but Oliver had said he would be the one to help me, so I let it be.

Oliver chimed in. "Sorry, Kate. I forgot to mention earlier. Mikey was in the Marine Corps before changing careers as a private security specialist."

"Private Security Specialist." I meant to keep the thought to myself, but it slipped out.

"Yes, I was assigned to protect you as we navigate the situation and handle any threats that arise," Michael said in an authoritative voice, looking at me straight in the eyes without blinking. If that look was supposed to scare me, it didn't. "Anyway, make sure you tell us the entire story," he added.

I looked at Hannah, and she nodded. Oliver nodded too. But I was sure they could feel the tension brewing inside me.

I took a deep breath. *Here we go.*

Chapter Three
JENNA
PAST

*I*t had been my final year, and I was working to complete my degree in psychology at Sierra Vista University. It was my first day as an intern for Dr. Dale Donovan, a professor of educational psychology, after he had to let the previous intern go. I walked in, nervous for my first day, just as another lady walked out of Professor Donnovan's office. She gave me the once-over as she carried a box of... stuff in her hands.

"Excuse me," I said as I held the door for her.

She smiled. "You must be the new intern," she said, her voice low.

I nodded, feeling awkward, then Professor Donnovan called me in. "Sorry, I gotta go."

"Good luck," she called out.

I smiled and then closed the door. After settling in at my desk, a man came in—actually, more like barged in. Dark hair, black sweatshirt pushed up to his elbows, and khaki pants with black loafers.

"Hi," he greeted as he strutted past me straight to Dr. Donovan's door without even stopping to say what he was there for.

"Uhm, hi, are you here for Professor Donovan? Is he expecting you?" I jumped up and chased after him.

He smiled. "You're new," was all he said, then opened the door to the Professor's office.

It's a good thing the Professor wasn't with anyone inside. I would've gotten in trouble.

As if I were committing a crime, he looked over his shoulder as I followed.

"I'm sorry, Professor, but he just—" I had tried to say when we entered.

"Hey," Dr. Donovan said enthusiastically from behind his desk, pulling his glasses down to his nose. "It's okay, Jenna. Sorry, I should have mentioned, this is my friend, Dr. Jim Miller, who often shows up unannounced. I gave up asking him to make an appointment, because he never does, so forgive him."

I would have thought Dr. Miller was too young to be Professor Donovan's friend. Professor Donovan was probably in his late forties, while Dr. Miller appeared to be in his early... thirties, maybe? But the Professor had all kinds of people coming in and out of his office—from students to colleagues of all ages—so Dr. Miller wasn't any different.

Dr. Miller smiled. I gave a faint smile back before excusing myself. I sat at my desk, somewhat annoyed. The man was Dr. Donovan's friend and all, but was it really that hard to say *hello* and introduce himself? Common courtesy, that was all. I started psychoanalyzing him, remembering what I'd learned from my Psych courses. Impolite, tactless, and his body exuded what? I thought, tapping the pen on the desk. I would have said confidence, but I changed my mind. *Arrogance.*

The intercom buzzed.

"Jenna, can you please grab some coffee from the shop downstairs? Thank you," Dr. Donovan said.

I picked up my purse and headed down to the campus coffee shop.

"Getting Professor Dale's caramel macchiato?" A lady behind me asked as I stood in line.

I turned around but quickly looked away. "Yeah," I replied with a faint smile. It was Professor Donovan's former intern.

She tapped my shoulder. "Make sure it's very hot. He likes his coffee boiling." She gave a slight chuckle.

I glanced over my shoulder. "Glad to know, thanks," I replied, giving her another half-smile as I moved forward to the counter and placed my order.

My friends, Tasha and Oliva, approached. Both had long, blonde hair and wore skinny jeans. Oliva was in a grey sweatshirt and brown knee-high boots, while Tasha had a pink blouse and wore beige flats. Oliva said something funny, and we laughed, then quickly hushed ourselves as other students turned to look at us. I turned around, and Professor Donovan's former intern smiled, then looked away.

"I'll see you later, okay? Call me," Tasha said as they walked away.

Another tap on my shoulder. "Hey, I was wondering. Perhaps you and I could get to know each other over coffee. I can give you some pointers about Professor Donnovan," the former intern offered.

"Uhm, that would be nice," I said, almost dismissively. I was in a hurry to get the coffee and return to the office, still trying to win the professor over.

"Anyway, my name is Deanna.

I smiled. "Nice to meet you. Sorry, Dina, I really have to get back to work." I inched away with a tray of coffee in my hand.

I heard her mumble something, and I nodded as I opened the door and walked out of the shop.

Chapter Four

JENNA

PAST

A couple of years later

The gallery I had opened in Temecula, California, hadn't been popular, but it had steady traffic. I rarely paid much attention to the visitors, but that day, when my door chimed, my eyes darted toward the man who had just entered, and they stayed there for a while. The man had a certain quality about him—*Confidence*. That's what he had—not too much, just right, well, so I thought. He carried himself well in his khakis, white shirt, and blue blazer. He wasn't very tall, around five-foot-ten, and was average-built. Every strand of his light brown hair was perfectly held by whatever gel he must have applied that morning. He was familiar.

The man sauntered, studying each framed image on the walls, smiling, frowning, and nodding as if in agreement with what each conveyed. He gave me a sidelong glance, letting me know he knew I was watching. In my defense, I was watching, but just trying to see if he needed help. Who was I kidding? I was totally checking him out; it was hard not to.

One of our associates, Deanna, approached him with a huge smile and started a conversation. From the looks of it, they knew each other. After a few minutes, she gestured for me to come over, and I did.

"Jenna, can you take care of my very important friend? I just need to finish with a customer. They want one of your *Wave series*." Deanna smiled and walked away.

I strutted toward the man in my black stilettos. "Hi! I'm Jenna Rivers." I greeted him, brushing the wrinkle away on my black and white A-line dress.

The man smiled and strolled past me to another set of images on the wall. Not that I was expecting him to be thrilled to hear my name; after all, I was only a newly emerging artist in the area—not too many people were familiar with my work yet, and, as it turned out, no one would be.

Most collectors who visited the gallery would have known my name; it was prominently displayed in the center of the place. Usually, someone would say something like: "*Oh, you're the artist...*" or "*Wow, it's nice to meet the artist.*" Some of them had said, "*I love your work.*" If he had heard of me or read the signs around the gallery, he surely wasn't impressed, or at least he wasn't showing any signs that he knew or had heard of me.

"This is an interesting piece." He looked at an image called "*The Loner.*" It was a photo of a man on a paddleboard in the middle of the vast sea, surrounded by a beautiful sunset, with his dog by his side. I intentionally composed the ocean's vastness so that the man on the paddleboard was almost invisible.

"If you look closely, you'd see he really wasn't alone, per se," I told him.

He leaned in closer to the image. After a full minute, a grin formed on his face.

"Would you look at that? There's a dog next to him," he announced gleefully.

"It's all in perspective." I smiled, hoping to land a sale.

He whirled around to face me. "Very interesting."

He continued to inspect the rest of the display, almost dismissing me, then he paused. "My meeting is just down the road—I'm early, so I thought I'd check out the gallery to pass the time. I'm glad I did. Lots of beautiful images here," he added, as he faced me again, looking straight into my eyes with his dark blue eyes. "I'm Jim—" He stuck out his hand, but quickly retrieved it. "Wait a minute. I know you," he said with a glint in his eyes. "Weren't you Dale Donovan's intern at Sierra Vista University?"

That's when I realized who he was—*Dr. Jim Miller.*

"Oh my gosh, Dr. Miller." I smiled. "Great to see you again."

He looked at me—not with admiration, but with a kind of puzzled curiosity. His brows drew together as he glanced around the gallery. "So... what happened with becoming a psychologist?" he asked, at last, the question I had tried to avoid.

My face heated. Unsure why. I had nothing to be embarrassed about. I had fully intended to start my own practice, but life took a different course. One day, I picked up my old camera. An old SD card was still inside. I had turned it on and went through the images. Suddenly, goosebumps were all over me. There was something about taking photos that made me feel complete—at peace. Since then, I'd taken my camera everywhere and photographed anything that moved me emotionally. Interestingly, after I passed the licensing exam, my parents gifted me a new camera, and that's when I knew. I didn't want to become a psychologist. I wanted to open my own gallery.

"Life," was all I could say. At that moment, I knew he was psychoanalyzing me, and I didn't care. "So..." I started to say, then looked toward where Deanna and a couple who were purchasing one of my pieces were standing. "Do you know Deanna?" I asked.

His eyes lingered on another framed photograph on the wall—a colorful array of petals scattered against a dark background. "Something like that," he replied.

I didn't push. He clearly didn't want to elaborate. "So, are you interested in this piece, Doctor? Perhaps for your home or your office?" I asked as I followed him, moving about the gallery.

"I'm a psychiatrist now," he said without even a slight glance in my direction.

Wow, that came out of nowhere.

He kept his interest in the images on the wall. At that moment, he was studying a macro image I took of a yellow lily, deliberately positioning the subject on the right, leaving the left space dark, contrasting with the only thing I captured—the lengthy part of the flower curving down, revealing a single drop on the tip, like a tear waiting to fall.

"Oh, I thought you always were."

This time, he glanced back and smiled. "*Was* a psychologist. *Now*, a psychiatrist," he said proudly, then looked down at his wristwatch. "Oh shoot, I'd better get going. I'm meeting some colleagues at the restaurant down the street."

His back was immediately to me as he started for the door, and I stood in the middle of the gallery, a little baffled.

I turned to head back to my desk when I heard him call my name. I paused, then walked back toward the door, where he stood waiting.

"My meeting will be done in an hour. Would you like to join me for a cup of coffee? I won't take a no this time; not that you'd ever said no before." He gave a faint smile.

There was something about his smile this time; it was handsome and captivating. It was one of those smiles that would make you lose track of what you were thinking or doing. I'd never noticed it before. I said yes to coffee and later justified it as spending time with an acquaintance who could become a client and land a sale. It was part of the job.

Later that day, I met Jim at a restaurant nearby. I was already seated at the back of the restaurant, but when he arrived, he asked the server to move us to a table by the window. Jim said it was the best seat, and we deserved to sit in the best spot in the place, so we did.

The server asked for our order, and I had asked for water, but Jim suggested we have a drink to celebrate seeing each other again. I thought it was a bit forward, but after contemplating it, I agreed. It had been a while since we last saw each other, and who would have thought that he would walk into my gallery after all this time?

We ended up talking, laughing, and having a good time. Jim was sweet and a gentleman. After several dates, I found out how affectionate he was; he would always hold my hand in public and kiss me in front of people. It was actually a little too much, but I did like the affection. Every week, he would send a bouquet of eleven white roses to the gallery, and the card would say *"just because"* or *"thinking about you."* It wasn't hard to fall for him. We started dating, and for months, I was the apple of his eye. I felt special.

"I am one lucky man, you know that?" he said one day while dropping an unexpected gift for me at the gallery—a blue box from Tiffany's. Inside was a beautiful gold pendant with his initials. It was gorgeous, but I thought it was odd that it was only his initials, not ours. He told me it was something for me to wear so I'd always be with him wherever I go. I've heard of people wearing their partner's initials, so I did, too.

Sometimes, something about his personality would nag at me, but at the end of the day, he would always show me how special I was to him, so I chose to ignore it.

He introduced me to his friends and was so proud of me, well, at first. Jim was loved by his colleagues, too. They praised him constantly for something he had done or accomplished, but he would brush it off with statements like, "Oh, stop it, Jenna might actually believe you guys." "You guys are too kind," or "I was just doing what anyone would do." But when the focus wasn't on him, he would bring up a situation where the limelight would return to him. Of course, I didn't catch on then. His enigmatic smile and tantalizing eyes blinded me. The man was brilliant—*that* I could give him.

I fell for him—hard, and it didn't take long before I became Jenna Miller, and not long after that, I was introduced to the *real* Dr. Jim Miller. I didn't know what I was in for, and by the time I did, it was too late.

Chapter Five

JIM

PAST

Jenna Rivers. I sat in my office between clients, thinking of our encounter the other day. I placed both hands behind my head and leaned back in my leather office chair. Jenna was just as pretty as I'd remembered her. She was supposed to become a psychologist; instead, she became an artist—*How odd.* And Deanna. What the hell was she doing at Jenna's gallery? I hadn't realized she and Jenna were friends. I wouldn't have put those two together. Jenna was brilliant, beautiful—the popular kid in college, and Deanna was...well, not so popular.

I shook the thoughts away as I tried to figure out my next move. There was no way I would let Jenna slip out of my hands again, not that she had the first time; I had never technically asked her out.

My thoughts went back to Deanna. *Deanna, Deanna, Deanna. What am I going to do with you?* Deanna and I, however, had "dated." The word made me nauseous. She wasn't my type, but the girl was persistent, so we decided we'd keep it our little secret.

"Hi, Dr. Miller," she greeted me with a huge smile one day as I entered Dale's office, where she'd worked. Professor Dale Donovan was a friend and a mentor.

"Hi Deanna." I walked straight into Dale's office.

It was the routine—until one day, when I stopped by, and Dale wasn't in. Deanna came into Dale's office and quietly shut the door behind her. One thing led to another. Since then, we'd been sneaking around behind Dale's back. Perhaps it was the thrill of sneaking around that made me keep seeing Deanna; it was the adrenaline, the secret we kept, because I was certainly not attracted to her—not anymore.

One day, I stopped by, knowing Dale wouldn't be in. And of course, we did what we always did. We were on Dale's leather sofa, making out, when the door suddenly opened. Dale stood there. His eyes were wide, sharp, and stunned. They said it all: the trace of my betrayal and the end of our friendship, *so I thought,* but all it took was for me to create some elaborate lie. *Deanna took me by surprise. I walked in as I usually do, sat on the couch, and waited for you. Then she came in, and just like that, she was on top of me. I was pushing her away when you walked in.*

Dale had bought it, and the next thing I knew, Deanna was a goner.

Chapter Six
JENNA
PAST

"**S**he's an artist, whatever *that* is, but she's happy with what she does, so I let her be," Jim had said to his colleagues as he laughed and sipped his brandy from a crystal glass, standing in the middle of our third social event of the month. That's how he told people what I did for a living— *an artist or whatever that is.* I once tried to explain to someone that I owned a gallery, and that was a huge mistake; it ended in an argument later that night, and Jim told me not to embarrass him in front of his colleagues again. I didn't understand. How could my explanation that I owned an art gallery embarrass him? Shouldn't he be proud? No, not Jim. "Being an artist is not an actual job. Anyone could take photographs and call them art. No degree needed," he would tell me. Somehow, I always justified his behavior.

I tolerated the evening. I was not much of a party girl, but Jim needed a muse for the night. Yes, not a *wife*, a *muse*. A lady in a long black body-con dress, standing confidently beside the man Jim conversed with, caught my attention. She gave me a look as if she understood how I felt. Boredom was on her face.

She smiled, unaware that in my head I was working out how she got into her dress to begin with. It looked pretty tight; I wondered if she could breathe.

"Hi, I'm Gayle." She extended her hand to me, and I shook it.

"I'm Jenna." I smiled.

"I know who you are. You are the envy of the ladies around here." She smiled. I couldn't quite tell if she was sincere.

Who was this lady, and what did she know about me? I got a little defensive, squinting my eyes as I felt my shoulders tighten.

"Excuse me, I need to go to the powder room," I said, sashaying across the room in the sage Ralph Lauren maxi Jim had surprised me with. My fingers brushed the fabric, still warm from the box he'd left on the bed that afternoon. I'd meant to wear one of my black dresses, the ones tucked neatly in my closet, but the moment I saw the box, I knew I wouldn't get away with it. *I can't wait to see you tonight. XOXO,* the card read.

What Jim wanted, Jim got. If I crossed him, then his silent treatment would ruin the day, like a petulant child who didn't get what he wanted. He would leave and not return until the next day. After several of those, I learned to avoid them to keep the peace.

"Jenna, where are you going?" Jim called out with a forced smile I knew so well. *How could I have been so stupid?* My chest tightened with nervousness. I knew I had no reason to, but my body reacted illogically when it came to Jim. I should have excused myself and kissed him on the cheek like he had always asked me to do. "A good wife is always polite," he would remind me. He would give me the rundown of how high society acted and how I should act. It was as if I'd never been to any high-class parties before meeting him, but there was no arguing with Jim Miller. He never failed to remind me that I was beneath him. I slowly got to know the real Dr. Jim Miller, and it wasn't long before I realized he wasn't the man I had married.

"I'm sorry, hon, I don't know where my manners were; I need to powder my nose," I said and gave him a quick peck on the lips. He smiled, nodded, and continued conversing with the gentleman as if he were permitting me to walk away. I could feel their gaze on me and knew they were discussing how *polite* I was as a wife and how lucky Jim must have been to have a wife like me. *Barf!*

Not realizing Gayle was next to me, I opened the bathroom door.

"Men," she blurted as she entered the bathroom before me. She pulled out a compact powder from her black sparkly Chanel evening clutch and started dabbing slowly on her face. Gayle was stunning, I thought as I studied her reflection in the mirror. She was older than me, I was pretty sure, but she was one of those women who really took care of themselves. The woman probably spent days in cycling class, ate nothing but salad, and had a strict and expensive nightly facial regimen. She had her long, black hair slicked back with gel, swept behind her ears, revealing two large diamond studs that contrasted with her bright blue eyes and flawless, shimmering skin.

Behind us were two matching green floral armchairs. She quickly claimed one, removed her red-bottom stilettos, and massaged her feet.

"These shoes are killing me."

Meanwhile, I watched her in the mirror, still wondering if she could breathe through her dress. But then she moved with surprising ease—it might not have been so tight after all.

"I can't wait to get out of this awful, chest-crushing dress," she announced.

I finally turned around and addressed her. "How are you able to breathe in that? It seems awfully snug," I told her, hoping I didn't sound judgmental.

"Oh, honey, if it were to me, I would wear pajamas and be just as happy." She smiled, still rubbing her feet, the left one this time.

"So... why do you wear it? I'm sorry, you don't have to answer that." I retracted quickly, embarrassed by my sudden tactlessness.

Unbothered, Gayle said. "Look at me. I look great. *I can't breathe; my feet hurt*, but I look *fa-a-a-bulous*." She batted her lashes. "I also make my husband look great."

If she was being sarcastic, I didn't catch it.

"I don't think I've seen you here before. Are you always present at these gatherings?" I asked, facing the mirror and dabbing a little powder on my nose.

"Oh, hon, these are hardly just gatherings. First, it's a charity event, which I'm all for. Second, it's a competition between all the big donors, which I suppose could be a good thing; third, it's a chance for the men to show off their wives, significant others, or whoever they decide to bring for the night, and I mean... *For. The. Night.*" She winked at me. "Lastly, it's a battleground for social climbers and a tournament for the ladies to see who's wearing the most expensive dress or jewelry and then post it all over social media as if people cared. Can't you tell? I *lo-o-v-e* these events."

The sarcasm—there it was. I suddenly liked the woman. I claimed the chair beside her, removed my heels, and started rubbing my feet.

"To answer your question, yes, I come to all these events, but I just had a baby three months ago, so I was out of the scene for most of last year's events. Thank God!" She rolled her eyes.

"You just had a baby, and your body looks like that? Wow!"

"Oh, don't be fooled, darling; I'm wearing one of those shapewear you see on social media nowadays."

"Still. You look fantastic."

"Thank you, Hon." She slipped her heels back on and leaned back, revealing her long, tan leg through the dress's slit as she crossed one leg over the other. "So, how is it being married to the most coveted man in Southern California?"

Her question took me by surprise. I knew Jim was popular, but most *coveted*. Really?

"It's great," I lied, giving her the best fake smile I could muster. Well, it wasn't really a lie because at times, it *was* great. It was great when he wasn't gaslighting me, when he wasn't condescending, when he wouldn't pick a fight just to have an excuse to walk out on me and stay somewhere else for the night or *nights.*

"I don't mean to be rude, Jenna, but I'm not convinced. I happened to know Jim before he married you."

My reaction might have given away my thoughts, because she quickly clarified what she meant.

"Oh, no, darling, not in *that* way." Her eyes widened as if offended by my insinuation. "He used to date one of my colleagues a few years ago—a friend and I know how Jim can be," she clarified.

"What do you mean?"

"Let's just say, my friend, didn't have good things to say about the infamous doctor." She lifted her perfectly shaped right brow.

Before I could ask for more clarification, my phone vibrated. Gayle glanced at it, gave me a side eye before standing up, and offered a hand to help me.

"Let's go, Hon, I'm sure your husband is already *missing* you." She gave me a wink. Her tone was full of sarcasm.

I was just about to walk out the door when I felt her hand on my shoulder. She handed me a card. "Just be careful and call me anytime. *Anytime. You understand?* Now smile," she said, sounding like a mother who had just finished scolding a child. She winked before we walked out of the bathroom and re-assimilated into the loud party.

Just be careful? My heart thudded as I played Gayle's ominous voice in my head. I shook the unsettling thoughts away as I followed Gayle, her heels clacking on the marble floor.

Jim was poking his head around, nodding absentmindedly to the older gentleman he was talking to—he wasn't happy, but I walked up, linked my arm to his, and forced a smile.

"I'm sorry, Dr. Miller. Your wife and I quickly hit it off and got carried away with our conversation. Didn't mean to take her away from you for so long," Gayle announced as she stood across Jim and me. She looked him straight in the eyes, as if they knew something I didn't.

Jim forced a smile of his own. "Dr. Lancaster," he said before glancing around as if looking for someone. "Shouldn't you be with your husband?"

"Aww, Jim, you know how Doctor Mark is. He's content..." She gently placed a hand on Jim's shoulder. I could feel Jim tense up. "And he trusts me," she said with a grin. "You should try it; it's invigorating," she added as she picked up a glass of wine from the server who had just passed by, lifted it toward us, and smiled before strutting away.

The glare in Jim's eyes was indescribable. His grip on my hand tightened, and I could sense he wanted to say something, but gritted his teeth instead as he watched her walk away.

There was tension between Jim and Gayle, which made me uneasy. Gayle was undoubtedly taunting Jim, but why? What did she know about him? She and her husband were doctors, too. We were at a medical fundraiser, so I assumed there would be many doctors around, but I just never pegged Gayle to be one. She looked more like a former model. But Gayle knew things about Jim. I wish I had asked her what she knew while we were in the bathroom.

"This must be the beautiful Mrs. Miller," the man Jim was talking to interjected, breaking the awkwardness.

I offered my hand. "Hi, I'm Jenna. Nice to meet you."

"I'm John. A pleasure to meet you, Jenna," he said with a strong British accent, keeping my hand in his longer than it should be.

John kissed the back of my hand before letting go. He was slightly taller than Jim. His salt-and-pepper hair, dark-rimmed eyeglasses, and dark suit, which I was sure cost more than anything I owned when I was single, made him look very distinguished. His eyes, which I assumed were blue, looked gray under the lights. John was a smooth talker, complimenting me from head to toe, making me blush—cringe at times, to be honest, but he wasn't fresh or anything like that.

Jim's arm tensed a little, but I was used to it, so I ignored it, not wanting to cause a scene. Once John and I finished exchanging pleasantries, he returned to discussing basketball with Jim.

"Did you see the Lakers game last night?" Jim asked, swirling his drink in his hand.

"Yes, great game! Did you see that buzzer-beater Luka made? That guy is simply amazing," John replied.

"Isn't he?" I chimed in. *Wrong move.*

I could feel the immediate tension in Jim's body. He gave a fake smile, and without taking his eyes off John, leaned into my ear and whispered, "You shouldn't be butting in on a conversation you know nothing about, Hon." He smiled again. "I'm sorry about that. It must be the champagne. Women and alcohol." Jim shook his head, smiling at John.

John nodded and gave an awkward smile.

I pretended the whole thing didn't bother me, stood beside him, and plastered a smile till my jaw hurt. Glancing around, I studied all the well-dressed attendees. I remembered when Jim and I were still dating, he told me some men brought escorts to these events, and I would try to spot them to pass the time, but as it turned out, I was bad at the game; there were some very classy and gorgeous escorts out there.

One dress caught my eye, well, everyone's eyes, especially the men. The woman stood by the large double doors, studying the room, then strutted slowly across the center of the ballroom as if walking a fashion runway during Paris Fashion Week. Suddenly, there was silence in the room as people watched her walk across the marble floor. Her brunette hair was tied in a messy bun, showing off her bare golden shoulders. She was tall to begin with, but the glittering gold Louboutin heels she wore made her even taller. She looked at least six feet tall.

She was stunning, but the dress, oh, the dress, made everyone's neck hurt from the quick turns, following her as she sashayed in the center of the ballroom in her gold, almost see-through gown with tiny black floral accents, only enough to cover her private parts.

The slit on the side of the dress went up her hips, accentuating her long, well-toned legs. When she approached where I was standing, I saw a nude bodysuit underneath the dress. *Wow!* I noticed Gayle in the corner, and she mouthed the same.

"Who is that?" I whispered in Jim's ear.

"That's Annabelle Morris. She's a model," a random lady next to Jim said before he could reply. Apparently, my whisper wasn't quite a whisper. I glanced at Jim. There was something in the way he watched her. It wasn't admiration; it was recognition, as if he'd already memorized her smile, the way she moved, the way she owned the surroundings. Suddenly, I felt a pang in my chest—it was never a good sign.

"She's gorgeous." My voice trembled.

"You look better, sweetheart," Jim mumbled under his breath without looking at me. His attention was fixed on the tall gentleman next to Annabelle. There was jealousy in his eyes; I could see it.

He finally snapped out of his trance, forced himself to straighten up, and kissed my cheek. He was always good at patronizing me.

The whole thing felt staged, as if he were justifying his actions. Of course, one older lady bought Jim's fake display of affection. "Aww, that's so sweet, Dr. Miller." She placed both hands on her chest. "You are one lucky lady," she added, smiling at me before returning her attention to Annabelle Morris. I could tell she disagreed with Jim.

Jim always complimented me in front of others, and everyone around us would make the same comments: *Dr. Miller is such a great man, so humble, and so generous. You are so lucky. It must be so great to be married to Dr. Miller.*

Yeah, lucky indeed. If only they knew.

Chapter Seven

JENNA

PAST

I had woken up to the sound of the front door shutting, and I instinctively tapped the screen on my phone, which was attached to the MagSafe charger. It was almost 2 a. m.—another late night. It had been happening often lately. The bedroom door slowly opened, and I could imagine Jim tiptoeing. I wanted to confront him, but I wasn't in the mood to hear one of his lies, so I closed my eyes and forced myself to sleep. It never came.

The next day, while he was in the shower, I noticed he had left his phone on the kitchen counter, which I thought was odd because it was always glued to him wherever he went. I picked it up. I was going to surprise him by adding our wedding photo to his empty profile. Suddenly, I felt a compulsion to go through his phone, but I decided against it. Instead, I focused on the photo I had just added to his iMessage profile. I was excited to see his reaction. When I heard the shower shut off, I put the phone back down—it buzzed. If I didn't know better, I would say my husband had bionic ears because he came out of the bedroom, rushing to get to the phone.

I picked up the phone, handed it to him, and sat on a barstool, smiling, as I waited for him to tell me how happy he was that I had added our wedding photo to his profile. Instead, he grabbed the phone from my hand, walked back to the room, and fiddled with it.

Dressed and ready for work, he came back out of the bedroom with a frown on his face.

Great! Bad news.

"Don't do that." He walked past me and poured himself a cup of coffee I had brewed earlier.

"Do what?" Surely, he wasn't talking about the profile picture on his phone. "Do what?" I asked again.

He tipped the white mug to his mouth, then paused. "Don't mess around with my phone."

"I didn't go through it. I only put a photo on your profile. It's our wedding photo. Look, we have—" I tried to say, trying to show him the photo on my phone.

"I know what your phone looks like. I don't like photos on mine. I message clients and colleagues. I don't want them seeing a photo of you—" He caught himself.

Jim spun around and placed the mug in the sink. "I meant you and me, of *anybody*. That's why I leave it blank. I want it to be professional," he explained.

I paused and pondered, and somehow, it made sense, so I let it go, even though I had suspicions about another woman. The late nights explained it all. The fact that he hadn't slept with me in months just meant he had been getting it elsewhere. Deep inside, I knew why I added our photo to his profile. I did it for my benefit, so that whoever he was texting could see that he was married.

I knew I shouldn't have violated his privacy. It wasn't like I was actively snooping, but there was this persistent, uneasy feeling in my gut that something wasn't right. I wondered if I was just being paranoid—even a little crazy. But then something would happen that made me question everything again: the way he always placed his phone face down, or how he'd step outside to take certain calls.

One morning, we were still in bed when I saw them—dark red and purple marks across his chest. Whoever left them hadn't even tried to be discreet. It was almost as if she wanted me to find them. And that's when I felt it: a rage I didn't know I had. It was the buildup of all the lies and deception, forming a tight, burning knot inside me—one that was finally threatening to explode.

"What is this?" I asked, touching the disgusting hickey on his chest.

"What? What is it?" he asked, rolling over to get up and look in the mirror.

Silence.

"That's a hickey," I said flatly, about to burst into tears. Not because I was hurt, but because I hated it when I was right.

"Don't be ridiculous! I got this from the shirt I bought last week. It rubbed against my chest when I wore it to go for a run." He looked at me—annoyed, almost offended. That was insulting. He pulled out a shirt from the drawer and walked out like I was the one who had crossed a line.

Me? Offend him? How dare he? The way he just walked away, like it was nothing. Like I'd imagined the whole thing. As if I were crazy, it made me want to scream. But then came the worst part—the part I couldn't explain. Why did I feel like

I was the one who'd done something wrong? Why did I feel guilty?

By the end of the day, I had convinced myself it was my fault. I was hurt—I couldn't deny that. I loved him. That much was true. But I let it go—for the sake of our marriage.

I knew I was being weak. I should've stood my ground. After everything—the way he'd been treating me—and now this? *Cheating? How could he?* I should have left him. I knew that. But I didn't. I couldn't. And I didn't even know why.

Months later, Jim caught the flu and spent a week in bed. I took care of him, of course. I prepared a meal, gave him medication, and sorted our mail so I could give him his, in case there was something important. One stood out; it was from a jewelry store. In fact, I thought it was mine, so I opened it. My stomach somersaulted, a feeling I got whenever something was amiss. Then I read the message.

Dear Dr. Jim Miller,

We at Bvlgari thank you for your recent visit to our store. We hope you enjoyed the necklace you purchased and look forward to seeing you again soon.

Michael Giovanni

Store Manager

My heartbeat quickened. I knew all the gifts Jim had given me, but a necklace from Bulgari wasn't one of them.

"You went to Bulgari?" I asked as I walked into the bedroom and gave him his mail.

"What?" There was a pause—too long to be innocent. It was the kind of delay that said more than words ever could, like he was calculating his next move.

Like he *knew* exactly what I meant... but couldn't figure out how I'd found out.

Jim was a master at covering his tracks. But it felt like the universe wanted me to see the truth—whether I wanted it or not.

I handed him the card.

He immediately opened it and read it. And just like that, he tossed it to the side.

"Junk mail." He curled his lips.

"Junk mail? It said, '*Thank you for visiting our store*,' Jim. You went there and bought something." I snapped.

His eyes widened, as if he were surprised I had raised my voice at him.

He glared at me. "Do you think I would spend that much money on a necklace? For another woman?"

Even though I knew the answer to his question, I mumbled, "I don't know."

My lack of confidence just fueled his anger. "You don't know? Is that all you can say? You don't know. What exactly do you know, Jenna?" He paused as if waiting for me to respond, but he continued, now standing next to the bed. "No, Jenna. You don't know anything. You dare to accuse me of things when you have no clue about anything?" He huffed and shook his head.

"I didn't accuse you, Jim. I asked—I simply asked." I picked up the scattered mail on the floor.

He rushed in front of me, and for a second, I braced myself—clutching the pillow on the bed, waiting for his heavy hand to strike, but it didn't come. Instead, shook his head and rolled his eyes in disgust before walking away.

I sat on the edge of the bed; the memory of the first time he'd hit me played on a loop in my head. It happened just after our first wedding anniversary. The ache in my chest deepened as I recalled how that special night had unraveled.

It had started perfectly—a candlelit, three-course dinner, a bottle of wine, and the restaurant's famous Crème Brulé for dessert. Jim gave me a diamond tennis bracelet; I gave him the watch he'd been eyeing for months. We were happy. On our way out, someone had called his name—a colleague from work, waving from the bar. We joined him for a quick drink. Jokes were exchanged, and I laughed at something his colleague had said, and that's when I noticed Jim's demeanor had changed.

Jim was quiet during our drive home that night, but as soon as we arrived, he threw his jacket on the couch and grabbed my arm.

"What the hell, Jenna!"

I was taken aback, unsure of what had just happened.

"You think it was right to joke around with my colleague, making me look bad?"

I had stepped closer to hug him, but he'd moved away.

I had reached for his hand. "Honey, we were just having fun," I tried to appease him, but he didn't want to hear any of it.

"Don't ever do that again," he'd commanded as he turned his back.

Then I made the mistake of having the last word. "Oh, my goodness, Jim; lighten up."

Before I knew it, the back of his hand landed on my cheek. I didn't even see it coming. His hand might have flown 100 mph before it crashed into my face. Gosh, it burned. Jim quickly pulled me into his arms, hugged me tightly, and apologized, tears welling up in his eyes. That night, we made up and made love. The next day, a beautiful bouquet of eleven white roses showed up at the gallery with a card that said: *I'm so sorry, sweetheart. Please know that it will never happen again. I love you very much—Jim.* That was when I knew: Jim's love came with pain.

It happened repeatedly after that, and a bouquet or a new piece of jewelry followed each time. I wasn't sure if anyone suspected anything; if they did, they didn't say a thing. Jim made sure he was an angel in front of everyone; as a result, no one would have suspected that Jim could ever lay a hand on me. I knew I should have left him a long time ago, but whenever I came around to it, I thought about the good times we had... *have.* I thought about moving on without him, and as odd as it may sound, I didn't want to. I loved him, so I convinced myself that he *was* sorry. That he just had a temper, and that it was somehow *my* fault for upsetting him and not obeying him. I couldn't bring myself to leave him.

A few weeks later, Jim started spending more time at his weekly poker games, stumbling in drunk around midnight. When I asked where he'd been, he'd just say, "You should be happy, I'm home early."

One night, feeling lonely and missing my husband's touch, I came on to him. I could tell he wasn't interested. I guess I should've been grateful he didn't turn me down. But I knew—of course I knew—he faked it, like I wouldn't notice. He didn't even try to be convincing.

I wasn't sure what hurt more: the lie or that he didn't care enough to lie well. That's when I realized something in me had changed. I couldn't stand up for myself anymore. All I could do was cry.

I was afraid Jim would leave me.

Chapter Eight

JENNA

PAST

One night after having dinner with his friends, Jim and I got into his black Range Rover.

"That was a fun evening," I said, breaking the silence. I knew he was upset.

"Yeah, it was, till you started speaking when you weren't supposed to. What's so hard to understand, Jenna? I told you. Do not speak when men are speaking," he said, looking straight ahead on the road.

"Just because you went to school and got your degree in psychology doesn't mean you can jump into a conversation with my colleagues. Plus, you're an *artist* now, remember?" He threw air quotes after saying the word *artist*.

He continued. "Stay in your lane. For crying out loud, Jenna, you aren't licensed. If you wanted to be a psychologist, you should've taken the exam, not that you'd—" He huffed then shook his head, "Never mind. All I'm saying is, quit butting into my conversations about work."

I spaced out for a moment, just staring at the brake lights ahead of us, wondering whether I should finally tell him the truth. That I'd passed my licensing exam. That I *am* a psychologist, but I chose not to practice. That he was a textbook narcissistic, manipulative freak, but because I was his wife, I decided it was vital to keep our marriage intact—I thought I could change him, despite the red flags I was trained to see.

I started to say something when Jim lifted his hand to adjust the rearview mirror, making me flinch.

A few weeks later, the gallery had landed a major account, and my client, Jason Adler, had invited us to dinner. Jason Adler was a special client, a real estate entrepreneur who had just bought a new condominium for which I supplied the art.

As usual, Jim was in one of his moods. His silence said it all. Jason was a good-looking guy; tall, dark, and handsome. I was not attracted to the man, but I was sure any woman would be, including my two colleagues, Ann and Deanna, who were ogling him. Jim noticed; it was hard not to.

Mr. Adler's family owned the restaurant we were in. It wasn't fancy, but it wasn't fast food either. I called it casual fancy. I enjoyed the food; that was what was important to me. Mr. Adler was a funny guy who got funnier with each shot of bourbon. He made jokes the whole night, and I could not stop laughing. At one point, when we finally had the time to be serious, I thanked him for the opportunity to display some of my photographs in his condominium.

Mr. Adler turned to me, grabbed my hand, and placed it between his. "No, Jenna, thank you. The pleasure is all mine. You are *one talented* woman. Your work is exceptional." He then picked up his glass and made a toast.

I glanced at Jim as I raised my glass. The look in his eyes could've frozen the wine in my glass—icy and accusing. He tried to mask it with a smile, but I didn't buy it; his jaw was too tight.

"To Jenna Miller and her fantastic colleagues."

Our glasses clinked; surprisingly, Jim joined.

"You are one lucky guy, Mr. Miller," Jason grinned at Jim before tipping the glass into his mouth.

I'm not sure why, but I could feel my associates staring at me, as if anticipating how Jim would react. Jim gave one of his famous forced smiles that *I* only knew about.

"You should slow down with the drinks, sweetheart. You know you shouldn't be mixing medicine and alcohol," Jim announced before placing his glass on the table.

What in the world? What medicine? I wasn't taking any medicine. He suddenly acted as if he were concerned about a condition I supposedly had.

I was about to ask him what was going on, but Jason stood.

"Thank you again, ladies and Mr. Miller, for—"

"*Doctor,*" Jim corrected dryly and stood.

"I'm sorry?" Jason asked, creasing his forehead.

"You can call me *Doctor* Miller," Jim clarified.

"I'm sorry. I didn't know you were a doctor. My apologies. Anyway, I must go. I just wanted to thank you all for the lovely evening." Jason placed a hand on my shoulder. "Jenna. I will be seeing more of you. I have another acquisition I'm working on, and I would like to discuss more of your artwork," he said.

My heart leaped. Another potential big - no, *huge* sale. "I would love that; thank you so much." I stood beside Jim. "Isn't that exciting, hon?" I held his hand.

He nodded, picked up his drink, and downed whatever was left in the crystal glass.

I could feel a glare toward me; it was Deanna's. I made a mental note to ask later, but just as Jason was about to walk away, he glanced back at me. "Jenna... I hope you feel better," he said with hesitation, like there was a question to his statement. I couldn't blame him; I, too, had some questions.

Before I could respond, Jim slipped a hand around my waist. "She's in good hands," he said flatly. "We should be going too, sweetheart. It isn't good for you to get stressed—you know how your moods can get." He grabbed my jacket from the back of the chair and draped it over my shoulders.

Embarrassed, I offered Jason a quick smile, then glanced at my associates, who looked just as confused as I was. I shrugged my shoulders at them as they stood and followed us out.

"What are you talking about, Jim?" I whispered, my tone placid, making sure not to question him aloud, that people would hear.

"Are you okay, Jenna? You didn't tell us you were sick," Deanna said from behind me.

Great. She heard. I side-eyed Jim, and his eyes were fuming.

My emotions got the best of me, and I glared at Deanna unintentionally. *That's because I'm not!* I wanted to yell, my blood boiling. Ann gave a faint smile, showing she was concerned but would rather not ask. She hugged me instead. I glanced back at Deanna. I tried to read her reaction, but couldn't. There was something in the way she looked at me. *Did she pity me? Did she know?*

"C'mon, sweetheart. I think it's time for your medication." Jim nudged me toward the parked car waiting outside.

"Ladies... " he nodded at Ann and Deanna.

"Jim," I called out, trying to stop him to get some clarification before getting in the car, but his grip on my arm was so tight that I could feel it go numb. He opened the car and practically shoved me in. When he finally climbed into the driver's seat and started the car, I didn't know what else to do. So, against my better judgment, I did what I wasn't supposed to do: I talked to him.

"What is going on?" I asked.

Silence.

The car jerked as he changed lanes. I glanced at his speedometer; he was going twenty miles above the speed limit. "Jim, slow down."

Still, it was the wrong thing to say. I should've known better, but I got nervous when people sped or drove angrily. "And what kind of illness do I supposedly have?" I tried *very* hard to hide my irritation. I didn't want another fight, but I was sure I wasn't doing a great job.

Silence.

Trying very hard to keep my composure, I smiled despite the migraine that was brewing in my head—the bright lights weren't helping either. I took a deep breath and tried again. I didn't want the whole thing to escalate into something big, but I needed to fix whatever it was I had done wrong in his eyes. "Did I do something wrong to upset you? If I—"

"What do you think?" he asked, his voice ice cold; it could freeze the breath in your lungs.

"Honestly, I have no idea. I'm confused. I thought we were having fun; then you started talking about me being sick and everything. What was that about? Ann and Deanna were worried."

"You *are* sick. You are sick in the head, and you don't even know it," he snapped.

"Why would you even say that?"

"Well, we all could see how you flirted with that Jason guy as I sat there," he blurted.

"We?"

"Yeah, *sweetheart... we.* As in your friends and I. Do you think they didn't notice how you have disrespected me and paid more attention to Jason?"

"Disrespected you?"

"Are you deaf? Or should I say it slower so you would understand?" He continued, this time talking slowly as if I was slow to understand. *"You. Have. Dis-res-pec-ted—"*

"Please... you don't have to be—"

The tire screeched as Jim turned the steering wheel so fast and pulled to the side of the road. "Be what? Be what exactly, *sweetheart?"* he yelled, turning his body to me, staring with a look unrecognizable since I'd known him. Whoever it was, it wasn't Jim.

I had to calm my nerves and take a deep breath. "Jim, I'm not sure why you're so upset. Mr. Adler is my client. That's all," I calmly touched his lap. He snatched my hand away.

"Sure, Jenna. You think I believe you? Do you not think he wouldn't take you to bed if he got the chance?"

"Jim! You're being ridiculous."

And just like that. WHAAM! Right across my face. I didn't even see it coming. I immediately tasted the blood slowly trickling down my chin and the side of my face.

Everything went hazy, and I didn't know what happened next. All I knew was that my heart was pounding, and I was walking alone on the roadside. I forced my eyes to open, but it was difficult; the bright lights around blinded me. There were honks from cars passing by, but none of them stopped. I kept walking, not knowing where I was headed. The surroundings felt familiar, but suddenly, a blur came over me, and I felt the world spinning.

Swooshing. I followed the noise. Barely, but I could make out a place to sit, so I felt around it. *Concrete.* I sat. The sound of the water splashing was loud and familiar, and I could even feel the mist on my arms. *Where was I? Where was Jim?* I could still faintly hear the cars passing by. The dizziness subsided a bit, and I slowly stood up. I could indistinctly make a dancing mist before me. I tried my hardest to scoop up a little water and splash my face. Stinging, I shut my eyes quickly, felt around it, and realized my left eye was almost completely swollen shut. *I needed to get back home.* Looking around with one eye, my heart pounded like it was trying to tear its way out of my chest, and I wanted to scream and cry. Tears formed in my eyes, and I quickly stopped them as soon as I felt them stinging. Unable to release my fear and tension, I felt helpless, and though it felt familiar, I still didn't know which way to go. Going east felt right, so I did.

Chapter Nine

JENNA

PAST

Murmurs from people I didn't recognize had forced me to open my eyes slowly, and the scent of antiseptic wafting in the air greeted me. I shut my eyes again at the glaring light above me, then took a deep breath and tried to readjust my vision. When I opened them, I looked around to see if I was finally home, just as a woman in blue scrubs entered.

"How are you feeling?" the nurse asked. "We called your emergency contact, and your husband, Dr. Miller, should be here any minute. I'm Mar by the way," she added.

I was so confused. *What happened to me? Where was Jim?* I could have sworn I was with him. I felt groggy, and the more I looked around, the more my head hurt, so I closed my eyes again.

"Oh, my God! Sweetheart! Are you okay?" Jim's voice jolted my good eye back open. *God, it hurts.*

He pulled a chair, sat beside me, brought my hand to his chest, and practically jumped as soon as the doctor entered the room. My vision was blurry, but I could tell it was an older gentleman with dark hair, streaked with gray at the temples, dressed in a white lab coat. I couldn't quite make out what he had on underneath—scrubs, something more formal. I closed my eyes to ease the sudden dizziness.

"Is she going to be okay? How's her head injury? Is it serious?" Jim said in a high-pitched voice I'd never heard before.

I was still confused, and I still couldn't remember exactly what had happened. I touched my throbbing head and felt the bandage on the side, then I heard the doctor's raspy voice.

"She will be all right. There's a laceration on her left cheek, a cut on her bottom lip, and she must have been hit with something on her right temple just below the hairline, but I can't tell with what. Her left eye is quite swollen; I'm not sure how she got that. If you were to ask me, it looks like someone has beaten up your wife," the doctor explained.

"God, who would do such a thing?" Jim asked, shaking his head in disbelief.

"We did a head CT, and everything is clear. Just some contusions."

"Did she tell you what happened?" Jim asked as both men walked out of the room.

The doctor shook his head. "I heard she walked here. We assumed she was mugged."

"And she doesn't remember," Jim said, sounding more like a statement than a question.

"It is not unusual for someone to have some temporary memory loss after a traumatic incident, you know that. I'm sure you see that a lot in your patients."

"Yes. Yes, I do. What about her medications?" he asked, taking a quick glance at me through the glass window.

"She was given some strong pain medication, but aside from that, all should be okay." The doctor lowered his voice, but I could still hear him. "I thought I'd wait for you, but have you called the cops yet?"

Jim steered the doctor farther away, but I could still see them nodding and looking back at me from time to time. Their voices started to fade. I wondered what he told them. If I were mugged, I was sure Jim had probably already called the cops, but where were they?

The doctor left, and Jim came back in, held my hand, and sat next to me just as another nurse came to check my vitals. She gave Jim a faint smile.

"Thank you so much for caring for my wife."

The nurse nodded. "All good, Mrs. Miller. I'll be back in a little while to check on you."

"Thank you," I tried to say, but my swollen lip made me sound like Daffy Duck with a mouthful of cotton balls. I almost laughed—if it didn't hurt so badly.

She glanced at Jim and then at me. "If you need anything, anything at all, you just press the buzzer."

With that, she left me wondering if there was more to what she said.

A displeased look formed on Jim's face. He shook it off before addressing me. "The doctor will administer some medication later to help you with the pain. It'll help you sleep. I should go back home and get some rest. I pushed all my morning sessions so I can be here as soon as you wake up, okay, *sweetheart*? The doctor said, you can go home tomorrow."

Something just didn't feel right. I reached for the bed remote, pressed the button to sit up, and asked. "Jim, what happened to me?"

"Sweetheart, you poor thing, you don't remember. You were mugged outside our home." He ran his fingers through my hair.

His touch made me cringe, as if it were foreign to me. I closed my eyes, trying to remember. When I opened them, I stared at the ceiling. "All I remembered was that we were on our way home from dinner... we were in the car... I think. I think I've upset you..." I shut my eyes again. "Then—"

"Yes, honey. We were out to dinner celebrating your deal with Ja—" He huffed. "With Mr. Adler, your client. We were celebrating your new deal with him, remember? You paid more attention to him and ignored me as if I wasn't there, so I was a little jealous, but you explained that it was nothing, and I felt better," he rambled, then smiled, touching my face.

Again, his touch repulsed me. I couldn't explain why. "I sort of remember it, but in bits and pieces," I replied.

"Then my phone rang, *remember*? In the car? A client was having a nervous breakdown, and I had to rush to the office and meet him. That's when I dropped you in front of the house. In fact, you insisted that I drop you off. I wanted to take you with me, but you told me a migraine was coming on and you wanted to sleep it off."

I kept my eyes shut, trying to remember him getting a phone call and dropping me off. Nothing was coming to my memory.

"*Sweetheart*, open your eyes," he tried to say, but his gritted teeth made it sound like a command, no matter how much he tried to hide it.

I opened my eyes.

"Listen to me, you just experienced a traumatic event. It is very common to be confused. You might even get your memory all screwed up. That's okay; I'm here to help you get better. Why don't you sleep now? I'll come back first thing tomorrow morning. In the meantime, make sure you don't speak to anyone about what happened until I'm here; we don't want you telling things that may not be true," Jim instructed.

He must have seen the confusion on my face.

"Because of your memory, *sweetheart*. Remember, a traumatic experience. That means you may get your memories confused. You should know—you were a psych major."

It was hard for me to discern whether he was trying to appease me or put me down. Still, I nodded, though I knew there was so much gaslighting behind his tone and the fact that he was emphasizing the 'sweetheart' part.

"Good girl. I love you." He kissed my forehead and then walked out of the room.

Outside by the counter was the nurse who had come in earlier. Her eyes followed Jim with what looked like contempt as he left. Then she glanced back in my direction. This time, her eyes dropped before proceeding with whatever she was doing.

Something wasn't right; I could feel it.

Chapter Ten

JENNA

PAST

I must have fallen asleep after Jim had left because the next time I opened my eyes, the same nurse from earlier was standing next to my bed holding a tablet. Though I felt the room spinning as I moved, I grabbed the remote and pressed the button to raise me so I could talk to her. She appeared to be in her early forties, with dark, attractive eyes, long black hair tied in a ponytail, and probably stood 5 feet 4 inches tall. The badge clipped on her scrub said—*Ragmar De Los Santos. What a unique name.*

"Mrs. Miller, it's time for your medication, but I thought I'd ask how you feel first. Are you in pain?" she asked as she checked the IV bag attached to me.

"A little, but it's tolerable. Didn't I get some meds when I got here?"

"Dr. Rhoda Kew prescribed morphine last night when you were admitted, but Dr. Miller, your husband, said you have been having trouble sleeping at home for weeks and made sure we give you another dose to help you sleep. He said you have had some bouts of depression on and off. Is that correct? I don't see it on your chart," she said, now scrolling down on the tablet's screen in her hand.

My head started spinning, and it wasn't from the injuries I'd sustained or the medication she gave me. *Why would Jim say those things? I wasn't having trouble sleeping. I wasn't depressed. So, what was he trying to do?* Bits of the evening started coming back. I remembered him saying I was sick—he said it at dinner. Was that how I ended up in the hospital?

Sensing my confusion, Mar set the tablet on the table next to me and closed the door. "Mrs. Miller. Do you remember what happened to you?"

"My husband said I was mugged outside our home," I replied, clutching the blanket to my chest.

"Were you?"

What kind of question was that? There was also uncertainty in her tone, as if she didn't want to offend me.

"I don't know. I can't remember. Why would you ask that?" I was taken aback by her question, and suddenly the temperature in the room seemed to have gotten colder.

"I am sticking my neck out here, and I could get myself in a lot of trouble, but I think there's more to your story than what you were told, Mrs. Miller. Do you remember being mugged?" This time, she didn't hold back.

I tried to recall and then shook my head.

"What was the last thing you remember before walking in here?" she prodded.

"I *walked* here?" I asked, furrowing my eyebrows, but immediately relaxed as I felt the pain in my head.

"*Yes*, you walked in, bleeding and disoriented, and before passing out, you mumbled something about being hit by someone. What was the last thing you remember?" she asked again, leaning in closer as she took a slow breath, as if she knew something I didn't.

"I remember having dinner with a client and some of my associates. Then Jim..." I choked on my words. "My husband and I drove home. I think we were arguing about something," I finished.

The nurse adjusted the blanket, which had slipped, exposing my right foot, then looked me straight in the eye. "Mrs. Miller..." She hesitated, then continued. "Do you know who hurt you?"

At first, I felt defensive about her insinuation. Then, I thought back on the few times Jim had slapped me, and that's when it all started flooding back. Even though I didn't want to, I nodded.

Suddenly, I could feel Jim's palm meeting my face, my ears ringing, and my head hitting something; it must have been the car door or the window. I was unsure, but whatever it was, it was sharp. There was blood. I could taste it, and there was blood trickling down my face, too. My heart raced as if wanting to burst out of my chest. Suddenly, I couldn't breathe.

"Who hit you, Mrs. Miller?"

The side of my head throbbed. I touched the bandage on my temple, trying to catch more air that suddenly had eluded me. Once I was able to take a few shaky breaths, I said, "I must have blacked out because the next thing I remember..." I swallowed hard, remembering the feeling I felt that night. My heart rate accelerated, causing the machine next to me to beep loudly.

"Take a deep breath. Slow, slow, Mrs. Miller." Mar placed an oxygen mask on my face.

My heart sank to the ground at my sudden realization. "Oh my God! Jim told me he dropped me off at home after dinner," I mumbled, pulling the mask to the side.

"Jim, as in your husband, Dr. Miller?"

I could feel the anger in Mar's voice.

"Yes, he *did* drop me off... But not at home. He dropped me off somewhere else. I don't remember where." I shut my eyes, trying to retrieve whatever information my brain would allow me, pulling the blanket up absentmindedly.

"I remember walking for a while, and then I got dizzy, so I sat on a bench... I think. I heard water, like a rushing fountain. I think it was behind me. Somehow, I knew the hospital was nearby, so I forced myself to walk a little further. I think—"

"You must have been dropped off at the park next block over. There's a fountain there," the nurse interjected.

I didn't want to, but I opened my eyes at the sudden realization. "Oh my God, you're right. He dropped me off at the Fountain Park. But why?" My eyes and face hurt as I squinted and wrinkled my forehead.

My husband hurting me, dropping me somewhere at night all alone, disoriented and bleeding, was tough to swallow. How could he have done that to me? My own husband.

I knew Mar could get in trouble for what I was about to ask her, but something in my gut told me she was trying to help.

"I want to leave now," I announced, snatching the mask off my face.

"Mrs. Miller, please don't—" Mar started to say as she attempted to place the mask back on my face, trying to calm me down.

"Jenna, please call me Jenna." A sudden burst of adrenaline rushed through me.

"Okay. Jenna, I understand you want to handle this alone, but there's help out there. You *can* get out of your situation. There are people we can call. You can stay in a shelter where you can be safe, but first, we must call the police."

"No! No police," I said firmly, knowing she was obligated to report such an incident.

Even though Jim hurt me, I still didn't want to see him behind bars. He was still my husband after all. I started to get up and fiddled with the IV connected to my arm. "Please. I don't want to go to a shelter. I want to leave," I begged.

She held my hand. "Is there someone we can call for you besides your husband?" Mar asked, defeat scribbled across her face.

I paused and thought of whom I could call. "Yes, I can call my friend, Ann." I looked around for my phone, but it wasn't there.

"Where is my purse?" I asked, searching the room.

"I don't recall seeing a purse with you when you came in." She let go of my hand and picked up an extra blanket that was on the chair next to me. No phone there.

Jim. He must've made sure I didn't have it with me. I let out a breath, shoulders sinking as I pulled the blanket down. I didn't even know what I wanted in that moment—just that I was flustered, unsettled.

"Jenna, if you don't want to go to a shelter, you can stay with me if you like; at least I can keep an eye on you, and then I can drop you off at your friends when you feel better. I'm clocking out at five; it's already a quarter till. We can go as soon as you're ready. We can't wait till the morning; your husband might be back by then."

Leaving Jim? My head screamed yes, but my heart whispered no. I should keep my distance until I figure out my next move, but what was my next move? *Divorce?* My spirit sank to the ground. No, I couldn't.

"Okay. I'll go with you."

Chapter Eleven

JENNA

PAST

It had been a few days since I left the hospital, and Nurse Mar had been gracious enough to let me stay in her spare bedroom. Part of me wanted to call Jim and let him know I was all right, but Mar was adamant that it was safer this way. Plus, I didn't have my phone with me. Jim must have taken it with him, together with my purse, or I must have left it in the car.

While Mar returned to work the following day, I stayed with her mother, Flor, short for Florentina. With a grown daughter and grandkids, Flor still looked young—in her late sixties, she told me, but she could pass for someone in their fifties. She was probably five feet tall with a short, platinum, wispy haircut—the woman was beautiful.

That morning, I walked out of Nurse Mar's guest room and found her mother in the kitchen, washing dishes. "Good morning," I greeted her.

"Good morning. I hope you slept well," she greeted back, smiling. There was something very welcoming about her.

"Oh, I did. Thank you," I lied. All night, all I did was think about what Jim had done and what I would do next.

"Please have a seat. Let me get you some breakfast. Mar dropped the girls off at school and went to the hospital. She'll be back right away."

"Flor, thank you so much for letting me stay here. I'm not sure if Mar told you about what's going on, but—"

"We don't keep secrets around here, dear. Not anymore, at least, but *your* secret is safe with me," she said with her sweet Filipino accent. I was familiar with the Filipino accent from my friends in Temecula and Hannah talking about her Filipino family.

The smile she had was contagious. She looked as if she enjoyed every little thing she did as she placed a plate of fried eggs, sausage, and fried rice in front of me. Her every move was a graceful dance in the kitchen; it made me smile, missing my mother. She would have taken good care of me, but I couldn't tell her what was going on. "Eat, you need to get your strength back," she said in a motherly tone, instantly making me miss my mom more. Gosh, I needed her at that moment. I wanted to call my family, but I couldn't yet. I couldn't take any chances. Flor must have seen the question on my face as I spooned some rice on my plate, slowly picked up a piece of red sausage link with my fork, and held it in front of me, studying it.

"It's a hot dog from the Philippines, and that's garlic fried rice. Trust me, it's good," she announced, smiling, revealing cute dimples.

"I've never seen a red-colored hot dog before," I confessed.

"It's weird, right? But it's good. We call it tender juicy in the Philippines." She laughed. I laughed with her; she was so cute. Flor was right; the food was great. We talked for a while, and our conversation led us to why Mar had been so adamant about helping me and why she hadn't thought twice about offering her home to me.

"It took a while before Mar decided to leave Manuel. It wasn't until her second daughter was born that she dared to leave the situation. Manuel used to hit her all the time in front of the girls.

"That's awful," I said, holding a cup of coffee Flor had prepared for me. She told me it was from a town in the Philippines famous for its coffee beans. It was a little strong for my taste, but it tasted good, soothing as it went down.

"You see, *my* Mar was a shy one. She didn't want to come with us when we migrated here years ago. She wanted to finish her studies in the Philippines, and when she finally came, we were so happy until she met Manuel. He was nice at first, but as their relationship progressed, I watched Mar cry more often. I told her to break it off with the guy, but you know how it is when you fall in love, nothing else matters." She shrugged as she wiped her wet hands on the towel hanging on the dishwasher. "Then she got pregnant. I told Mar I'd help her raise her baby, but she wanted a family."

"No wonder she wanted to help me so badly. I'm glad she got out of that situation." I sipped my coffee, feeling grateful and sad at the same time—a woman, a mother, had to go through something awful like that.

"It wasn't easy, and it took a while. Mar forgave that bastard repeatedly. He was always so sweet to her after doing some damage to her face, but I could see right through him. I told her if she didn't leave him, she would end up dead one day, and that rattled something in her brain because one day, she just left him, but Manuel followed and promised her he would change.

When that didn't work, he would threaten her, but my Mar didn't back down. She filed for a restraining order and worked with the police. She then got involved with a women's group for battered women. They helped her get away from him, and finally, he signed the divorce papers, and Mar got full custody of the girls."

Hearing Mar's story made me wonder if I was as strong as she was. One thing I was thankful for was not having kids to worry about. I wouldn't know what to do if I had to go through this with my children. I let the thoughts go as I remembered that I'd been wanting to ask about Mar's name.

"Flor, how did Mar get her name? It's unique," I said, breaking our conversation from Mar's awful experience.

Flor smiled. "In the Philippines, it's common to put two names of people who mean a lot to you, like your parents or grandparents. *Rag* is part of my dad's name, and *Mar* is part of my husband's father's name. So, we named her *Ragmar,*" she explained, chuckling.

Interesting. I nodded and smiled.

"Your husband was at the hospital bright and early, as I suspected. He was pretty upset to find you gone," Mar announced as she waltz into the kitchen in her plain clothes, making me whip my head around.

My chest tightened. "Did he say anything?"

"Oh, he had plenty to say, all right. Aside from insulting the nurses, he also threatened to sue the hospital. Accusing us of patient negligence. He quickly shut up, though, when we showed him that you checked out voluntarily," Mar said, feistiness in her tone.

She set some brochures on the counter in front of me, picked up a piece of a hot dog from the table, and took a bite. I brushed my hand on one of the brochures. *What to do when you suspect Domestic Violence.* The sudden realization that I was one of these women left an unexplained feeling inside me. No one expected these things to happen to them. I had always thought I was a strong and independent woman who could stand up for herself, but when I fell in love with Jim, something in me changed as if I wasn't in control of myself any longer.

"Those are the shelters you can stay in if you decide to leave him, which I strongly encourage you to do. I know it's easier said than done, but you should really think about it." Mar gently placed a hand on my shoulder. "I'll help you. Here are some phone numbers of people who could help us if you decide to file a restraining order or... file for divorce." She pulled a sheet from the bottom pile of papers she had placed before me.

"Thank you. I really appreciate this," I said sincerely, despite feeling off. I didn't believe in divorce, and I had never thought I would be in this situation.

"Of course. If there's anything you need while you're here, please let us know."

"Actually, there is one. Can I borrow a phone?"

Mar's reaction changed in an instant, and she gave me a suspicious look. "Jenna—"

"No, I'm not calling Jim. I need to call work and let them know I won't be around for a while. Don't worry, I'll inform them of the situation." I reassured her.

She smiled reluctantly and handed me the phone. I punched the gallery's number, and after a couple of rings, Deanna answered.

"Hey, how are you feeling?" she asked, her voice was an octave too high than what I was used to, sweet and shaky, like she was trying too hard to sound concerned.

The question threw me off. There was no *What happened to you? Where are you? Why weren't you at work for days?* Her question was *How are you feeling?* as if she already knew something had happened to me.

"How—" I started to say.

"Jim called the other day, saying you were taken to the hospital. That you were mugged or something after our dinner with Mr. Adler," she explained, almost sounding like she was bored with me. There had always been something I couldn't quite put my finger on about Deanna. She'd only been at the gallery a few months, but I'd noticed her moods swinging up and down, though she always managed to pull herself back together. There was a watchfulness in her, like she was constantly waiting for something to go wrong. Or for someone to catch her in the middle of a lie she hadn't told yet.

I pulled my attention back to Deanna on the phone.

"I'm doing okay, Deanna. I will, however, be out for a while—"

"Where are you?" she interrupted. I tightened my grip on the phone and let out a breath. Her interruptions weren't a surprise; it was Deanna's annoying flaw. I had to constantly remind her not to interrupt when a client was speaking, but at times, there was no stopping her.

"I'm still at the hospital." I lied, giving a fake smile as if she could see me—a habit.

"Ann and I will come and visit you after work."

"Deanna, listen. My doctor required me to rest. So that means no visitors. I'll text you when visitors are allowed, okay? But for now, can you and Ann hold the fort while I'm gone?"

"Of course. Jenna, I'm sorry this happened to you. Ann and I are really worried about you."

I could hear some rustling noise and pictured Ann pressing her ear to the phone next to her.

"Is Ann next to you?"

"Umm... yeah, she is," Deanna replied with some hesitancy. Deanna somehow had the notion that we were the best of friends, even though Ann had been with me since I opened the gallery. Still, from time to time, I sensed Deanna's jealousy toward her.

"Can I talk to her?"

Silence.

"Hey, Jenna. Are you okay? I'm so worried about you," Ann finally asked after a long pause.

Right away, I noticed the difference in how she asked and how Deanna did. Ann sounded genuinely concerned about my well-being. "Ann, I'm okay. I will be away for a while, as per the doctor's order. Anyway, I asked Deanna if you guys can hold the fort while I'm gone."

"Jenna, you didn't have to ask, you know that."

"I know, but I want to make sure I told you. You know how Deanna can be." She knew I meant that Deanna can be flaky.

Deanna and I talked again for a bit, and after we hung up, something felt... off. There was something in Deanna's voice that bothered me. I couldn't pinpoint what it was. Before she hung up, she told me she loved me; that was new. Ann and I had always told each other that, but not Deanna. Then she said she'd take care of the gallery, not to worry, and for me to take my time. It almost sounded as if she was excited that I would be gone for a while.

A knock on the door shook my thoughts aside; Mar and I exchanged looks.

It couldn't be.

Chapter Twelve

JENNA

PAST

"Stay here," Mar said.

I hid behind a bookshelf and watched Mar through the mirror on the wall. She opened the door. I listened to their exchange.

"Why would she be here? No, I don't know where she is," Mar said.

Then I heard Jim's voice. He was calm, but I knew deep inside he wanted to yell at Mar. I could see his jaw muscle tensing.

"I know she's here. Someone from the hospital told me she walked out with you, nurse... *Mar,* is it? What kind of name is that? Anyway..." There was a pause as if Jim waited for Mar to retaliate to his petulant insult, but no words came out of her; I was sure her eyes said it all. I've seen it at the hospital when she watched Jim leave. If looks could kill, Jim would have been dead.

I wanted to give her an 'attagirl', but instead, I found myself holding my breath, waiting for Jim's response.

"If you don't tell me where she is, I will be forced to file a kidnapping charge, and you will go to jail. Do you want that?" Jim threatened.

Mar wasn't shaken. Instead, she gave a huff and a devious smile. "Go ahead, call the police, Dr. Miller. Then I can tell them how you beat your wife and left her on the streets to wander alone in the middle of the night," she said, her voice controlled and steady.

Silence.

She knew she hit the right spot.

Jim took a deep breath and exhaled forcefully. "Preposterous. Jenna suffered from dissociative fugue. Often, she wanders around, not knowing where she is or who she is," he hissed.

Dissociative fugue? What?! Why would he say that? I wanted to dash out and confront him, but I held my breath and waited for whatever else he said.

"Are you serious?" Mar hissed, clearly not believing the BS she had just heard.

"Who would believe you anyhow? I'm a pillar of the community. A philanthropist, and you are just a—"

"A *what*, Dr. Miller?" She scowled at him. "*A nurse? A woman* who would stand up and fight for what is right? Say whatever you want to say, Dr. Miller. You won't get away with this." Mar retaliated.

Jim laughed, a laugh that grated on my nerves like nails on a chalkboard, and though I knew it was his way of disguising defeat, I knew it was about to get personal. I sank lightly, barely able to stand at the thought of what Jim could do.

That was it. I couldn't let Mar be involved with our mess any longer, not when she'd been through a lot. She'd been through this before, and I couldn't let her go through it again, especially when she had a family to protect.

I straightened my shoulders, at least I tried to, and took a deep breath. Then I stepped out from behind the shelf. "I'm here," I said, hoping my voice didn't tremble as much as I felt it did.

Jim's eyes were on me as Mar's head jerked in my direction.

"Jenna. You don't have to—"

"It's okay, Mar. I have to go back home sooner or later," I said softly, blinking hard to keep my tears from falling.

"No, you don't." She insisted as she came closer, grabbing my hands.

"I'm so sorry. I shouldn't have gotten you involved in my mess in the first place. Don't worry, I'll be okay."

With that, I hugged her and walked toward Jim. He smiled, looped his arm in mine, and grinned, showing Mar he'd won the fight.

I looked back over my shoulder and couldn't help but finally shed a tear for Mar's kindness. "Please tell your mom I said thank you," I said over my shoulder as Jim practically dragged me to the car.

She nodded, looking defeated, but something in me knew she understood.

Chapter Thirteen

JENNA

PAST

Months later, I lit some candles and dimmed the lights; it was romantic, at least I had thought so. It had been a few months since the last incident, and yet I kept in touch with Mar and her mom in secret. They still tried to convince me to get away and would always tell me I had a place in their home whenever I needed to escape, but the last few months since that awful day had been great. Jim had been very affectionate and sensitive to my needs; it felt like the first few months after we got married. Maybe he learned his lessons, I told myself.

I heard the door close, followed by his footsteps, so I took off my apron and straightened myself in my newly bought yellow floral maxi dress. When he opened the door, he studied the room, kissing me on the cheek, and looked me up and down, checking my outfit.

"What's going on?" He smiled, bewildered.

"I made a special dinner for you. We are celebrating."

"Celebrating what?"

"Why don't you sit down?" I pulled a chair for him to sit in.

He walked past me and walked toward the bedroom instead. "Let me get comfortable, and I'll join you in a bit." He looked over his shoulder toward the table I had set up. "Bring out the wine. We can't celebrate whatever it is we're celebrating without wine."

When he came back out, I was already at the table. I poured a glass of Merlot and placed it in front of him.

Jim eyed my glass and furrowed his brows. Jim wasn't fooled.

"Cranberry juice," I replied to his unasked question.

"Are you sick?"

Jim had become more attentive when I wasn't feeling well, which confused the heck out of me. If he truly cared about how I felt, which at certain moments it really felt like he did, then why had he allowed himself to hurt me as he had? I shook the thought aside and reminded myself that he had changed and that we were moving on.

"I'm fine." I smiled. "In fact, I am more than fine... I'm pregnant." I sounded overly excited and hopeful, but deep down, I was also worried about how he would react to the news.

Jim stared at me. It wasn't quite the response I'd hoped for, but I had heard that some men just didn't know how to respond to this kind of situation, so I gave him time to absorb the news, holding my breath.

Finally, I saw a twinkle in his eyes as his lips curved into a smile. "Are you serious?"

Whew. I nodded and smiled.

Jim shot up from his chair and pulled my chair a little too fast, so I instinctively braced myself, holding my stomach.

"I'm sorry. Did I hurt you?" He backed off a little, then gently placed his hand on my shoulder. "Come here, babe. I just want to hug my beautiful *pregnant* wife. I'm going to be a dad." His voice was full of comfort, gentleness, and... love.

"It will be a boy." He touched my flat belly. I was only about six weeks along, not enough to show the sex yet, but Jim was convinced, nevertheless. I didn't know how to react to that. I felt uneasy at how he unequivocally claimed the sex of our baby.

A couple of weeks had passed, and I started to worry. *What if it wasn't a boy? Would he still love our baby?* This question haunted me. Jim had adamantly claimed it was a boy and had referred to our baby as such since I told him. If I were to have a girl, what would he think? I dreaded the thought of how he would react.

"You'd better watch what you eat; you're getting big," he told me as I was trying to zip up my pants. I was at the beginning of the second trimester, and my pants started to get a little tight.

"Hey there, son. You'd better stay strong and healthy. Don't let Mommy take all the nutrients, okay? We don't want her fat, anyhow."

I forced a smile, trying my best not to deserve a blow to the face, even though my hormones had kicked in and wanted to scream at him. Yes, I was still cautious, especially in the last few months. Jim had been under a lot of stress at work, and I wondered when the next blow would come. Even though he hadn't shown any signs of anger lately, it still felt like waiting for a ticking time bomb—it could explode at any time.

Chapter Fourteen

JENNA

PAST

Jim had been very supportive. He'd been serving me hand and foot. He loved talking to my belly—to his *son.* A knot in my stomach formed every time he referred to our baby, his son, almost confirming my fear of having a daughter. I just had a strong feeling that I was having a girl.

The TV blasted in the background while Jim and I sat on the couch with my feet on his lap, Jim rubbing my feet.

"Roland!" Out of the blue, he blurted out.

"I'm sorry?"

"Roland. That's the name of our son. Roland, after my grandfather," he announced.

"Jim, don't you think we should discuss this?" The knot in my stomach was back. I thought it was my baby protesting as if to say, *I'm a girl, daddy.* "I had been thinking of names, too, but we haven't really discussed it together."

"What's wrong with Roland?" He frowned, and his grip on my foot started getting tighter than I would have liked.

"Nothing. Roland is nice, but I think we should come up with other names, you know? So, we have options," I mumbled, trying to pull my foot out of his hand, but he held on. I told myself he wouldn't hurt me. I was carrying his child, but there was still fear inside me, knowing that this time, if he laid a hand on me, he wouldn't just hurt me, he'd hurt my baby, too.

"Okay. What other names do you have in mind?" he asked, relaxing his grip a little.

"What about Eugene?"

"Eugene? Nah, I think Roland would be a much better name for our son. *Roland Miller*. It has a nice ring to it. Plus, he would be named after my grandfather, who was a great man. A great psychiatrist like me," he explained, his eyes focused on the TV, but I knew he hadn't been watching whatever show was on.

Jim did tell me about his grandfather and how great he was. He told me how his grandfather started from nothing and made a name for himself, just like he did. According to him, his grandfather inspired Jim to become a psychiatrist.

"What if we're having a girl?"

His grip became tighter again.

"I'm pretty sure we're having a boy," he declared, dropped my legs on the couch, got up, and made himself a drink before heading to his office, slamming the door behind him like a petulant child.

A few weeks later, I found myself pacing outside the clinic after my prenatal appointment.

Congratulations, you're having a girl, my obstetrician had announced as she moved the transducer around my bulging belly. I was overjoyed, and tears fell down my face as I watched the image on the monitor, but why did I feel like I'd done something wrong? My happiness was replaced with fear, and my stomach churned. I dreaded going home. I didn't know how I would break the news to Jim.

I finally gathered the courage to step out of the clinic, and just as I opened the door, Jim did, too. The heat in his eyes stopped me cold, like a dragon about to scorch everything in its path.

He stepped aside and waited for me to exit the clinic. "Why didn't you tell me the appointment was moved to today?" He tried to conceal his emotions as another couple walked out the door after me.

"I did," I said in a low voice as I rushed to the car, trying to avoid a scene. "I even told you I would meet you here, remember?" I lied. I lied because I didn't want him with me when I found out the gender of our baby. I lied because I was pretty sure we were having a girl, call it mother's intuition.

"No, Jenna. You didn't tell me that. The appointment was supposed to be next week." He gritted his teeth.

How he found out I had an appointment today, I wouldn't know. My chest tightened.

"So?" he prodded as if I should have provided him with more information.

I knew what he was asking, but I just couldn't. "Everything is fine. The baby is healthy," I said as I opened the driver's side door and climbed into my car.

"Did you find out the baby's gender?" he asked, holding the door open.

My heart thudded. "No. Not yet. It's too early," I said calmly, trying not to stammer, my hands gripping the steering wheel.

To my surprise, he let it go, bent down, and kissed me on the head. "I'll see you at home."

Trying to distract myself, I called my mother as soon as I got home. She was so excited, telling me a few tricks to get over the morning sickness I was still having. She mentioned her plans to see us soon and how she would spoil her future granddaughter. After almost an hour on the phone, I told her I missed and loved her, and she said the same before we hung up. I had never mentioned anything about Jim.

I decided I needed to relax after my encounter at the clinic and with Jim, so I drew a bubble bath to help ease the pain I was starting to feel in my legs. I wasn't that big yet, but my body was reacting to the changes already. I lit a few lavender candles and played soothing music, trying to forget the day I had. I played the image of my daughter on the sonogram in my head; she was beautiful. I dimmed the lights, unrobed, and slowly slipped into the tub. My hands rested on my belly, instinctively protective. I lay my head on the white rolled towel I placed on the tub's edge and closed my eyes, hearing my baby's rapid heartbeat in my head. The warm water and the lavender milk bath I had poured earlier helped me relax as I submerged my whole body in the water, but no matter how I tried not to, I kept wondering how Jim found out I went to the clinic.

I felt guilty about finding the gender without him, but I was just too afraid of how he would react. I thought I'd find out first and then slowly get him used to the reality. Instead, I lied when I knew better. Jim knew that by the second trimester, one could already tell the baby's gender. After all, he went to med school. There was no going back now, so I took a deep breath and tried to forget that part of the day.

Suddenly, I was underwater, struggling to breathe. I fought the heavy hand pushing me and tried to get my head above water, coughing and spitting the water that I had swallowed, and then my head went back under. It took all my strength to push the hand away the second time, and when I finally did, I woke up screaming, sweating, if that was even possible underwater. My heart was going a million beats per minute, and I gasped for air as if I were still underwater. I had fallen asleep, and it was all a dream. *Thank God.* But it felt real, and I couldn't help but feel like an impending doom was about to happen.

I forced myself to calm down as I lay in the tub holding my belly. I was still pregnant. The dream was so vivid. Thank God it was all but a nightmare. A terrifying nightmare. Suddenly, the water had turned cold, and the bath no longer felt relaxing, so I stood and decided to tell Jim about our daughter, perhaps to apologize for not telling him about the appointment. I was still standing in the tub naked when the door flung open.

"A girl!" Jim yelled, gritting his teeth.

"Jim, Honey—" I snapped my head in his direction.

He leaned in closer. "You found out, and you didn't tell me! A girl. *A girl*, Jenna?!" He screamed, sounding as if having a girl was some fatal disease.

"Yes, Hon, we're having a girl. Aren't you happy?" I started to rise from the tub, but his anger hung in the air; it held me down.

"Why didn't you tell me?"

"Can you hand me my robe first, please?" I pointed to my white robe hanging on the wall.

He didn't flinch.

"Answer me," he growled. His eyes were burning with contempt and... I couldn't believe it—*disgust.* That's what I saw on his face as he realized we were having a daughter—he was disgusted. Right then and there, my heart broke into pieces.

I fought back the tears that were threatening to fall at any moment. "I was afraid. You were so adamant that we're having a boy that I was scared—"

"*Scared?!*"

I flinched.

"Scared that what Jenna? That I won't love our baby because it's a damn girl? Do you really think I'm that big of a monster?"

I wanted to say yes.

"Jim." I tried to soothe him and tried reach for my robe. Suddenly, a bright light came through the window, and my chest tightened.

"Don't Jim me, *Jenna.* You lied to me. Do you think I'm stupid? That I wouldn't know? I'm a doctor, Jenna," he yelled, yanking the robe away from me as I stepped out of the tub, and just like that, my foot slipped, slamming my back onto the cold, hard tiles, just as the rain poured and the thunder bellowed.

Jim just stood over me as I tried to brace myself to stand, and that's when I felt it—wetness trickling down my legs. I closed my eyes, took a deep breath, and prayed that it was just the water from the tub, but I knew better. I could feel it—*Impending doom.*

"No! No! No! Jim, call 9-1-1!" I cried. "Call 9-1-1!"

Jim stood frozen, contemplating what to do next, fury still etched on his face as I lay on the cold, wet floor.

"Jim! Help! Please help!"

Another roar shook the room, forcing him to snap out of whatever trance he was in, and he slowly walked out the door with the phone in his hand.

Yes, hello. I came home, and I found my wife on the bathroom floor. I think she slipped while trying to get out of the tub... No, she's conscious, but she's bleeding. She's pregnant.

Suddenly, the tone changed. *Please hurry! I don't want to lose our baby girl. Please hurry! Send the ambulance to 98 Fieldbrook Court. Hurry!*

Chapter Fifteen

JENNA

PRESENT

*M*y hands were now enveloped in Hannah's. I hadn't realized tears were flowing down my face as I told the worst part of my story, for the first time.

"You didn't tell me," Hannah whispered.

"I know. I couldn't." I stood to look for a tissue, but Oliver immediately handed one to me.

"I'm so sorry, Kate—Jenna. You've been carrying this load inside you all these years." He shook his head. "Trust me, this guy will pay," Oliver added, a juxtaposition of empathy and anger emanating from his words.

Michael was silent. He just stared at me, but I could see the compassion in his eyes. I could also see... anger. Anger that he seemed to be trying very hard to keep inside.

"Thank you." It was all I could say.

How could I possibly explain that I missed a baby I never met? That I dreamed of my little girl every night? That I pictured her face, wondering how she might look today?

"Honey, we can continue tomorrow if you want—"

"No, I'm okay. Let's get it over with." I didn't think I could start again after telling them the worst part. I wanted to finish, and I hoped I wouldn't have to tell another soul again.

Hannah nodded as she squeezed my hands. "So, how did you end up in Sacramento?"

"After I found out I lost my baby girl, I decided Mar was right. I should've walked away from him a long time ago. It was difficult this time around because Jim learned from his mistake the first time and never left me in the hospital."

"And the doctors believed it was an accident?" Michael asked, dumbfounded. His tone was sharp, though I knew he didn't mean to snap at me.

"At first. Until Mar showed up with the cops later," I said softly, now tracing the rim of my wine glass.

"The nurse," Hannah said, and I nodded. "Was he arrested?"

"He was questioned, but they said there was no evidence of abuse. It was Mar's words against Jim's, and Jim was known to the community. He knew all the doctors at the hospital, so they believed his lies."

"Bastards." Oliver downed his newly poured whiskey.

"So, what happened next?" Michael asked.

"Jim decided to work from home. He must have decided not to see patients in person because no one came to the house. But I knew he had to leave sooner or later. He must have finally gotten bored one day because he grabbed his golf clubs one afternoon and walked out the door without saying a word. That's when I took my chance. Nurse Mar and some others from her group had been ready for weeks, just waiting for my call. At first, I moved to Moreno Valley, hoping he wouldn't find me there, but he did."

"Please don't tell me you went back," Oliver said with a contemptuous tone, but I understood.

"No. One day, on my way back from the grocery store, I saw him walk up to the apartment where I was staying, so I immediately got back in my car and drove away. I found a hotel, called Mar, and stayed the night. The next morning, they were at my door with everything I needed, including a new driver's license. I don't know how they got it so fast, but they did, and I didn't ask."

"How and when did you find out he found you here?" Michael asked, placing this empty glass on the table.

"I don't know when exactly or how, but I know he did. I started sensing his presence everywhere. I could feel someone watching me as I walked back to my car after work, and even at the apartment when I got home. I could feel his eyes on me; it gave me the creeps, but I had never actually seen him. Then, I've been getting hang-up calls, and finally, there have been flower deliveries at work and my apartment—flowers that I knew would only come from him: eleven white roses."

Hannah shook her head slowly, then knitted her brows together. "Why eleven?"

"He said a whole dozen was cliché. I'm sure it was his way of being neurotic."

"Wait, why stay in California? Why didn't you go out of state, where it would be twice as hard for him to find you?" Ol asked.

I sighed and let my gaze fall. "I couldn't get myself to move far away. Part of me was here. I wanted to stay around here to be close..." A lump formed in my throat, and I was unsure if I made sense to them. I looked up, and I could feel tears running down my face.

"Your baby," Hannah said softly, and all I could do was nod. "Oh, sweetheart," she added, holding back her own tears.

"Jim won't let go of her urn. He hid it from me." I choked on my words. "I was a mess for weeks. I couldn't eat, I couldn't sleep, I just wanted to stay in bed and cry."

I wasn't sure if Hannah and Oliver or Michael would understand. No one could understand the pain of losing an unborn child you loved so much unless they've been through it themselves. But it hurt. It hurt so badly that I didn't even know how to live anymore.

"Jim left me alone initially, but as time passed, he lost patience. He grabbed the urn and told me it wasn't healthy for me to keep seeing it. He said he'd give it back once I started taking care of myself again. So, I forced myself to get up, forced myself to eat even though I couldn't keep the food in me, yet I ate, but he still didn't tell me where he hid the urn. I had no choice but to leave my baby girl."

I wasn't sure if it was from his drink or what, but Michael's face turned red. "I think we've heard enough."

"You should get some rest. You're safe here," Hannah nudged me to go to my room. "I am so sorry you had to go through that alone. I wish you had told me, but I understand why you couldn't," she said before pulling me into her arms.

"Savannah Love," I whispered.

"I'm sorry?" Hannah pulled away from our embrace and stared into my teary eyes.

"Savannah Love was my baby girl's name."

Chapter Sixteen
MICHAEL
PRESENT

The more I listened to Kate, the more my blood pressure rose. I tried to stay composed, but her story could make anyone furious. To distract myself, I focused on her face instead, watching her expressions, hoping to learn something about her beyond the painful story she was trying to tell.

Oliver had never mentioned how beautiful Kate was. All he'd said was that I was in for a surprise, and he'd never really elaborated on that. I quickly deduced, after seeing her standing next to Hannah at the parking garage, that she was probably five feet six inches tall. Definitely an intriguing woman. Her hair, which flowed down to her shoulders, was red and orange—unsure what was going on with that, but somehow it didn't take away from her beauty. Her tantalizing brown eyes glistened as she told her story, whether it was from the light above her or the welled-up tears, I couldn't tell, probably both.

I imagined her pale white skin was soft. Kate wore a massive pair of eyeglasses, and I caught her studying me from behind that god-awful pair—clearly a disguise. Yet even with the façade, her beauty and sex appeal radiated through the room, making me wonder what she truly looked like beneath it. Also, seeing her made me wonder how anyone could treat her the way her husband did. The thought made my blood boil. It took all my strength not to punch something as I listened to her tell her dreadful story. I could see she was in so much pain. Women are to be cherished, cared for, and loved—especially a woman like Kate or, as I had been told, *Jenna Miller.*

I quickly snapped out of it before my mind took me somewhere it shouldn't have. I was there to help this woman. It was just so damn hard to control my anger as I listened to how awful he'd treated her, but studying her face wasn't the proper diversion.

When my cousin Oliver called and asked if I could do him a favor, my answer was instantaneous: yes, because I could never say no to my favorite cousin. However, I said no when he told me what it would entail: going out of town with a woman trying to hide from her husband. It sounded like a babysitting gig to me.

"C'mon, Cuz, hear me out first. She needs protection, trust me. Her husband is a psychopath who has been stalking her. She's a good girl and a great friend, and you're the best at what you do. I need your help," Oliver explained.

I gave my cousin the benefit of the doubt and had him fill me in on this Kate lady. Suddenly, I found myself behind the steering wheel, following my cousin to the Grand Hotel, where they had placed Kate. After hearing part of her story, something in me churned. I usually required a whole backstory from clients before taking them in, so that I knew what or who I was dealing with. For the most part, I was never bothered by them or got involved; I provided protection, which was my job.

Kate's case was unlike any I had handled before. I'd protected high-profile politicians, witnesses in criminal cases, and even celebrities from the paparazzi, but Kate was different. She was special. Not just because my cousin Oliver had asked me to protect her, but because there was something special about her. I had to remind myself I was there to protect her; this was a job. She needed my service, *my* protection. But the more I studied her, the more I listened to her, the more I realized how beautiful she was, and how fragile she was at the same time. I had to focus; I couldn't jeopardize anything; her safety came first.

Midnight came, and I remained awake. After hearing Kate's entire story, my chest wouldn't stop pounding. I stared at the ceiling, trying to replay everything I had heard earlier in the night. How could someone do such a thing to someone, especially to a woman like Kate? *Jim Miller.* The name made my spine stiffen, and my fists clench. Who could sleep?

Then there were those pleading eyes—Kate's pleading eyes. I couldn't get them off my mind. There was pain in those brown eyes, and it bothered me. *Why did it bother me so much? Why did Kate affect me so quickly?* I shut my eyes tightly, hoping for a couple of hours of sleep, but it just never came. So, I grabbed my laptop and typed *Jim Miller.*

I found a few photos on the internet, but nothing suspicious or anything that would indicate this man was a stalker. In fact, some of the articles I found said the opposite: he was a philanthropist, loved by many. There were pictures of him at charity events, handing out oversized checks, smiling beside local politicians. Testimonials praised his generosity and his commitment to community work. He didn't look like someone who followed women home or watched them from across the street. But I wasn't buying any of it. His eyes told everything I needed to know; this man was a scumbag.

I kept scrolling, hoping to find older photos, perhaps from his high school or college years, but came up empty. Aside from a few posts from other people on social media, there was nothing from him directly. *Odd.* For someone who loved the limelight, he didn't have much to show. Well, that didn't say much. I didn't have social media either, but then again, I didn't like attention.

I jotted down some notes to give to Derrick, my private investigator. If anyone could find information about somebody, it would be him.

Chapter Seventeen
JENNA
PRESENT

I woke to the sound of chatter outside my room. I must have been more exhausted than I realized—it was nearly eight thirty in the morning when I checked the time on my phone. I stayed in bed a bit longer, letting the coolness of the sheets comfort me as I replayed the long night I had with Hannah and Oliver, and... Oliver's cousin, Michael. I wondered if he'd stayed over. There *was* an extra room. I shook the thought away and let myself sink into the soft mattress, just a while longer.

The night before was intense. It was the first time I had told anyone that I had lost a baby, not even my parents knew. I just ran away without any explanation. I did tell my mom that I will someday tell her everything. I suddenly felt a strong urge to be in her arms and let all the tears that had been building up fall—*someday soon.*

Pulling the blanket away, I decided to get up before I ended up spending the rest of the day in bed crying. I brushed my teeth, dabbed a little tinted sunscreen on my face, applied lip gloss, and brushed my now below-the-shoulder-length wavy red boxed-dyed hair. I paused to study myself in the mirror. I thought about cutting my hair short again. I didn't particularly like the color on me anyway: it was patchy—some areas bright red, others dark, and a few almost orange.

I skipped the blue contacts and stuck with my natural brown eyes. I wore a black-and-white floral skirt that flowed below my knees, a red shirt, and an oversized mustard-colored long-sleeve shirt left unbuttoned. White knee socks, chunky black loafers, and what Hannah and Oliver called my "God-forsaken" eyeglasses completed the look. Before stepping out of my room, I applied scented lotion to my hands and arms.

"Good morning; how did you sleep?" Hannah smiled in her yellow floral dress. She looked beautiful, making me miss the way I normally dressed. She sipped what I assumed was chai tea with ginger powder—her favorite drink.

"Good, surprisingly," I replied as I walked to the cart where a neatly arranged silver pot, platter of fruits, and croissants waited for me. I picked up the pot. "Is this coffee?"

"Yes, I hope it's still hot; there's hot water there also if you'd rather have tea," Hannah said.

I heard the balcony door slide open behind us as I poured water into a white porcelain cup.

"Alright, we got a plan,"

I turned at the sound of his voice—Michael approached and stood next to Ol. They were about the same height, six feet three inches. Michael made those ripped black jeans, the dark blue short-sleeved button-down shirt, and the once-white tennis shoes exude an unexpected elegance and class. It must have been the chiseled jaw, well-trimmed beard, and those dark, piercing brown eyes that flickered under the sunlight beaming through the glass window. His dark, curly hair was tied into a man bun. If it were under different circumstances, I'd actually find him attractive.

"How did you sleep?" Oliver asked.

Probably realizing I was in a different universe, Hannah, holding a mug, nudged me, snapping me out of my trance. "Hey."

"What?" I asked.

"I said: How did you sleep?" Oliver asked again with a grin.

"Oh, good," I replied with a sudden, high-pitched voice I had not heard before.

"Good morning," Michael said. He paused as if trying to sniff something in the air. "Is that Jasmin I smell?" he asked.

I stared blankly.

He stared back.

"Jenna," Hannah called out.

"Yes. Yes, uhm, it's my lotion." *There goes that high-pitched voice again. What the heck is going on with me?* "And... I mean, good morning to you, too," I added. I suddenly could feel my face heat up. "I'm so sorry," I stammered as I turned my attention to the cart in front of me and pretended to study the fruit platter.

I could feel him smiling behind me.

Goodness gracious, could this guy be any more handsome? His smile looked like it could melt a lady's undergarments. Okay, Jenna, get a grip.

Oliver picked up a white mug from the tray and poured some coffee into it. "Let's all sit down and formulate our thoughts. Mikey, we'll follow your lead."

Mikey. What a cute name for a massive man. I caught Hannah's gaze, and she had a wicked grin painted on her face as she watched me watch *Mikey. Busted. Surely, she must know how gorgeous this man is.* Oliver was handsome in a GQ kind of way, but his cousin was a different story. He was ruggedly handsome. Rough, but elegant if that even made sense. The thought suddenly sent a shiver down my spine, and it wasn't a good way. Could I really trust this guy? Suddenly, the idea of me not trusting my judgment scared me. What if he were just like, Jim?

"You're in good hands, Jenna. Mikey's good at what he does." Hannah said.

"Good?" Michael asked, as if he were insulted.

"All right, he's great at what he does," Hannah said, smirking.

He smiled. "That's better."

"Wait, are you guys leaving?" I asked nervously, rising from my seat as I watched Oliver and Hannah collect their belongings.

"We have to get back to the kids, but I'll be in touch. Oliver will be in and out to check on you guys. Don't worry, you'll be fine," Hannah said, reassuring me.

"Take care of her, Mikey," Oliver said.

"Yes, sir," Michael replied with a boyish smile, revealing a deep dimple on the right cheek.

"Guys, maybe this isn't a good idea after all," I said, my voice trembling, feeling uncomfortable trusting a complete stranger.

"Soon, there will be no more running and no more hiding," Oliver said.

"Are you sure, Ol?" I asked, smiling faintly.

He placed a hand on my shoulder. "Trust me, kid. Have I lied to you? Mikey is family, you can trust him."

I glanced back to where his cousin was sitting. "Okay, only because I trust you."

Ol smiled. "By the way, I wonder what the real Kate looks like," he said, pretending to think, rubbing his chin.

I smiled.

"Hon, if I didn't know any better, you sound like you're flirting with my best friend," Hannah said, tilting her head to the side, lifting an eyebrow.

"I've just been..." Ol paused, waving his hands around my face like a magician. He continued. "Amused by the interestingly shaped magnifying glasses you wear. Hopefully, you won't have to do that any longer."

"Thanks, Ol. I owe you."

"Thank me once we get your husband in jail. Keep the door locked."

"I got this, Cuz," Michael called out from the couch.

"I know you do. Good luck, though," Ol said with a faint laugh.

"What is that supposed to mean?" I asked, furrowing my brows.

"She can be a handful," Ol said as Hannah pulled him out the door.

"Love you, Jenna," Hannah said before they headed through the hallway.

"Love you, too," I replied before closing the door behind me.

I joined Michael in the sitting area. His legs crossed, obviously waiting for me. We chatted for a bit, getting to know each other and letting me know he'd been working with an investigator to find out more about Jim.

Before we knew it, it was well into the afternoon, but we wouldn't have known it if my stomach hadn't growled. As soon as he heard the unfortunate betrayal of my stomach, he glanced at his watch and rose from his seat.

"Let's get something to eat," he said, heading toward the door.

"I'm sorry about that," I said, embarrassed.

"About what?" He tried to conceal a smile.

What a gentleman.

"Wait, but are we supposed to leave the hotel?" I stopped before I reached the door.

"You're with me. If you're not comfortable, we can stay on the hotel premises. There are a couple of restaurants here."

"I suppose that's okay."

"You *suppose*?" This time, he smiled—dimples and all.

That smile would get me into trouble if I didn't watch it. It was a smile that could make anyone lose their train of thought. He opened the door and held it for me. He raised his arms as I approached the door to make way, making me flinch. Stunned, I quickly stepped back.

"I'm sorry. I didn't mean to startle you," he said with a slight panic in his voice.

For a moment, I just stood there speechless, my heart racing.

"Jenna, I'm so sorry."

I blinked, and realizing I wasn't in danger, I replied. "It's okay. It was a reflex."

"I totally understand. Next time, I'll be careful with my sudden movements, but *please* know I would never hurt you. I would never hurt a woman. It's a cowardly thing to do."

I nodded.

"Would you rather stay in?"

"No, let's go. I'm okay."

"Wait a minute, before I forget. Hand me your phone."

I scowled. "What for?"

"We need to make sure Jim can't track you."

Without protest, I rummaged through my purse, took out my phone, and handed it to him.

Michael removed the battery and the SIM card and handed the phone back to me.

I looked down at the disassembled phone in my hand. "What do I use now?"

"It's better if you don't contact anyone for now," he said, looking me in the eye, as if searching for understanding.

"I understand."

Chapter Eighteen
JENNA
PRESENT

We rode the elevator in silence, with me thinking that I needed to calm my nerves and trust Michael if I expected him to keep me safe. The door chimed on the fifth floor, where one of the restaurants, *Prego,* was located. The place wasn't big and the bartender at the bar on our left nodded as we walked in. We walked past several open tables covered with white linens. It was dark inside, and only one table was occupied by a couple also having a late lunch. They had an outdoor dining area, and Michael decided we would eat out since the weather was favorable. Outside were just a few white round tables with wicker chairs. We both ordered water to start, then I ordered a club sandwich, and Michael asked for the Reuben.

"So, you own an art gallery? That's pretty cool," he said as he sipped his iced water.

"I did." I pulled a tiny bottle of hand sanitizer from my purse, squeezing some into my palm.

"Have I seen your work?"

"I doubt it. I was an emerging artist, and I just started to get some attention when Jim happened," I explained nonchalantly, not making a big deal of it.

"Do you miss it?" He leaned back on his chair.

"I do. I miss traveling and taking photos of everything beautiful. I miss editing and turning them into a piece of art."

The server came with our food.

"Wow, this sandwich is massive. How am I going to eat this?" I said, laughing. "I don't understand why restaurants pile up their sandwiches into a giant tower that you can barely get your mouth around," I added as I tried to flatten the tower in front of me.

"Tell me about it." He grinned before biting his equally massive Reuben sandwich.

I sliced my sandwich in half, then cut the half into little bite-sized pieces.

He knitted his brows together. "Interesting."

"It's just easier," I said as I took a small piece of my sandwich and ate it.

"So, why'd you stop?" he asked, wiping off the mayo on the side of his mouth.

"Stop what?"

"Taking pictures."

"I just lost interest." I glanced down, somewhat embarrassed.

"Hey, none of that. If we work together, there's none of that, okay?"

"None of what?"

"Shyness, embarrassment, whatever you call it. I'm a friend as much as your protector, so please, none of that," he said, looking straight into my eyes. "Understand?" he added as he shoved another huge bite into his mouth.

"Yes, sir," I said, smiling. "So..."

He looked at me, and I couldn't help but notice his brown eyes. "Yes?"

"You're... *my* protector?"

"At your service." He winked.

And there it was—just like that, I could swear my bra straps snapped themselves.

I had to divert my attention. "What if Ol or Hannah calls?" I asked.

"They'll call me," he said.

I nodded.

"Okay, what's your mom's number?"

"My mom's? Why?" I asked, confused.

"I assume she'd be the one person you would want to talk to, right?"

And he was right. I needed to talk to my mom soon. I gave him the number and watched as he keyed the number into his phone.

"You didn't even ask me what my mom's name is. What name did you put it under?"

"Secret," he said, giving a small smile before handing me the phone. "Here. Only your mom, you understand?" he said, his gaze sharpened with intent.

I nodded. He knew it was vital for me to, at least, let my mother know I was safe. I smiled, and I moved on. "So, tell me something about you," I said, trying to get to know *my* protector.

Picking up the white linen from his lap, he wiped his mouth and took a sip of water before answering my question. "Well, as Ol said, I was in the military, then opened my own company a couple of years after I left the Marines."

"Why did you leave?"

He shrugged. "It was just time."

I could tell he wasn't ready to discuss his time in the military, so I left it alone. "So, this company of yours, what exactly does it do?"

"It's a security agency for high-profile clients."

"Wow, I feel special," I said, picking up the little bite-sized pieces of my sandwich I had cut while listening to him.

"You are," he said quietly under his breath.

"I'm sorry?" My heart quickened.

"I heard you are... *special*, that is. Hannah and Ol spoke highly of you."

"Oh." I didn't know what to say to that.

He studied me. "They do, you know," he said, knitting his brows together as if trying to convince me of something I had known all along.

"I know they do. That's why I feel guilty getting them involved in my mess."

"Oh, trust me, Ol wouldn't have it any other way; that's why he called me. That guy rarely asks a favor."

"Now, I *really* feel special."

He smiled again. "So, tell me more about you."

I wondered if the questions were part of the job. "What do you want to know?" I asked as I finished eating, folded my napkin, and placed it on the table.

"How old are you? Let's start with that," he said, pushing his plate to the side before leaning back and waiting for my answer.

"You know it isn't polite to ask for a lady's age, right?"

"Oh, c'mon." He smiled, his dimple distracting me for a second.

"I'm joking. I'm twenty-nine. How about you?"

He just stared at me.

Chapter Nineteen
MICHAEL
PRESENT

I contemplated whether I should reveal my age to Jenna. If I did, then she'd know that it was my birthday. "I just turned thirty-three." It just came out.

"When?" she asked.

Of course, she would ask. I cleared my throat. "Today." *Geez, Michael, don't hold back.*

Her eyes grew wide. "What?! Today is your birthday, and you're here with me? Working?"

"*Protecting,*" I clarified.

She rolled her eyes, "Okay, fine, *protecting*. We need to celebrate," she said, scanning the place, her head swiveling.

"What are you doing?"

"We need cake," she said casually, reading the small selection of desserts on the menu.

I snatched the menu from her hand. "No, we don't. I'm thirty-three. I don't celebrate birthdays anymore."

She snatched it back. Her sudden move took me by surprise.

"Nonsense. Everyone needs to celebrate their birthdays," she said as she continued to study the menu. It made me smile.

The server approached.

"Can we have the molten chocolate cake, please? And uhm, can you also please bring a match or a lighter?"

Lighter? A match? But she didn't ask for a candle. What is this woman up to?

The cake arrived, and she immediately fiddled with her purse. After a few seconds, she pulled out a small, unused white birthday candlestick, stuck it in the center of the single-sliced chocolate cake, lit it, and pushed it in front of me. "Okay, make a wish," she said with a smile.

I knitted my brows and looked at her. "So, you randomly carry a candle in your purse?"

"Well, I like to be prepared." She tilted her head to the side and stared at me. I stared back, smiling, and she quickly averted her eyes from me before continuing. "And hey—it looks like it came in handy today," she added, her tone light and cheerful.

"You are one intriguing lady," I said before closing my eyes and blowing out the candle.

"Happy birthday, Michael," she said in a soft voice that affected me, but I was unsure how. A shiver ran down my spine.

"Thank you, Jenna. I don't remember the last time I did that."

"Did what? Blow out a candle or make a wish?" she asked with a twinkle in her eye—completely unaware of how her small gesture had shaken me or what her question meant.

"Both," I said as I looked up. The lips... my eyes landed on those plump, kissable lips. *Focus.* Since we sat down, I had tried to convince myself that I was doing well. That I was focused and not distracted by the perfume she wore, subtly wafting in the air every time she moved, the way she tossed her hair, or the way she licked her lips after a bite, which she just did again. *Damn it, Michael, focus!*

Then this whole birthday cake, randomly pulling a candle from her purse, and making me make a wish. I knew then there was something special about this redhead. I couldn't even remember the last time I had a birthday cake and made a wish. Who was I kidding? Of course, I remembered. It was three years ago. My wife, Zoey, had surprised me with a crookedly stacked, two-tiered, round chocolate cake for my birthday. Zoey wasn't much of a baker, but she'd tried. On top of the melting cake were thirty lit candles.

"Come on, babe, make a wish," Zoey had said with her unforgettable smile.

I blew out the candles and made a wish like an eight-year-old boy.

"What was your wish?" she'd asked.

"I'm not telling you," I'd jested.

"Come on, tell me. Please?" She'd begged, pouting those lips I missed so much.

When Zoey begged, there was no denying her anything. Her gorgeous blue eyes imprisoned me. "I wish that time would go quickly so I can finish my next mission and be with you again," I said, kissing her forehead.

She'd smiled. That was all it took before part of the cake landed on the floor as I pulled her close to me, claimed her lips, and dragged her to the other room. Our bodies bumped into the walls and the table, knocking down the rest of the cake and spreading it all over the kitchen. We didn't care. We were married. And we were in love.

Zoey understood my job, but I could see the stress it put on her every time I left for a mission. She had bravely faced the uncertainty of my whereabouts and the months of being unable to reach me. I had decided I couldn't do it to her any longer. I was on my final tour, planning to request a transfer upon my return, but I was too late.

Chapter Twenty
JENNA
PRESENT

I watched Michael lost in his thoughts. *What, blow a candle or make a wish?* My question played in my head, but his answer went straight to my heart, tightening it. *Both.* I wondered if I had crossed the line with the whole cake scene. I was getting ready to apologize when the waiter returned.

"Excuse me, Mrs. Miller. Someone wants me to give this to you," the waiter announced, handing me a folded napkin.

"What?" I asked, my tone curt, but I couldn't help it. *How did he know my last name?*

Michael took the napkin from the server's hand and read it.

"I'm sorry, you're Ms. Miller, right?" The waiter asked, confused.

Hearing the waiter say my last name made all the hair on my body stand up. This could only mean one thing: Jim was around, but I didn't feel any eyes on me. There was no hair standing up on my body. Had I let my guard down?

Michael stood, now with a gun in his hand, which I hadn't noticed before, and studied the surroundings. I also scanned the place; there were only two other tables besides ours, one with a couple and the other with a family with kids, the same people who were there when we first arrived. I checked. Something I had done ever since I started running. I didn't see Jim, but that didn't mean he wasn't there.

Michael unfolded the napkin.

"Hey, that's my message," I protested.

"Who gave this to you?" Michael asked the server, towering over him as he folded the napkin and handed it to me.

The baffled young man took a step back. "The lady at the bar, sir," he replied. "Is everything all right?" he asked.

The poor thing looked terrified. I would be, too, if a six-foot-three, one hundred and eighty-five pounds of muscle towered over me and scowled. "I'm sorry, yes. Thank you," I said, trying to appease the young server.

The bar. The server said the lady was at the bar, but I didn't see anyone when we came in. Jim was sly, and I wouldn't put it past him to pay someone, like the server, to pretend a woman had sent the note, just to throw me off. But after reading the note, I relaxed.

I had just started toward the bar when I felt Michael's grip on my arm.

"Where do you think you're going?"

I stopped, turned, and placed a reassuring hand on his shoulder. "To the bar. It's okay. It's a note from a friend of mine."

"How can you be sure it's from her? And who is *Gayle?* Can she be trusted?" The series of questions made my head spin, but I knew he was just doing his job.

"Yes, I met her at one of the charity balls Jim and I—"

"She's also a friend of your husband? I don't think this is a good idea. What if—" he started to say.

"It's okay, trust me," I said, touching his arm to convince him I knew what I was doing. Suddenly, I was aware of how muscular his arm was. I quickly removed my hand.

"I'm going with you," he announced, snapping me out of my thoughts.

I didn't protest. He walked closely beside me, and I almost reached for his hand, a habit I had with Jim. *Pull yourself together, Jenna. You're not here on a date. Distraction*, I blamed it all on his muscular arms. Why did I have to touch it?

Michael looped his arm around mine. *Well, so much for trying not to think about his muscular arm.*

"Stay close to me," he said. "By the way, how did she know you're here?"

"I texted her yesterday. I remembered she knew—"

His eyes widened. "You did what? You shouldn't have done that," he said, his tone disappointed.

"I'm sorry, but it's okay, she knows things about Jim before we met, I thought she could give us some information," I explained.

He huffed, then shook his head.

As I walked next to him, I could smell the combination of what I assumed were his cologne and deodorant—a sweet, woody, spicy mixture wafting in the air, sending my womanly senses into overdrive. As we neared the bar, only an older man in a suit, talking on his phone, and the bartender, polishing a wine glass, were there.

"No one's here," Michael said.

"Hold on," I said as a tall lady strutting in from the lobby caught the corner of my eye. Her dark hair was pulled back tightly with gel in a high ponytail, and she wore a grey A-line skirt and a baby blue long-sleeved blouse with a slightly revealing neckline. As she approached, I could hear the clicking of her four-inch Manolos and immediately took in the Chanel #5 perfume that had wafted through the air. There was no mistaking it; it was Gayle.

"I knew that was you," she said casually, pulling me into a slight hug and giving me graceful air kisses as the French people do.

"Great to see you, Gayle," I said as I hugged her back, making sure I didn't wrinkle her expensive blouse.

Michael holstered his gun. "Let's head back to the lobby?" he said, gesturing for us to follow him, and we did. Michael paused and offered Gayle a hand to shake. "I'm Michael, by the way. Jenna's friend."

"*Friend. Sure.*" Gayle winked at me before taking Michael's hand. "Pleasure to meet you."

We continued walking.

"I'm so glad you're okay. Why did it take so long for you to call me? I texted you earlier by the way," Gayle said, placing a hand on my back as we walked.

"I'm sorry; there was just a lot going on." I looked at Michael.

"Like moving away without letting me know?" she said, tugging my arm to stop me, and lifting a brow. "Well, I don't blame you. I probably would, too," she added, shrugging a shoulder and side-eyeing Michael as we continued our walk through the lobby.

Gayle was always so forward, but I loved that about her.

"So, what have you been up to? Jim said you were staying with your mom for a few months to heal from... You know." She didn't have to say it; I knew she was referring to me losing my baby. "Of course, I didn't believe it. Something's always up with that man," she finished before rolling her eyes.

"Hey, why don't we go back to the room and have some drinks?" Michael suggested before I could reply.

"Ah, so, you guys checked in," there was a teasing tone in Gayle's voice.

"It's not like that, I'll explain later," I said. "So, do you have time for a drink?"

She glanced at the multi-toned, diamond-clustered Rolex on her wrist. "I actually have an hour or so to kill. Why not?" she said, flipping her ponytail flamboyantly.

Once we were back in the suite, Michael took out a bottle of Rosé and poured a glass for Gayle and me as we sat in the living area. Michael didn't waste time asking Gayle some questions.

"So, you said Jim was always up to something. What do you mean by that?"

Gayle looked at me as if to ask permission.

"Michael is my..." I pondered the description. *What was he? My security? My bodyguard?* "He's my protector," I said.

I thought Gayle would burst out laughing, but she didn't flinch.

"Understood," she simply said before slowly sipping her wine.

"My husband and I attended the annual Red Ball last year, and of course, Jim was there, but I was surprised to see someone else with him. I haven't seen or heard from you for months, so I asked him right in front of his date, the infamous Annabelle Morris, where you were," she said, looking at me with a brow raised.

Gayle paused and gently grasped my hand. "Darling, I will not be gentle about this because I know this doesn't bother you. Right? It doesn't bother you, or *does it*?"

I could feel Michael's eyes on me, waiting for my reaction.

"Of course, it doesn't," I said, and it was the truth. "Annabelle is not a surprise to me; I had a feeling there was something between them the first time I laid eyes on her," I added.

"What did Jim say?" Michael prodded on.

"Of course, he lied," Gayle answered with conviction. "He said Jenna was at her mother's and that she and Annabelle agreed that she should attend the ball with him this time. Ha! Like I was born yesterday." She scowled. "I called you a few times, you know, but your phone was disconnected. I got worried. I started asking around and heard a few different stories: *He filed for divorce, you left in the middle of the night with another man, and that he has been looking for you*, and my favorite was—"

"What?" Michael asked eagerly.

"That Jim had to commit her. Of course, I knew better, especially knowing Jim. I dealt with patients like him."

"What do you mean by that?"

"That he's a pathological liar; narcissistic to say the least," she explained in a disgusted manner. She reached for my hand again, and her tone changed into a warm and apologetic way. "I never got to tell you what I knew about Jim, and I deeply regretted it. I wanted to; trust me, but my husband told me to keep my nose out of your business. Of course, I didn't listen. I tried to contact you even when you were still back in Temecula so I could tell you."

"What? I didn't get any calls from you," I said, shooting up from my chair.

She pulled back with an air of aristocratic disdain, letting go of my hand. If I didn't know her, I would have been offended, but that's just how she carried herself. "I texted and called you several times, darling. Wait, here, let me go through my phone," she said, rummaging through her texts as if she needed to prove to me that she had actually called and texted, but I already believed her.

She showed me the texts she'd sent me and all the unanswered calls she'd made from her phone. There were several, but I never got any of them.

Rage brewed inside me like a volcano ready to erupt as I handed Gayle's phone back to her. There could only be one explanation: Jim had been checking and deleting my calls and messages. I wondered how many other calls and texts he had deleted, and from whom? And why would he do such a thing? My anger must have been evident because Michael came to sit next to me.

"You okay?" He placed a hand on my shoulder.

I gulped the last of my wine before answering. "Yeah," I said flatly, staring into space. "I mean, I knew he was checking on me, but I didn't know he was erasing my texts," I added as I fought the tears ready to gush out of my eyes any moment.

Michael held the bottle of Rosé and asked if I wanted more. I nodded. This whole thing was just too much. I could use more drinks to mask my anger.

"Anyhow, I knew something was off," Gayle said, crossing her leg and then leaning back on the chair gracefully.

"Great disguise, by the way. *Awful*, but a great disguise, nonetheless," she said, drinking the last of her wine.

I smiled.

"You haven't told us what you knew about Jim," I reminded Gayle, holding my breath as I anticipated her response. I glanced at Michael, who was just as eager, if not more, to hear what Gayle was about to reveal.

"Oh yeah. When he first moved to Temecula, he dated one of my friends. She discovered early in the relationship that there was something unusual about Jim. He was very sweet in the beginning, then suddenly turned into this secretive, jealous, and controlling freak — her words, not mine. Anyway, she'd mentioned it to me a couple of times. One day, she came to the house, and I saw a mark on her hand; it was faded, as if it had healed, but I could tell it was from someone's tight grip. I knew then that Jim had hurt her, but she denied it. Not till a couple of months later, when I saw her again, did she tell me she had broken up with the psycho. *Again,* her words, not mine."

My head started to spin; anger was building up even more, if that was even possible. If I had just received Gayle's texts, I would have left Jim a long time ago and wouldn't have gone through what I had. But then again, there were several times when I could have left him but didn't, so ultimately, it was all my fault.

"Thanks for trying to warn me. That means a lot," I told Gayle.

"Oh, darling, I wish I were able to sooner," she replied, reaching for my hand.

I nodded, understanding.

"So, which one is it?" Gayle asked, lifting a brow.

"What do you mean?" I asked.

"Where have you been? Did you go to your mother's, or did you leave him at night with another man?" She turned her attention to Michael and smiled.

"Neither. I ran away—*alone*," I said, surprisingly choking on my words.

Her demeanor changed, dropping the playful attitude. "Oh God, he hurt you, too, didn't he?" Gayle said, anger plastered on her face.

"More than you know," Michael answered, his voice low, almost strained. His jaw tightened as he looked at me. But there was something else in his eyes—something softer. I could be wrong, but I was pretty sure I saw sadness. His answer surprised me. Deep inside this burly man was a soft, empathetic soul.

"Oh, darling, I'm sorry. I mean, I had the suspicion, but you know..."

I understood. She probably didn't want to get involved in our drama, especially since her husband was Jim's colleague.

Michael must have sensed my uneasiness because he quickly changed the subject. "Okay, so here's the deal. You didn't see Jenna. You didn't talk to her. We must figure out how to keep her safe from her husband for now. That's number one on the agenda. Until then, she must hide," Michael announced.

"Of course, I understand," Gayle confirmed. "Will I see or hear from you again?" She directed the question to me.

I glanced at Michael.

"I know you want to, and we will make arrangements later, I promise, but for now, no one should have her contact information. We will reach out to you later, Gayle. We'll let you know that Jenna's all right, which she'll be, because I'm here. Once we get Jim, everything will be back to normal," he said.

Normal, whatever normal was. I didn't even know anymore.

Gayle simply nodded, worry still etched on her flawless face. She glanced at her watch and stood. "Oh, I'd better get going." She pulled me into a tight hug. "Take care of yourself, darling, and once you get the bastard, you call me, you hear? You still owe me that coffee," she said before kissing me on the cheek.

We walked Gayle to the door, Michael holding it open for her. Before she walked out, she addressed him, "Please take care of my friend."

Chapter Twenty-One

JENNA

PRESENT

We stayed in for dinner, and after, Michael and I spent some time on the balcony. The sky was a little cloudy, but the night lights from the surrounding buildings shone brightly, and the air was cool, carrying a hint of damp earth and river water. I tried to hand him a glass and gestured if I should pour some wine.

"I would love to, but I think I've had enough," he said.

"Oh, come on, just one?"

"No, thank you," he smiled.

"All right, suit yourself. It's probably better not to, anyhow. It's the weekend, and there are usually speed traps around," I said as I poured the wine into the glass and took a sip, suddenly realizing I was already feeling a bit tipsy, so I mostly held the glass and toyed with it, swirling the liquid inside instead of drinking it.

A slight grin formed on his face.

"What?" I said, furrowing my brows.

"Did you think I was going home?"

"Well, yeah. Aren't you?"

"Jenna, do you think I would leave you here alone? What kind of service do you think I provide?"

That question took a different route in my head, and I absentmindedly scanned his physique. Oh goodness, the wine was definitely doing its job, releasing my inhibitions.

"Jenna," he called out, trying to bring me back from my trance.

"Huh?"

"I said I'm staying here."

"Of course you are. I knew that." I lied.

I saw him grin as he walked toward the railing, looking down at the garden below.

"Don't worry, I'm sleeping in the other room," he said with a chuckle, not looking at me.

"I knew that." I lied about that, too. It wasn't as if I thought he'd be outside the suite, standing next to the door, guarding me like I'm some Princess or something. Of course, he'd be utilizing the spare bedroom. I absentmindedly took a sip of the wine in my hand and quickly placed it on the side table before I drank more. Two glasses of wine were my limit, and I'd reached that—*A while ago.*

Michael eyed me, but before he could say anything, his phone vibrated in his jeans pocket, and he quickly took it out to answer.

"I have to take this," he announced, walking into the room beside mine.

With nothing else to do, I cleaned up, picked up the used wine glasses on the table, and brought them to the kitchen sink. I wondered why he didn't take the room Hannah and Ol used the night before; it was bigger and had a king-size bed. The room he chose had two double beds.

I could hear him from the kitchen, but I couldn't make out the conversation. Then it dawned on me, *girlfriend*. He was a handsome guy; *of course, he had a girlfriend.* That's why he had to take the call in private.

I heard the door open and close, so I quickly turned on the faucet and rinsed the glass I held.

"Jenna," he called out. "Jenna," he called out again.

"In the kitchen."

"How long did you date your husband before you married him?" he asked, standing beside me.

The question took me by surprise. Why did he want to know that information? Then it hit me.

"Not long. Do you want to know if it's time?"

The confused look on his face was indescribable.

"Time for what?"

"To propose to your girlfriend." I smiled, waving my wet left hand to him, wiggling my ring finger. Gosh, I was tipsy.

He shook his head and squinted like I'd gone crazy or something. "Sit with me, will you?" he said as he walked to the living room and sat on the white sofa.

I dried my hands on the towel and followed. As I walked toward him, I admired the gorgeous Sacramento skyline through the spotless glass window. "Why so tense?" I asked.

"How long did you and Jim know each other before you got married?"

"Not long. A few months, why? What is this about?"

"Please have a seat."

He patted the space next to him, but I plopped myself down in the chair across from him instead.

"That was one of my colleagues on the phone. I had asked them to do a background check on your husband—"

Fearful of what he'd found out, my tipsiness vanished with his announcement. Suddenly, he had my attention. "And what did you find? Did he spend time in jail? Did he hurt someone? Oh gosh, has he killed someone?"

He shook his head slowly as if to tell me not to jump to conclusions. "Not really," he replied hesitantly.

My heart started pounding, and suddenly I had the urge to stand up and face Michael, as if doing so would make me feel better once I found out what Jim had done. "*Not really?* What kind of answer is that? It's either that he'd *been* in jail, *killed* someone, or not. Which one is it?" I snapped unintentionally.

I expected him to react and snap back at me, but he didn't flinch. In fact, his face softened, and I braced for what was to come next. Usually, when people did that, they'd drop an exploding bomb. I held on to something invisible.

"Well, *Jim Miller* has not killed anyone or gone to jail, but—"

I sighed in relief.

"Oh, thank God," *Wait, he said—but.* "But..." I urged him to continue.

He stared straight into my eyes as if saying, *Brace yourself.* "I'm not sure about *your* husband."

I sat back down, trying to soak in what Michael had just said, clasping a bright yellow throw pillow to my chest. I automatically went back to the day I met Jim, the dates we had been on, and the wedding. *The wedding.* The thought made my heart spasm. Our wedding was small. We both agreed on a small, intimate wedding, but looking back, he was more insistent on inviting only a few people. A few, meaning my parents, my sister, Kayla, his best friend, and his dad. That was it. I didn't even think anything of it then.

"Jenna," Michael placed a hand on my shoulder.

"His name isn't Jim Miller," I said flatly.

"I'm afraid not."

"Do you know his real name?"

"Not yet; we're still looking into it."

"How could I have been so naïve?" I asked rhetorically, standing up again and pacing the room like a caged animal waiting to be fed, my heart racing.

"People like him know what they're doing and are very sophisticated. Don't blame yourself. It's *not* your fault," he said, watching me pace around the entire living room.

"So, the real Jim Miller. Do you know anything about him?"

"James W. Miller was killed in an accident in 2000. To our knowledge, no living family members have been identified. According to my colleague, he bounced from job to job in different parts of Minnesota."

"*Minnesota*...Was he a psychologist?"

Michael shook his head.

"But Jim had credentials. It was all displayed in his office. I don't understand. He saw patients."

"Did you see him with patients?"

I paused, realizing I'd only been in his office twice. "Once before we were married, and once after. Jim was always adamant about keeping work and home separate, so... not exactly. There was one time he brought me in to show me the art he'd bought from my gallery. That was early in our relationship.

"The other time?" Michael asked, joining me in the kitchen, where I had ended up from my nervous pacing.

"A few days after we got back from our honeymoon in Hawaii, he said he needed to stop by his office to pick up a patient's file."

"Does he have a secretary or administrative assistant?"

"Yes, Karen. *Karen*, something."

"Have you met this, *Karen*?" Michael asked, leaning his back against the bar counter.

I moved away from the kitchen and began pacing the living room again. "Yes, she was there when we stopped by the second time. I've also spoken to her on the phone a few times. Jim would ask me to call her or vice versa."

"He asked you to call his secretary?"

"Yes. Why is that surprising? This is not making sense." I snapped, frustrated. "Jim saw patients. I saw his credentials, he, he," I was lost for words. I tossed the pillow I was hugging on the chair. Then, I picked up another one; I wanted to cry and scream at it, but I didn't want Michael to think I'd lost it.

"Was this random? Different times, weeks, months of the year?"

"What?" I asked, lost in my thoughts.

"You, calling his secretary, were they at random times?"

I wasn't quite sure where his mind was at or what he was thinking, but I tried to recall. "It was early in our marriage. He had asked me twice or three times... I think, within a month. Karen had also called me several times, following up on whether I had received the gifts Jim had asked her to send."

I stood at the patio sliding door without opening it, simply staring at the flickering lights outside.

Michael stood next to me. He, too, stared outside, at what I didn't have a clue. "Did you get any weird feelings about her?"

"Not really," I said softly. Then I let out a deep breath.

Michael furrowed his brows and nodded. I could tell a lot was happening in his mind, and I wished I could help more, but I also had questions of my own, like, *who in the world did I freakin' marry?*

"I don't know if this is odd per se, but at one point in my conversation with Karen, she started telling me how long she'd been working for Jim, how great a boss he was, and so on. Mind you, I didn't ask. I didn't really think anything about it; I just thought she was a bit of an oversharer."

Michael was keeping notes of everything I said on his phone.

"Do you know what Karen's last name is?"

I shook my head.

"Karen probably isn't her real name. Even if we tried to look her up, it would be hard. Guys like Jim are smart; they will try to hide all traces of evidence," Michael said, placing his hand on my shoulder as I let out another huff.

"Tell you what, why don't you get some rest? We will get you a new phone tomorrow so that you can call your mom and dad."

I looked at Michael, thoughts racing through my head: Questions—lots of questions. Frustration was simmering inside of me. The idea that I was so stupid as to have fallen for someone I didn't even know. Perhaps Michael would read my mind and suddenly blurt out, '*Wake up, it was all a dream.*' But, no, it wasn't a dream. I had married a psychopath.

I took my gaze off Michael, who stood patiently waiting for me to say something coherent. "I don't know if I can sleep," I said, finally, slowly trying to digest everything I just learned. My heart tightened as I remembered my Savannah. I held back my tears as I tried to push the sliding door open, but his hand covered mine, stopping me.

"I know. Try at least. This is just the beginning; we will figure out our next step tomorrow. I'm sure you're tired. Especially from all that pacing you just did; I know I am—just from watching you," he said, smiling.

I let out a faint laugh, knowing I would be facing a long night ahead.

Chapter Twenty-Two
MICHAEL
PRESENT

I paced around my room, hoping that my heartbeat would slow down. Listening and watching Jenna, who was weighed down by the betrayal she felt as I told her about the piece of crap of a husband she had, made me want to hunt the coward myself. I plopped on the bed without turning it down, staring at the ceiling fan, thinking of the redhead in the next room. My heart sped up, and I shot up from the bed. *I needed a drink.*

Walking quietly, I went to the bar and poured myself a bourbon. I wanted ice, but I didn't want to make noise in case Jenna had fallen asleep, though after the news I had given her, I doubted that she had. Suddenly, I found myself standing in front of her room. I lifted a hand, contemplating knocking to see if she was awake. I didn't know what time it was, but I knew it was at least midnight or past that. I headed to the balcony instead. The night was relatively quiet, even under the Sacramento skyline. The river below danced peacefully, with the lights bouncing from the buildings and the surrounding bridge. Suddenly, I wished Jenna were standing next to me.

I tried to occupy my mind with every movement before me, but something kept pulling my attention back to the woman inside. I wondered how she looked asleep; I imagined her lying peacefully on the bed, eyes closed, tucked inside the comforter, red hair on the white pillow—*beautiful.* I took a sip of the drink in my hand, instantly sending warmth through my body as it went down my throat. I tried to part from my thoughts but couldn't stop thinking about her.

I hadn't looked at a woman like that since Zoey. Perhaps it wasn't an attraction—not exactly. The idea that she was vulnerable, that her monster of a husband had taken advantage of her, stirred something in me. I decided that's what it was—her needing me.

Most of my clients acted as if they knew better than I did. They demanded and dictated whatever they thought they needed—and it always ended in disaster. *Why hire a security detail if you think you can protect yourself better?* But Jenna was different. She didn't just want protection; she needed it. And more importantly, she trusted me, well, not until Oliver said I could be trusted. I couldn't blame her; she'd been hurt by the one person she trusted most. I couldn't afford to fail her. Not this time. Not after everything she'd been through.

I swallowed the last of my drink and went back inside. I glanced at her door, and for some reason, I felt the need to stay in the living room just in case she woke up and needed me. I grabbed the pillows and blanket from the room next to hers and camped in the living room, placing my gun on the table next to me.

The hours dragged on, and the next time I looked at my phone, it was nearly five in the morning. I was used to sleepless nights during my military days, and of course, after Zoey. *Shower*—that's what I needed, so I picked up my gun, went to my room, got in the shower, and stood under the cold water.

I stood there, hoping the water would wash away my thoughts of Jenna, but with her just next door, and me standing there naked, it was hopeless. I'd been in the same room with other women before, but this time, it felt different. The thought of Jenna next door while I stood naked in the shower made my body tense. *What the hell is going on with me?* It's not like I hadn't been with a woman since Zoey—though it had been months. There was something about Jenna. A kind of magnetic energy I couldn't ignore. Must be the red hair, I smirked to myself.

After a few minutes, my skin began to wrinkle; I stepped out, wrapped a towel around my waist, and started getting ready for the day ahead. Just as I was about to leave my room, my phone buzzed—it was Derrick from work. *Good.* Now, I could focus on the job at hand, not on the woman next door, but then again, they go hand in hand—*I'm screwed.*

After speaking with Derrick, I was torn about whether to tell Jenna; she'd been through so much, and giving her more bad news made me uneasy. I was unsure why her case affected me so deeply. I had protected other female clients before, but their stories had never affected me as deeply as Jenna's did. Perhaps it was because I saw a little of Zoey in her. I could hear my grief counselor saying: *Could it be that you are trying to absolve yourself from not being there for Zoey by protecting Jenna?* That's what he said when I took more female clients who needed protection, so I tried to prove him wrong, of course. I focused on serving male clients who required my services. The next time we met, he'd asked: *Are you trying to prove me wrong, or are you now avoiding female clients to avoid disappointment in case you fail?* I couldn't win.

The memory ignited a fire in me: *breaths, deep breaths.* I forced myself to wrench away from my thoughts. I didn't care why I did what I did then; what was important was now—*Jenna.* She needed me, but I had to tell her more bad news. It wouldn't be easy.

Chapter Twenty-Three
JENNA
PRESENT

A sliver of light started to come through between the curtains. I didn't want to get up. I wanted to sleep—sleep for days if I could, but I couldn't, so I pulled the comforter off me, slid into my furry slippers, and headed to the bathroom. The first thing I did was stare at the ginormous gold-framed mirror. *God, I looked awful.* Dark circles formed around my eyes, not to mention they were swollen from the tears I'd shed all night.

The white, spotless, oval Jacuzzi tub was calling my name, and soaking in it would surely ease all the knots that had formed on my neck and shoulders, but as I stared at it, my chest started to spasm. I didn't know if I could ever get into one again after what had happened. I shook off all the bad memories, turned on the shower, and let it run for a few minutes to reach my desired temperature. I finally stepped into the marbled shower stall big enough to hold a Coachella, and immediately, the hot water from the waterfall rain shower system mounted on the ceiling, the three body sprays on the wall, and the massive hand spray all worked in unison, soothing and massaging every inch of my stressed and tensed body; it felt amazing. I could stand there all day, and maybe, just *maybe,* I would forget that I married a total stranger who was now stalking me.

When I finished, I turned off the shower and let the revelation about Jim go down the drain. I'm sure Michael had this all under control. *Michael.* The thought of Michael outside my room, waiting for me, suddenly made me aware that I was naked. My thoughts took me somewhere else, but I quickly shook it off. The last thing I needed was the idea of being involved with another man while still married and trying to get my life back.

I grabbed the towel, wrapped myself in it, dried my hair straight, and finally slipped into a pair of ripped, straight-cut jeans, a red and white knee-length flowy floral dress, and topped them with an oversized purple plaid long-sleeve shirt; it wasn't my style, but I had to be creative, especially if we had to go out in public. I washed my hands before inserting blue contact lenses, applied a slight blush on my cheeks, dabbed pink lip gloss, and finally stepped into a pair of yellow chunky clogs before leaving my room.

The sun was shining into the room, and Michael stood on the balcony, a phone plastered to his ear. My first thought was that he was checking in with a girlfriend, perhaps telling her he was staying in a hotel with a female client. *Would he, though? Would he tell his girlfriend he was staying with me in a hotel?* Of course, it was only a job for him, so I was sure he would tell his girlfriend or wife about me.

He turned around, paused as he looked me up and down. I twirled, just to mess with him. He smiled and gestured that he would be a second before pointing to the glass-topped dining table next to the living room. He must have woken up early and ordered room service. I smiled back as I picked up the silver coffee pot and poured some into the cup next to it, then lifted the silver cloche, which revealed a variety of croissants. I picked up what looked like a strawberry one, tore a piece, picked up the cup of coffee, and took a sip.

"Good morning!" Michael greeted me as he walked in, placing his phone in his pocket.

He looked better today than yesterday. He wore a plain white shirt and dark denim jeans—yeah, that was it—simple yet... attractive. His hair was again tied into a ponytail, and his beard was freshly trimmed. He looked younger, which was ironic because he had just had his birthday.

"Good morning," I managed to say while I chewed and wiped the strawberry filling off my mouth.

"Sleep well?"

I tilted my head to the side.

"I'm sorry. If it's any consolation to you, I didn't either," he said.

"You didn't?" I sipped my coffee.

He shrugged. "I never sleep on the first day of staying in a new hotel."

"Of course."

"I'm sorry?"

Oh shit, did I say that out loud?

"I meant, of course, you didn't. No one does." I turned my back so he couldn't see how my face had turned red.

He walked past me into the kitchen and grabbed a glass of water.

"Blue, huh?" he said before leaning back against the sink, taking a big gulp of water, his eyes flickering as he stared at me, waiting for my answer.

"I'm sorry?"

"Your eyes. They turned blue," he said before returning to the living room and sitting on the sofa. "I like your natural brown better."

I couldn't believe he noticed the color of my eyes.

"You're very observant," I said, bringing the cup with me as I sat across from him in an accent chair.

"Part of the job." He leaned forward and put the glass on the table.

"As a protector?"

"That's right," he said, creasing his forehead, studying me. "What?"

He shook his head and smiled. "Nothing, just admiring your *OOTD*."

"What's wrong with my outfit? You disapprove?" I asked, pretending to be offended, though the 'real' Jenna wouldn't have worn the outfit either. Not that it didn't look good; I've seen others who could pull it off, but it just wasn't my style. My style had always been simple—classic—jeans, a neutral-color shirt, sandals or tennis shoes for casual days, and a nice sheath dress or A-line skirt with a blouse and three-inch stilettos would usually do the trick for a more semi-formal attire. I liked pieces that felt timeless, things I could wear repeatedly without worrying about trends. "Wait, did you just say *OOTD*?"

He laughed and then took a sip of water before responding. "Yes, I keep up with the current lingo. I'm still 'hip' like that."

"The fact that you just said *OOTD* and then followed it with *hip*," I smirked.

Water shot out of his mouth like a malfunctioning sprinkler.

We both laughed so hard; it felt good, actually, and I needed it. I was starting to feel more comfortable around Michael. I picked up a box of tissues from the table next to me and handed it to him. "Are you okay?" I asked, trying to contain my laughter.

"Yeah, thanks. That was funny," he said as he patted himself dry.

"So, you don't approve of my *OOTD*?"

He glanced up from wiping his shirt and gave me a piercing look as if to say, *Don't mess with me,* but it was in a joking way. "I don't think it matters whether I approve or not; if that's your style. I just think it—" He looked away before continuing. "Never mind."

"What? You think it's what? C'mon, spit it out. It's what?" I said, then froze, realizing what I'd just said. "Oh, shoot! No pun intended," I added, laughing.

He smirked, his beautiful brown eyes flickering as the sunlight hit them at just the right angle.

"I just think your choice of wardrobe takes away from your beauty," he said with a more serious tone.

What was I supposed to say to that? I was sure my face was as red as the strawberry filling in the croissant I had earlier.

"Part of the job," I managed to say.

"Touché."

I was glad for the momentary distraction we had. I was pretty sure it was intentional on his part to keep me from thinking about my situation. But, suddenly, the air between us shifted.

"Anyway," he started to say.

Just as I said, "So, what's the plan? Did you find out anything new about Jim?"

"Not yet. We're working on it. He's good. He's avoided detection, probably even had help. Either way, nobody stays that invisible without a reason. We will find something," he said confidently.

I could tell Michael was expecting me to react, but I inhaled deeply and remained calm. "I don't even know the name of the man I married. So, was the man who attended our wedding even his father?" I sat on the chair and wondered.

Michael shrugged. "I don't know. If I were to bet on it, I would say no. That's the bad part," he said and paused as if contemplating whether to continue or not.

"What's the bad part?" I asked, my chest tightening in fearful anticipation.

"I also had Derrick look into the people who stood by Jim at your wedding, but the names you gave me didn't turn up anything. I'm sorry, Jenna," he said, sitting on the sofa across from me.

I stared into space. Jim was a manipulative liar, yet deep inside me, I still wondered if anything in our relationship was real. *Did he even really love me? Would he have loved our child?* Suddenly, I was jolted out of my thoughts when the doorbell rang. I stood up immediately, questioning Michael with my eyes.

"Relax," he said, standing and raising both hands. "I's Ol and Hannah. They just texted, saying they were on their way up."

He walked past me to the door as I exhaled in relief and followed him. He looked over his shoulder, gesturing for me to stay behind him.

The door opened. "Hey," Hannah chirped as she pulled me in for a hug. "How are you?"

"Well, it could be better. I just discovered that my years with Jim—or whatever his name is—were a big fat lie." I rolled my eyes as we all walked back to the living area.

"We heard. So sorry about that kid," Oliver said, patting me on the back before walking with Michael to sit. "So, what's the next step, Cuz?"

I pulled the sheer curtain closed to shield my eyes from the sunlight, but plenty of light still came through the massive glass window.

"You're right, I don't think it's safe for us to stay here. I met one of Jenna's friends yesterday, and if she recognized her with that..." Michael paused, looked at me, then at Oliver.

"That crazy disguise she has?" Oliver smirked. "Hey, your eyes are blue again," he added.

Michael shook his head and laughed with the kind of flair that said, *Can you believe it?* "Yes, *that* disguise."

"What's so wrong with my disguise?" I protested like a little kid, pouting my lips as both men mocked my looks.

Michael snapped his gaze away as soon as I caught him staring at my pouting lips. I quickly let them relax, suddenly embarrassed by my action. My chest started to pound. He was looking at me, at my lips, and his eyes—ooh, his eyes had that dark, unreadable pull that made it hard to breathe. Like he was seeing something he wasn't supposed to want, yet his eyes said otherwise.

"I think it's..." Hannah paused, as if searching for the right words to describe the way I was dressed. "Oddly adorable," she finished with a smile that conveyed between innocent and teasing.

I grabbed a throw pillow and tossed it at her, laughing. "Not you, too. My own best friend?"

"Oh, c'mon, kid, we're just teasing you," Oliver said.

Michael interjected, bringing the seriousness back into the air. "Anyway, as I was saying, if her friend, Gayle, recognized her, it won't be difficult for Jim to do the same, even with those... *blue eyes*," he said, squinting as if my blue eyes distracted him for a second. "I'm sure he did love her once, and if he did, there is no way he wouldn't recognize those beautiful eyes even if they're disguised."

I slowly shifted my head and looked at Hannah. *Beautiful? Did he just say, I had beautiful eyes?*

Hannah grinned.

"I agree. So, what's your plan?" Oliver said, draping his arm on his wife's shoulder, oblivious to his cousin's comment, and I think Michael was, too, honestly. I waited for him to correct himself or at least look embarrassed by his comment, but neither happened. He continued as if he didn't just compliment my eyes.

"I think this guy is extremely unpredictable—dangerous. He seems to have all kinds of connections, and I'm sure he's gotten away with a lot. I'm more worried about the threat. 'If I can't have you, no one can.' That's a threat, and who knows what he'll do to Jenna. We can't let our guard down, not when we don't know what he's capable of. Right now, we need to find another place to stay while my team gathers more information about Jim. Preferably, out of state."

Michael glanced at me, searching my face for understanding. "I know you want to stay in California, but this is for your safety."

I nodded in response, thinking of what Jim was capable of, but unsure of all the plans.

"Until we find out more information, I think we need to find a place to lie low," Michael added.

"Green Ridge," Hannah blurted out.

"Green Ridge? Are you sure?" Ol asked, turning his attention to his wife.

"Yes, I can talk to Sally and see if she can help us," Hannah replied.

"Where is Green Ridge?" Michael asked.

My eyes met Michael's. "Virginia."

Chapter Twenty-Four

JENNA

PRESENT

"Virginia? That's perfect. How quickly can you arrange a place for us to stay?" Michael asked, looking at Hannah.

"I can do it now," Hannah replied as she stood and picked up her purse to rummage for her phone. When she found it, she walked to the kitchen and made the call.

Us? As in, Michael and me? In Virginia? The romantic place Hannah couldn't stop talking about? I didn't know how to react to this. I knew he was there to protect me, but that smile, that demeanor, that physique was all so distracting, and with all that in the *love state*? Oh, boy, I'd be in trouble. Oddly, there were butterflies in my stomach, and my heartbeat suddenly rose as if I was nervous. My feelings were all over the place. I waited for Hannah to finish her phone call so I could scold her.

"We would have to meet with Derrick first," Michael said.

I glanced at Oliver, who was grinning at me.

"What?" I asked.

"Have you been to Green Ridge?"

"No, why?"

"It's very romantic," he said, lifting his brows a few times, his eyes sparkling, teasing.

I glanced at Michael to see if he had heard his cousin's stupid remark, but he was busy scrolling on his phone. *Good.*

"Stop it." I playfully punched Oliver's shoulder. "We're hiding from a lunatic who *may* or *may not* have the desire to kill me, not have a romantic getaway," I added sarcastically, glancing around for Hannah. "Hannah, take care of your husband; he's being ridiculous," I said.

He smirked. "Tattletale," he replied playfully, then immediately changed his tone, stood, and draped his arm over my shoulder, as if consoling a little sister. "This is serious, Kate, I know. Had I known your situation before, I would have hunted that bastard husband of yours. But we're here now, and your safety is my concern, and there's no better person to keep you safe, well, aside from me and Mikey," he said. "I just want to make you laugh, you know, so you're not scared. I know how scared you are."

"I know, Ol. You're a good friend."

"All taken care of. Sally has a room ready for you guys," Hannah announced as she waltzed back into the living room.

Michael and I glanced up at the same time, exchanging looks. I spoke first. "*A room?* You mean *rooms,* right?"

Hannah grinned, as if I had just caught her doing something mischievous, and then turned serious when Michael squinted at her. "There's only one room for the next week or so, but she said once one opens, one of you can move. There are two double beds in the room, if that helps," she added.

"*Right*," I said, giving her a suspicious look. Then I checked how Michael was taking the announcement. Blank. His face revealed nothing.

"What about another place? I'm sure there are plenty of Airbnbs there or a hotel with connecting rooms," I offered as I watched Michael scroll through his phone, probably searching for hotels in Green Ridge.

"Listen, we know Sally and her kids. I think you guys will be more comfortable at Serenity Manor. Plus, she knows the Sheriff there," Ol chimed in.

Michael glanced up from his phone and stared at me as if waiting for my approval.

I shrugged.

Michael put his phone away. "Fine, tell your friend, we'll take the room. This is better. I can keep an eye on you," he said with a take-charge tone, looking in my direction.

"I already did," Hannah replied. She looked at me, trying to give me her straightest face.

I glare at her, knowing what my best friend was up to. I stood, walked toward Hannah, and grabbed her arm, leading her to my bedroom.

Hannah sat on the edge of the bed, and I sat next to her.

"What are you doing?" I asked, glaring at her.

"What?" she asked, trying not to laugh.

I rolled my eyes. "I know what you're doing. Green Ridge, where you and Ethan had your anniversary? You told me how romantic that place was. Why would you suggest that place?"

"Jenna, honestly, it was the first thing that came to mind, plus I thought it's the perfect place. We have friends we trust there; we know the area, and it's far from California. Yes, it so happens that the place *is* romantic, and Virginia *is* for lovers," she said casually, like she wasn't doing anything wrong. "But that's not what I had in mind, trust me... now that you mention it, who knows?" she finished, lifting her brows at me.

"Who knows what?" I asked.

"Who knows, you and Michael might hit it off," she grins.

"He has a girlfriend," I announced.

"He does?" She sounded surprised.

"Doesn't he?"

"Oh, I don't know, I don't think so. If he did, Ol would have told me," Hannah said.

"Ugh. Hannah, why does he have to be so dang distracting?" I covered my face with my hands.

"Ha! I *knew* it. You think he's attractive," she said, practically bouncing on the bed.

I put a finger to my nose. "Shhh, they might hear us. But honestly, have you seen him?" I whispered with a quiet laugh, wrinkling my forehead, acting like a teenage girl with a crush.

"Yeah, I know," Hannah sighed in agreement.

"Hey! You're married. To his cousin," I reminded her teasingly, though I knew she wouldn't find anyone more attractive than the man she married. "Are all of Oliver's relatives that attractive?"

Hannah's eyes widened as if shocked by my question, "Gosh, no!"

We laughed out loud until a knock on the door forced us to stop goofing around.

"Are you two okay in there?" Oliver called out behind the door.

We burst out laughing again, and I felt so lucky to have friends like Hannah and Oliver, especially at times like these. I didn't know what I would have done without them.

Hannah stood and opened the door for her husband. "Yes, Hon, we're okay. I'm just making Jenna laugh."

Oliver smiled at his wife, and my heart spasmed. Jealousy? Not over Oliver, but jealousy of what Hannah and Oliver had. I thought I had found it with Jim, but as it turned out, it was all lies. *One day, I'll find someone who will make me smile the way Ethan had— and now Ol made Hannah smile.*

"By the way, we're back to calling her Kate, according to Mikey," Ol said.

Chapter Twenty-Five

MICHAEL

PRESENT

I scanned the plane, searching for anyone who looked re-
motely suspicious; even though I had checked numerous
times, once as we arrived at the airport, inside the airport,
when we boarded, and now, one couldn't be too sure.

Kate had fallen asleep as soon as she settled into the seat
next to me. I couldn't blame her; I'd be exhausted, too, if
I'd just found out that my marriage was all a lie. Honestly, I
probably wouldn't be able to handle it. She was stronger than
I.

I watched her sleep. She looked so peaceful, resting her
head on the window with her left hand supporting it, just like
Zoey used to. I still couldn't believe someone could hurt this
lovely lady. I shook the thought away, grabbed a folder out of
my backup under the seat, and studied Jim's file again.

Jim's file was thin. There wasn't much to know about him,
except for his life in Temecula, but I needed to learn as much as
I could about this guy so I could understand who I was dealing
with and what he was capable of. I stared at the copy of the
restraining order Kate had filed, and that was pretty much

it, except for a few articles and notes Derrick had written. Skimming through the notes, I quickly realized that this man was good. Nothing stood out, aside from the fact that we knew he had stolen someone's identity.

Jim Miller graduated from the University of California with a degree in psychology and later became a psychiatrist. He was even a member of the board. Jim was referred to as a philanthropist in an article I was reading—*narcissist* was more accurate. I picked up a photo of him and immediately felt the tension forming at the back of my head. I wanted to erase the smug look he had on his face with my fist.

We hit a slight bit of turbulence, and Kate shifted in her seat. I instinctively place a hand on her shoulder, which I didn't think she felt, because she went right back to her original position. I shut the folder in front of me and placed it back in my backpack. I leaned back, hoping to join Kate in her journey to oblivion, but no matter how hard I tried, I just couldn't. Kate's hand on her lap, which I assumed was smooth and soft, caught my attention. I wanted to touch it. It reminded me of when Zoey and I would travel, whether in a car or on a plane; I would always hold her supple hand. A lump formed in my throat as memories of her surfaced, pulling me back to the days we spent together. I missed Zoey.

I glanced at Kate and couldn't help but compare her to my wife. They were different in some ways, yet similar in others. Zoey had been pretty, but Kate was beautiful—if that made any sense. Zoey was tall, while Kate, from my estimation, was about five-five or five-six. Kate was slender, and my wife had curves—but both had been equally sexy.

What was I doing? I shouldn't be comparing them; it wasn't fair.

I thought about Zoey instead. Gosh, the woman had been too wise for her own good. She had a heart of gold, always trying to help anyone who asked. I loved that about her, but at times, it became too much. I felt like people had started taking advantage of her—but that possibility had never crossed her mind.

I thought about her smile. Zoey had the most beautiful smile, and when she laughed—God, it was contagious. She didn't care who was around, or where we were, for that matter. If she wanted to laugh, she did—wholeheartedly.

The plane started to descend, and the turbulence shook my thoughts away. I touched Kate's hand softly, not wanting to startle her again like I did the last time at the hotel. And I was right—her hand was as soft as the clouds outside our window.

She smiled, a little dazed, almost looking like she didn't know where she was.

"We're about to land," I said.

"Already?"

I replied with a nod.

She placed a hand on her forehead as if feeling for a fever. "Gosh, Michael, I feel awful—"

I quickly straightened up. "Are you okay? You're not feeling sick, are you?" I wanted to touch her hand, but I restrained myself.

"Oh, gosh, no. I meant, I feel awful that I fell asleep on you. What a boring company I turned out to be," she explained, her cheeks slightly rosy.

Zoey used to get nauseous when we flew. I just assumed.

"Don't worry about it, kid. You have lots more time to make it up to me." I smiled.

Within a few minutes, we touched down at Dulles International Airport. Again, I scanned the surroundings. All good as far as I could tell. After getting our luggage, we went to the car rental and picked up our reserved SUV. Last I checked, the drive to Green Ridge was less than an hour, but we would be hitting rush hour soon, so I knew that could change.

I had forgotten to take a whiz before we left the airport, so we stopped at a coffee shop just outside the airport. I looked at Kate as I was about to enter the bathroom.

She wrinkled her forehead. "What? Don't tell me, you want me to go in there with you," she said, almost sounding disgusted.

"Of course not!"

She laughed. "Go! I'll be right out here."

"Stay put and keep talking to me," I said, my voice firm as I pulled the door closed. But just before it shut, I caught her rolling her eyes. I couldn't help but smile.

Kate ordered hot tea before we left. That was another thing she and Zoey shared—they both loved their tea.

Chapter Twenty-Six
KATE
PRESENT

When we exited the coffee shop, we ran to our rented Hyundai Tucson; it had started pouring out of nowhere. "Oh my gosh, where did that come from?" I asked, rushing into the car in case thunder and lightning followed. I wiped my face on my sleeve.

Michael studied me but didn't ask questions. "I have no idea, but those raindrops felt like the size of a quarter," he said, fumbling for something from the backseat. His backpack. He took out a shirt and handed it to me.

"Here, you can use this to dry yourself."

I stared at the neatly folded, crisp white T-shirt.

"It's clean."

I started rummaging in my brown purse. "I know, but it's your shirt. I might get makeup on it. I'm sure I have a packet of tissues in my purse."

"Nah, it's all good. I'll wash it later."

I put my purse away, took his shirt reluctantly and, slowly, wiped my arms and patted my face with it. Immediately, the scents of laundry soap, fabric softener, and his cologne greeted my nostrils. My mind wandered.

"Are you okay?" he asked as he watched me take in his intoxicating shirt.

"What?"

A boyish smirk formed on his face. "I said, Are you okay?"

Suddenly, I realized I was still smelling his shirt and quickly pulled it away from my face. "Yes. I'm okay. Thank you. Here." I tried to reach and wipe the rain off *his* face.

He tried to grab the shirt but accidentally grabbed my hand instead.

"I'm sorry," we said in unison.

Awkward.

Glancing away, he wiped his face and tossed the shirt in the backseat. Within a few minutes, we were back on the road in silence. I had no idea what had just happened, and, to hide my embarrassment, I dug through my purse for a piece of Dove chocolate. When I found it, I removed the lid from my cup of tea, unwrapped the piece, and dropped it in.

He gave me a side eye.

"What?"

"Chocolate in tea?" he asked, perplexed, keeping his eyes on the road.

"It's good. Wanna try?" I said with a pep in my tone, offering my cup to him.

He shook his head. "I'll take your word." He smiled. "So, do you know these people we're staying with?"

"Not really. I met them once, at Ol and Hannah's wedding, but that was it. I'm surprised you didn't meet them."

"I didn't meet you there, either."

"That's true. I don't know how I could have missed you," I said, then regretted it after I heard it.

"I don't know how I could have missed *you.*"

Silence.

I looked out the window as we drove, watching the trees roll by. Some were still bare, but others had begun to wake with small green buds pushing through—signs of life just starting to show. A few trees were dotted with white blossoms I didn't recognize. Scattered among them were bursts of color: soft pinks, pale greens, touches of purple and yellow. The sight of it all lifted something in me. As the mountains and valleys came into view, I felt lighter, wishing I had my camera with me. The scenery was beautiful.

The cologne he wore made me feel certain things; it didn't make me nauseous or trigger a migraine like others usually do. Something about a guy and the right cologne that makes my heart skip a beat. Michael wore grey denim jeans and a simple white pullover sweatshirt. I was also digging the man bun, which surprised me, because I had sworn I'd never entertain a guy with long hair. Yet there I was, finding him attractive.

We'd only been back on the road for a few minutes. Michael was so focused on the road that he didn't realize I was gawking at him, *or did he?* Well, I didn't care. I wanted to study his features. *What is his story? Am I right? Does he have a girlfriend, or did I assume that? He definitely has a girlfriend. With those piercing, brown eyes, chiseled jaw, and red, kissable lips? Who wouldn't? He's also my protector, and I hardly know this guy, and just because I trust him now... somewhat, doesn't mean...*

"What?" he asked, pulling me out of my thoughts. *Dang.*

"What?"

"You're staring. Do I have something on my face?"

"Oh, no, I was looking past you. Trying to see what's on the other side." I leaned forward as I lied.

He smiled with a flair that said, *I saw you.*

Busted.

"So, have you ever been to Virginia?" he asked, trying to save me from my stupidity.

"No, first time. You?"

"A couple of times, but never been to Green Ridge. I heard it's a beautiful small town."

"It's romantic," I said. I regretted it the moment I heard it. *I really need to work on my impulsiveness. Note to self.*

"I'm sorry?" he asked, surprised, even though I knew he had heard me clearly.

"Hannah told me it's romantic. I wouldn't know. Hannah said. You know Hannah? My best friend? Oliver's wife?"

"Yes, Kate. I know who Hannah is." He smirked, nodding his head as if amused by my blabbering.

"Hannah and her late husband, Ethan, spent some time there," I managed to add, cleaning up the mess I just made.

His demeanor shifted. "I heard about Ethan. Such a tragedy."

"Yeah, it was." I looked out the window, remembering how great a man Ethan was.

His phone vibrated, interrupting my thoughts.

"Are you gonna get that?"

He shook his head. "I'll check it later."

Girlfriend. It was *definitely* a girlfriend.

I looked out the window, and the rain had subsided. The sun was peeking through the clouds, revealing a partial rainbow. Part of the sky had turned bright red as the sun started to set. I sighed and wished I had my Sony a7 IV with me.

"Beautiful," I whispered.

"Indeed."

I looked at him, about to say something, then realized he was not looking at the sunset, but at me.

I immediately felt my face heat up like a match that had just been lit. He shifted his gaze back to the road as if nothing had happened, but I saw it. I saw the way he looked at me.

Miles later, we finally entered Green Ridge.

"Well, would you look at that?" he said, grinning at the sign that greeted us: *L-O-V-E. 'Virginia is for Lovers.'*

Chapter Twenty-Seven

KATE

PRESENT

Serenity Manor was just as Hannah described; the area was massive. The two-story manor stood surrounded by trees, some no more than dead trunks, but beautiful in their own way. Michael parked the car, and as I stepped out, standing admiring the place, the scent of fresh-cut grass drifted through the air, welcoming us. To my left, next to the manor, was a gated swimming pool with a fountain of some kind, and just behind it, to the right, I spotted a horse behind the fence. The place was amazing.

I turned around and saw Michael unloading the car, so I tried to give him a hand, but he didn't want my help. Still, I grabbed a smaller bag with my purse, and as we were taking out our luggage, Sally and her daughter, Nichole, came to greet us.

"Hi, welcome to Green Ridge," Sally said, with a welcoming smile.

"Hi, Sally," I greeted back. "I'm not sure if you remember me; we met at Hannah and Oliver's wedding," I added as she came closer. She hadn't aged since I last saw her. Her hair was still short and dyed silver. If I recall correctly, she was in her late fifties or early sixties—either way, still beautiful.

"Of course, I remember you," she said, pulling me in for a hug.

"This is Michael, my..." I paused, unsure what he was to me: *a bodyguard, protector...*

"Her friend, also Oliver's cousin," Michael quickly chimed in as he offered his hand to shake Sally's.

A friend. That was nice. I would have gone with protector, but I guess we're friends now.

Nichole hugged me. Nichole was beautiful. She looked like a younger version of her mother, just with longer hair and taller. They even had the same-sized dimple on their right cheek. The way Nichole looked at Michael was amusing. I could tell she thought he was handsome. She stood in front of Michael, beaming as if she'd just seen the man of her dreams. I couldn't blame her; I'd felt the same way the first time I saw him. Well, didn't see him as the man of my dreams, but it was undeniable that the man was in fact attractive.

"Nichole," Sally called out, bringing her daughter back to earth.

"Yes. Sorry, I'm Nichole," she said finally.

"It's nice to meet you, Nichole," Michael said, returning Nichole's smile before giving me a side eye.

"Let's get you guys settled in," Sally offered.

"This place is beautiful, Sally. *Huge*," Michael said, glancing over his shoulder as we followed them into the wooden double doors.

"It's about fifty acres of land," Nichole said.

"Wow," Michael said, clearly impressed. I was, too.

As we stepped into the manor, we were greeted by a spacious foyer with a beautiful white staircase to the right. I looked up to the glowing crystal chandelier hanging in the vaulted ceiling. Sally and Nichole were in front of us, walking on the maroon floral Persian rug beneath our feet. The house was nostalgic giving the space a sense of history and quiet luxury, just as Hannah described. The property was huge, but the house was a descent size, not quite a mansion, but big.

"So, I'm sure Hannah explained that all four rooms in this Manor are taken, except for one. It has two queen beds. Hannah said you guys won't mind," Sally announced as she climbed the stairs.

"Hannah said that?" I asked.

Sally turned around. "I hope that's okay. I told Hannah about it," she said, panic in her eyes as if she was worried Hannah had not explained the room situation to us.

"It's okay, Sally. Hannah *did* tell us. We'll be fine, *right*, Kate?" Michael asked, tilting his head toward me in a questioning nod.

"Oh yes, we'll be fine. I'm sure you guys have a partition board we can use, right?" I said, throwing a glance at Michael.

Sally was about to answer, but saw Michael roll his eyes. She grinned, then continued walking up.

As we reached the landing upstairs, Nichole pointed to the hallway on our right.

"That hallway has one bedroom tucked away from the others. It's the largest room in the manor. That's where Ethan and Hannah stayed," she said with a faint smile, but her smile quickly faded. I'm sure she remembered the tragedy that had happened to Ethan.

We gave each other a weak smile, as if to say we both miss Ethan and that he was now in a better place.

To our left were two white doors separated by a large painting of a black stallion. One door had a gold sign in cursive that read, "*Mountain.*" The other had a similar sign, called "*Valleys*". The one across was called *Hills*. We turned the corner into another hallway, where another door, called "*Rivers*", was located. I smiled at the name of the room and pointed it out to Michael, who narrowed his eyes slightly.

"My maiden name," I said, smiling.

"Oh, that's right," he smiled back, "Meant to be." He winked.

The wink. Great, the wink. Stop that!

Sally opened the door and held it open for us to enter. The room wasn't big, but the bright light filtering through the large bay window made it look more spacious than it was. A white lamp rested on a matching side table between the two queen beds; each crowned with a gray rustic headboard. Crisp white linens covered the beds, tucked neatly at every corner, and each bed was adorned with four matching pillows. A tall dresser, matching the bedroom set, stood in the corner by the window, which was dressed in light gray curtains—sheer and blackout. On the dresser sat a glass pitcher of water and two glasses.

After Michael took in the room, he looked at me, mouthing something I couldn't quite get. I furrowed my brows, and he mouthed them again, this time, slowly. I finally got what he was trying to say. *No TV?*

I shrugged and smiled.

"The bathroom's right there," Nichole pointed to a sliding door. The bathroom was just as pretty as the bedroom. It had a white, porcelain, free-standing tub next to a large, spotless window that offered a view of the expansive, fenced yard and the Blue Ridge Mountains. To the right, I could see a lake in the distance, its surface catching bits of sunlight. Pretty. I caught my reflection in the giant silver mirror and instinctively tucked my hair behind my ear, then brushed my hand over the two white robes hanging beside a shelf stacked with rolled towels and tiny bottles of toiletries.

"We are around most of the day and live down the road, inside the compound. If you need anything, don't hesitate to pick up the phone," Sally said as she stood by the door.

"Breakfast is from seven to nine-thirty. We serve both at the library and the dining room downstairs," Nichole added.

"Have fun and enjoy your stay," Sally said before closing the door behind them.

I found Michael by the window. I could tell he wasn't admiring the view but studying the surroundings. I guess it was part of his ritual as my protector. I let it go, rummaged through my suitcase, and grabbed some things.

When he turned around, we looked at each other in silence.

"Well, this is a first," I said, finally breaking the silence as I walked into the bathroom, bringing my toiletries.

"What's a first?"

"Me sharing a bedroom with a stranger," I said, peeking through the door.

He smiled. "We shared a hotel room last night," he replied as he walked into the bathroom with me. "Nice," he said. "Are you gonna stand there while I use the bathroom?"

I gave a small, exasperated huff. "You could've warned me." I slid the door shut behind me. The door swung open again, making me jump.

He flashed a mischievous grin I've never seen before. "Just checking."

I rolled my eyes.

He shut the door with a chuckle.

I heard the water running as I walked toward the window. *Did we just have a moment there?* I brushed the thought aside as I took in the backyard. There was a lake on one side of the massive lawn, a few red maple trees, and several other trees. Below us, just a few feet from our room, was a pebbled path lined with shrubbery, leading to what looked like a garden with various colorful flowers. I spotted another house from afar; it must be where Sally and her family lived.

"I'll take this bed," he said when he exited the bathroom and sat on the one close to the window. "I hope that's okay. I need to have full visibility of the room, especially the door," he added.

I narrowed my eyes. "I don't mind, but why? The room isn't that big. You can literally see everything from either bed?"

"Just my thing." He shrugged.

I shrugged, too, and decided not to pry. "So, are you going to check for a monster under my bed?" I asked instead, lifting the skirt of the bed near me.

He stared at me with squinting eyes. "Are you mocking my job?"

I forced a smile, then quickly grew serious. "I'm sorry, I was just joking."

He grinned. "Just joking."

I rolled my eyes. "So, what now?"

"What do you mean?"

I glanced at my Apple Watch; it was almost seven. "Well, should we get dinner?"

"Oh dang, I suppose we should. Let's drive around and see what they have," he said as he picked up the car keys from the night table and headed for the door. "Shall we?"

I grabbed my purse from the bed and stepped out the door before he closed it behind us.

"Hannah said there's a small town about fifteen minutes from here, called Front Royal. We can go there if you like," I offered.

"Sounds good. And Kate?"

"Yes?"

"I know this is a romantic place, but... I'm here to keep you safe. To protect you... I just have to throw that out there," he said, acting as if he was uncomfortable.

He was uncomfortable, and I was dumbfounded. Speechless. The audacity!

"Are you for real?"

"I'm sorry, I'm not saying—"

"Clearly you're full of yourself," I said.

"Ouch. I was just making sure we didn't."

"Oh, trust me, we... *I* wouldn't." I huffed and walked out the door.

He ran after me in the hallway. "Hey," he called out, reaching for my arm. "You can't walk away by yourself. I'm sorry, it probably came out the wrong way."

I paused, turned around, and stared at him. "Fine. Just so we're clear. You're here to protect me, and I'm here to be protected," I said flatly, then continued to walk in front of him.

Chapter Twenty-Eight

KATE

PRESENT

*T*he drive downtown was quiet. I was still annoyed by his assumptions, but as we entered Front Royal, I relaxed. The place was a quaint little town, the kind of town that invited you to slow down and breathe.

Michael found a parking spot by the street next to a park. They weren't kidding about this place being for lovers, as everywhere I looked, there was some '*LOVE*' sign. One particularly large sign was displayed in the middle of the park, featuring an artistic design in blue, yellow, and red. We decided to walk around and see what the town had to offer. While walking next to Michael, I glanced around and almost reached for his hand. I glanced at him, still a bit irritated by his comment earlier.

It was a typical small town with small shops, but something about the atmosphere there... I couldn't quite put my finger on it. A few couples were walking up and down the well-lit streets, holding hands. I spotted one, who I assumed was well into their eighties, and across the street, a young couple was sitting on a bench next to another '*LOVE*' sign. I smiled. I could see why Hannah felt this town was romantic. Every few feet stood a lamp post, making the streets bright and beautiful. Some establishments were already closed, but a few bars and restaurants were still serving.

"What do you think of this place?" Michael asked as he stopped in front of a brewery and checked it out through the transparent window.

"As long as they serve food."

We walked in and were immediately greeted by friendly staff and live music from a man on the corner playing the guitar and singing his version of "*Lean on Me*" by Bill Withers. I only knew the song because my parents used to sing it around me. I relaxed some more.

We decided to sit outside under a canopy. There were several tables, and most of them were occupied. Michael asked to sit facing the establishment's door. I was noticing patterns from him. At the hotel in Sacramento, he took the room closest to the door. At the manor, he chose the bed where he could see the door; now, he wanted to sit so he could face the entrance. I thought about asking him, but I decided against it. I was hungry, and I needed food.

Michael ordered a massive cheeseburger topped with fried onions. It looked good, but I had to be in the mood to eat a burger, so I smiled at the waitress. "Greek salad, no olives, and a side of tofu bites." She nodded with a smile, tucked her pad into her pocket, and walked away.

"You know the olives are what make that salad Greek, right?" Michael said, sounding almost offended.

"I thought Olives were from Italy?"

"Well, both places love olives, but from what I understand, olives were first cultivated in Greece."

"Look at you, Mr. Wikipedia."

Not long after, the waitress returned with our food.

"You *do* know I'm part Greek, right?" he said before tilting the beer bottle to his lips.

"*Again,* I thought you were from Italy," I said as I popped a piece of tofu in my mouth.

This time, I was serious. I knew Oliver's family was Italian. I didn't think they were part Greek, too.

"My mom is quarter Greek," he said before biting into his burger.

"Now it makes sense," I whispered.

"What makes sense?"

I've always thought Greek and Italian men were good-looking. Now mix the two, and you have this Adonis-looking man in front of me. But I couldn't very well tell him that.

"It makes sense that you knew what you were talking about... *Olives.* About olives, I meant," I stammered, then decided to shove a forkful of lettuce into my mouth so I'd shut up.

I could tell my sudden lack of articulacy amused him. He lifted his beer, took a sip, and gave me a half grin as he stared. Suddenly, I felt naked, and my heart thumped. I didn't know how to take it. He wasn't smiling; he wasn't really grinning—what was he doing? Ugh, whatever it was, it suddenly sent nerve-pulsating sensations all over my body. I glanced away and started playing with my food, and when that didn't take my uneasiness away, I picked up the glass of Rosé and downed half of it.

"Are we okay?" he asked.

I nodded.

"So, what are we doing tomorrow?" he asked, breaking the tension between us.

"About that. I was going to ask you about our trip here while we were on the plane, but then... You know," I smiled, embarrassed that I fell asleep right away.

"You needed the rest. I understand," he said softly. Then just like that, he shifted, straightened himself up, and conducted the conversation more seriously, like we were in a business meeting or something. "The plan is for us to lie low, away from Cali and your husband. Hannah suggested that we come here so that you can relax and keep your mind off the situation..."

"I sense *a but*."

"*But...* we also need to be vigilant. Your husband—"

"Ex," I interrupted.

He looked me straight in the eyes. I couldn't tell whether he was bothered that I interrupted or if he was questioning what I just said. Either way, he continued.

"Your *ex*-husband is smart. There's a reason why he hasn't been flagged all these years despite his appetite for attention. That means he's also unpredictable. We need to be prepared. I'm not sure what he's capable of or what he would do, but if I were him and I was married to you..." He paused, leaned forward, beer in his hand.

I waited. Suddenly, my heart skipped a beat.

He let out a deep breath, leaned back, and continued. "I wouldn't stop till I find you. But let me make this clear..." He paused again, then took a sip of his beer.

"Nothing can happen between us," I said acidly. Not because I wanted something to happen between us, but because of his... I wanted to say arrogance, but he wasn't really being arrogant. He was just... doing his job.

He squinted, then shook his head. "Our motives would be different. He's a narcissist, and that means his motivation will be purely for his benefit, even if he ends up hurting you and anyone else. Do you understand?"

Maybe I was just taken aback by his comment earlier. I nodded.

"My *job* is to *protect you*, and I will do everything to keep you safe, but you have to trust me. You must listen to me without hesitation," he said firmly, but I could also sense the uneasiness in his delivery. It was as if he were guarded, not wanting to offend me again. This must be how he conducted his job in the military, probably more intense, but I got it. He was responsible for my safety.

"I trust you," I said, surprised that I said it without hesitation, but I did, I did trust him.

"Do you?" he asked.

"Yes, I do," I answered sternly.

"If I tell you to get up and run out now, would you?"

I looked around, my heart dropping. "Why, why? Should I get up?" I asked, looking straight at him, afraid that if I looked back, I would see Jim.

He just stared at me, waiting.

I adjusted my seat and grabbed my purse, ready to get up.

"Relax." He gave me a faint smile and touched my hand on the table. It wasn't romantic—just a gesture to let me know I was safe. "You don't need to get up and run right now, but if we get into a *situation,* I will need you to trust me. If I say run, then no questions asked—run."

I gave a small, silent acknowledgement.

Chapter Twenty-Nine
MICHAEL
PRESENT

I woke up, and, aside from the light inside the bathroom, the room was still dark. I knew it was already at least five thirty because that was the time I've been getting up lately, since what happened with Zoey. I'd wanted to sleep some more, but just couldn't. Usually, I would either go for a run or work out, but I couldn't do that. I couldn't leave Kate alone.

I propped myself up with pillows and glanced at the bed next to me. I could make out Kate's figure. She was lying on her left side, and my eyes automatically traced whatever curves I could make out. Starting from her shoulders, my eyes traveled down to the dip of her waist. I paused there for a minute and wondered how it would feel to hold her there. My eyes continued to glide down to what I imagined were her slender legs, one over a pillow. Suddenly, my mind wandered, thinking about how it would feel for me to lie next to her with my leg over her soft body as I did with Zoey.

"Good morning," she greeted me in a soft voice. Then, she pulled a red cloth off her head and away from her face, startling me.

I was wrong; she had been lying on her right side, facing me. That's not good. I should have known exactly how she was positioned. "How long have you been awake?" I asked, suddenly feeling guilty about where my eyes and thoughts had been.

"Enough to watch you study me." I could hear the slight amusement in her tone. "Everything okay?" she asked as she stretched under the covers, making me wonder what her body looked like underneath.

"Yes, everything's okay. I was just wondering what that thing on your head is?" I managed to lie.

She pulled what looked like a red bandana and waved it around. "This? I use it to keep my hair in place while I sleep; they go all over the place."

I nodded, unsure what to think of it. "I thought it was your hair. Do you always wear that when you sleep?"

"Not always. I have natural waves, and they fall flat or end up sticking out in every direction, like they can't decide what kind of hair day it's going to be, especially when I started cutting them myself," she said, with a soft yawn, running her fingers through her hair, wiggling inside the blanket, and propping herself up. "What time is it?"

I picked up my phone from the nightstand and checked the time. "It's six thirty," I said.

"So, what are we doing today?" she asked.

"Up to you. Whatever you want," I replied, placing my phone back on the table.

She snickered. "Be careful what you wish for."

"Bring it on," I teased.

She smiled.

I took a breath and cracked my neck from side to side. "Hey, can I ask you a question?" I asked, my voice faltering.

"Sure, what is it?" she replied.

I cleared my throat. "Were you and my cousin a thing?" I asked, my chest tightening, as I instantly regretted the question.

Kate shot straight up. "What?!" she exclaimed as she propped herself and turned on the lamp between us. The sudden brightness caught me by surprise; I had to shut my eyes, accidentally knocking the lamp down and almost falling off the bed as I tried to catch it.

"Oh gosh, I'm so sorry," she said, now sitting on the side of the bed, facing me. "Michael, are you okay?"

I decided to milk the situation, blinking as if I couldn't see and touching my forehead like I had hit it on something. "I don't know."

"Let me see," she tried to pry my hand off my forehead.

I smiled. "I'm okay, just yanking your tail. But you did blind me," I said, now back propped up on the bed.

She shook her head as she climbed back to her bed. "You're in the Marines, and you cry over a bright light?"

"Ouch! Are you calling me a baby?"

She tilted her head to the side, a playful spark in her eyes. "I didn't say that." She fiddled with the lampshade, then looked back at me with a softer expression. "For what it's worth, this bulb *is* bright. Do you want me to turn it off?"

"No, it's okay. I think my retina will survive," I said as I straightened under my blanket. "So?" I prodded. I wasn't sure why I did it again. I should've just let the conversation go. Because what if she said she liked my cousin? What if she told me they did have something, then what? I wasn't quite sure where my question was headed and why I had to ask.

"Oliver? What would make you think we had something?"

I faced her. "Do you always answer a question with a question?"

"No, I don't, and to answer yours, *no*, we did not have *a* thing. Now, can you answer mine?" she said as she pulled the comforter and wrapped herself in it like a little girl cold in the winter.

"Because Ol sure talked a lot about you. That's all," I replied, now staring at the ceiling.

"Really? What did he say?" she asked, almost excitedly, as she shifted to her side to face me.

Her enthusiasm took me aback, and I rolled to my side to face her again. I wasn't jealous, but for some reason, her excitement made me feel a certain way. *Did she like Oliver?* It wasn't like there was something she could do about it. My cousin was very much in love with his wife—her best friend.

"That Hannah was trying to fix him up with you, but you weren't interested," I said, resting my head on my hand.

She mimicked my position. "Believe me, the lack of interest was mutual. Not that he wasn't attractive or anything, but I just knew he had feelings for Hannah. It wasn't hard to see."

"Yeah, my cousin wears his heart on his sleeves, that's for sure."

"And even if he *was* interested in me, I couldn't. I just couldn't start a relationship based on a lie," she added as she sat back up.

"I can respect that," I replied, matching her movement.

"What else did he say about me?" she prodded. I guess my confusion was evident because she quickly added. "I just want to know how he saw me because I had to act differently, you know. I thought it would be smart to have a different persona, just in case."

"He did say, you were kind of..." I held back, not wanting to offend her.

"What?!" Her eyes widened. It was so adorable.

"Weird?" The word came out as a question.

She laughed; I couldn't help but chuckle.

"*Weird*, yeah. *That* I was. It wasn't easy, you know. But I thought, I'd act quirky, *hip* as you call it, and young so that if anyone asked—"

"They'll describe you as such, and your ex-husband wouldn't think it was you," I finished, placing my hands behind my head.

"Exactly. I really wasn't sure if it would work, but I needed to do something."

She looked me straight in the eyes, and the warm golden light from the lamp between us made her brown eyes sparkle. The sight sent a rush of electricity through me, and for a moment I was grateful she hadn't turned the lamp off when she asked—grateful, too, that I was hidden beneath the blanket. *Shake it off, Michael.*

I'd never been affected by a woman like this so quickly since Zoey. Perhaps it was because I felt as if I knew her already from all the things Oliver had told me. Ol was trying to help me move on from my wife, and I never really entertained the idea, even about this *awesome* gal named Kate. *She's pretty, but she tries to hide it. She's a redhead—most of the time.* I didn't know what to make of that statement, but I didn't ask because I wasn't interested. *Blue eyes, has a great personality, a little quirky and talkative, but she has a good heart. I think you'll like her.* That's how my cousin had described her.

Kate was a job. Nothing more—or so I thought until I spent time with her. *With Jenna.*

It was those damn candles she carried in her purse. *Who does that?* After I blew out the candle, she stuck on a slice of cake on my birthday, something shifted. Kate had this *instantaneous* hold on my heart. It was quick. I didn't know why, but she just... did. I told myself it wasn't in a romantic way. Just that, she was nice and that she made an impact on me; that was all.

But the more I got to know her, the more I realized she wasn't anything like Oliver had described. Pretty? No, she's beautiful. Oliver said she talked a lot, faster than a bullet, but that wasn't my experience. In fact, she was soft-spoken. He said she dressed oddly—and okay, that part was true. Everything was oversized. She was a total mess of patterns. Polka dots and stripes thrown in just because. And the gigantic glasses? Yeah, she wore those too. But it was all a disguise. The loud clothes, the chatter, the mismatched energy—it was armor. And her purse? According to Ol, it was like a treasure chest of strange things, but after seeing the birthday candle, I wondered what other wonderful things might be inside.

"So, can *I* ask you a question?" She leaned forward and then faced me.

I braced myself. "Sure."

"Does your girlfriend know you're staying with a woman in the same room?"

I kept my gaze on the ceiling, knowing this conversation would lead to Zoey. "What makes you think I have a girlfriend?"

She leaned back. "Do you always answer questions with a question?" she said, grinning.

"Touché," I said, buying time, thinking whether I should even discuss it. "I don't have a girlfriend, I..."

She covered her mouth with her hand and quickly sat back up. "Oh my gosh, I just assumed. Of course, you're married. Does your wife know?"

I let out a slight laugh. "I don't have a wife either," I said as I tensed under the sheets. I hadn't spoken about Zoey in a long time. "Not anymore."

The silence that followed was deafening.

"I'm so sorry, Michael. I didn't mean to pry into your personal stuff. How long have you been divorced?" She quickly clasped her mouth. "What is wrong with me? Never mind, you don't have to answer that."

"It's okay. We didn't get divorced. She passed away three years ago," I managed to say without choking. It wasn't easy. I had always steered away from conversation about Zoey, but it felt easy with Kate. I could tell I made her feel uncomfortable. "It's okay, Kate. You didn't know." I added, trying to abort the awkwardness.

She slowly wiggled out of her comforter, got up, and sat on the edge of my bed. She touched my knee from outside the blanket and shook her head. "Michael, I'm not always this tactless, I promise. I usually don't just assume, but—"

"You don't need to explain. I totally understand. It was the reason I left the Marines. I blamed myself for what happened—"

"We don't need to talk about it if you don't want to," she said, her eyes shimmering from sudden tears. She was full of compassion, and it made me want to share more.

"We were married for almost three years. Also, married to our jobs for more than that. Zoey was a criminal defense attorney. Both our jobs were not easy; we knew that from the start, but we were both ambitious. But we also had an agreement, you know? We agreed to focus on our jobs for a couple more years, then, after that, we would focus on our marriage and build a family; we just couldn't wait to be married. But being in the special ops... I was away more than I was home, and most of the time, I couldn't tell her where the Marines were sending me. Then Zoey had a change of heart. She wanted me home more, and because I couldn't just abandon my job, it took a toll on our marriage."

"Oh, Michael. I'm so sorry," she said, now holding my hand.

I let out a slow, heavy sigh as I glanced down at our hands. "I tried. Honestly, I tried. I submitted my orders for transfer, but it was just taking so long. Then I was sent away again, this time for months. Zoey understood. She knew I was working on the transfer. We were okay. While I was away, she was busy doing her job, as usual, defending criminals, and I had no clue her last case involved some dangerous gangs. Apparently, she'd been getting some death threats at work. I was away, and she couldn't confide in me. Then one day, my superior just told me I had to go home right away. I knew something was wrong."

Her grip on my hand got tighter as if anticipating what was to come next. My shoulders tensed, so I took the deepest breath I could take in before I continued. "Zoey was found in her car outside our home. They said she overdosed, but Zoey never touched drugs. She wouldn't even take ibuprofen for her migraines, for crying out loud. I always had to force her to take medicine, and they tell me she took drugs? OD'd? BS!" I shook my head as I instinctively pulled my hand away from Kate's grip and ran my fingers through my hair. "Oh, I'm sorry, I didn't mean to—"

Kate scooted up and hugged me. "No, I'm so sorry." This time, I could feel her tears on my shoulder.

We sat there hugging each other for a while. It felt good. I could feel Kate's compassion emanating through her heartbeat. I had not opened like that with anyone since Zoey died, not even with my grief counselor, not like that, and it felt so damn good, but I still couldn't and shouldn't be attracted to her.

Chapter Thirty

KATE

PRESENT

What in the world? I couldn't believe what Michael had just told me. The poor guy had been through so much. I wouldn't have thought he carried such a burden. It was almost like he hadn't expressed his feelings before. After hearing about Zoey, I understood why he was so adamant about protecting me. His job meant something to him, protecting others the way he couldn't do for her. It must have been very hard for him to open up to a total stranger like me, but I could tell he needed it. Our hug felt natural, and I could feel his heartbeat mimicking mine. I knew I had to get his mind off things. And I had to be nicer, despite the constant reminder that he was just my protector, because now, I understood. He was my protector, but he was also protecting himself.

"What about going downtown and checking it out during the day? I'm sure there's plenty of stuff to do there," I said as I pulled away from our hug.

"As you wish." He wiped his eyes discreetly, and watching him, broke my heart.

"Look, it's almost seven thirty," I said, looking at my phone, attempting to divert his thoughts. "We'd better get ready if we want to make Sally's breakfast."

He glanced toward the bathroom. "You go first." He stood and started rummaging through his suitcase.

"You know there are empty drawers there, right?" I said, pointing to the chest of drawers, before closing the bathroom door.

***

When we arrived in the dining room, it was already full. All five wooden, oval dining tables were occupied. One table was occupied by a young couple feeding their toddler a banana, and the other by a man in a suit. Perhaps he was in town for business. I wondered what type of job would bring him to such a small town, but I immediately dismissed the question as I noticed the three ladies drinking mimosas at the table across from him.

They stopped talking, and all eyes were on us, well, on Michael. I couldn't blame them; I'd be gawking too if I were with them. Just like when he got out of the bathroom earlier this morning, my heart almost stopped.

He wore nothing but his denim jeans. People often referred to a fit abdomen as having a six-pack, but I counted eight, so I guess Michael had an eight-pack. His hair was loose from its usual manbun; I thought he had curly hair, but he didn't—it was slightly wavy and flowed down his face. He apologized for not having his shirt on as he rummaged through his suitcase and pulled out a black shirt to put on. I thought that was adorable.

The ladies started giggling like high school girls, but as I turned to watch Michael's reaction, there was none, as if he was used to it or perhaps oblivious to how good-looking he was and the effect he had on women. *Very interesting*. I liked a man who wasn't full of himself, but I had to keep my feelings in check. As he had reminded me, he was there to protect me, no matter how romantic our scenery may be.

Suddenly, Sally called out our names, forcing me to part with my thoughts. I turned around to see her walking across the room.

"Join us in the library. There's a table waiting for you there," she said as she strolled across the room, carrying a tray of food. We followed her lead and found three smaller wooden dining tables inside. In the center was a beige, floral Persian rug. By the wall in front of us was a tall, white armoire with glass doors; blue, floral vintage China and tea sets were displayed inside it. On each wall were shelves of books. It was bright outside, but the curtains blocked some of the light, making the room warm and cozy.

We took the empty table by the window next to a couple, probably in their sixties or seventies; I couldn't really tell. The woman smiled as she saw us walk in. She had that warm smile that reminded me of my mom and my aunts. I could almost tell immediately that she was a kind person; she just exuded kindness—the kind that didn't need to announce itself, you could feel it—exactly like my mother. I felt a sudden wave of nostalgia, missing my mom so much. I made a mental note to call her when I could.

As we stood next to our table, the man nodded and smiled.

"Good morning," the woman beamed.

I smiled back. "Good morning," I replied politely as Michael, and I claimed the table beside them.

"I'm Joe, and this is my wife, Gina." The man said before sipping from his mug. "Is this your first time here?"

"Yes, sir," Michael answered before offering his hand to shake Joe's, then his wife's. "I'm Michael, and this is my girl-friend, Kate."

We exchanged pleasantries, but deep inside my brain was stuck on Michael calling me his *girlfriend*. I knew what Michael was doing, but it took me by surprise.

"Well, you will enjoy it. We've been coming to this area for years and have stayed in this manor since it opened. Sally and her kids are great people," Joe said, sipping from a white porcelain cup.

"Where are you from?" Gina asked.

I was about to answer when I felt a light squeeze on my thigh from under the table. I glanced at Michael and hoped that the couple didn't see my hesitation. Michael was quick to answer.

"South Carolina," he said.

The couple beamed, especially Gina.

"Ooh, we're from South Carolina. Whereabouts are you from?" she asked before taking a bite of her bread.

I almost choked on my orange juice. *"Please know what you're talking about,"* I prayed, suddenly unsure if Michael knew anything about South Carolina.

"Are you okay, dear?" Gina asked; apparently, I wasn't as discreet with my reaction.

"I'm okay, the pulp got to me," I managed to lie.

"Greenville, we're from Greenville," Michael provided. "Are you okay?" he asked, turning to me and softly touching my back.

"We're from Charleston. I heard Greenville is beautiful, though," Gina said before smiling at her husband. "We should go sometime. I don't know why we haven't when it's what... three, four hours away?"

"We should. In the summer," Joe replied.

"Reedy Park, downtown, is great to visit. There are also other parks and reserves in the neighboring towns if you're into that type of thing," Michael provided before winking at me.

I should have known. I'm sure he'd been in these types of situations before, making sure he knew what to do and what to say. Then there was the wink. Hannah used to tell me that guys winking at her made her feel all silly inside, and I had mocked her for it. Winks just didn't do anything for me; in fact, I thought it was kind of fresh for a guy to do such a thing, *till now.* His wink had brought out a different reaction from within me. I made a mental note to call Hannah later and scold her for bringing this winking nonsense to my attention.

It had been a while since I'd chatted with other people aside from people at work and, of course, Hannah and Oliver. It was a pleasant change of pace. Joe was very knowledgeable, not only about Virginia and what the place had to offer, but also about places they had been and experiences they'd had.

"Well, you two lovebirds, enjoy your stay. Make sure to check out some of the wineries around; they're great!" Joe patted Michael on the shoulders on their way out.

"I know why we didn't tell them where we're really from, but why South Carolina?" I asked.

"It was the first place that came to mind, the last place I traveled to, and Kate, I know I said, you were my girlfriend—"

I smiled. "I understand. Anyway, South Carolina? For work?" I asked.

"Yes, and visited my cousin. Ol's brother, Caleb."

"Oh, that's right. I forgot he has a brother there, he's the doctor, right?" I sipped the English breakfast tea from a pretty, floral, porcelain teacup.

He nodded, picking up the last piece of bacon from his plate, and took a bite and continued to chew in silence, staring into space.

"You okay? Something on your mind?"

He took a drink of water before answering. "Just thinking of your case and why it's taking so long for Derrick to get back to me."

There was a hint of regret and frustration in his tone, and I thought of how in the dark he might have felt when Zoey died, being out on a mission far away, unable to protect her.

"I understand," were the only words I could say.

"Are you ready?"

I nodded and grabbed the purse that I had slung over the back of the chair before we sat.

"Did you enjoy breakfast?" Nichole emerged just as we got up from our chairs.

"Yes, it was delicious," Michael and I said in unison. We immediately exchanged looks and smiled.

"Great minds think alike," Sally said, grinning as she joined us. "I promised Hannah I'd take good care of you two, so please, if you need anything, don't hesitate to let Nichole and me know," she added.

I hugged Sally and thanked her.

Minutes later, we were in our rented vehicle.

Chapter Thirty-One

KATE

PRESENT

We pulled into the driveway of Rappahannock Cellars, a charming, beige wooden building nestled in the middle of the expansive rolling vineyard. After parking the SUV in the open lot next to the building, we exited the vehicle, and as usual, Michael scanned the area before we headed to the entrance. Immediately, we were greeted with wafting sweet aromas of crushed grapes—fruity, tangy, and earthy.

I smiled at Michael as we walked the planks beneath our feet, which creaked with each step. Suddenly, the creaking stopped as we neared the counter, where a man who appeared to be in his late twenties stood behind, entertaining people with his knowledge of wines. Some were swirling the wine in their glasses, while others were sniffing the aroma it released into the air. When it was our turn, Michael and I approached. The man, with dark hair and blue eyes, enthusiastically provided us with the necessary information. We quickly learned that the distillery next door also sold and served gin, vodka, and brandy.

"Would you want to try the spirits next door?" I asked Michael as we stepped to the side to let others have their turn.

"I think I'll stick with wine, for now. We can check it out on our way out."

With drinks in our hands, we settled on the rooftop. We found an empty two-seater round bar table close to the edge of the open area. We didn't sit; instead, I set my purse on the chair and stood at the edge, gazing out at the view. It was a sunny day, and the Blue Ridge Mountains surrounded us, serving as the backdrop for the plantation of grapevines below; the view was magnificent. Lots of greenery under a bright blue sky. I'd been to several wineries, but for some reason, as simple as the place was, it exuded an intimacy that made the time slow. Suddenly, I could almost hear Hannah's voice saying, *Romance.* She was right, especially with a man like Michael next to me. If only we were actually there on a date...

"What do you think?"

"It's beautiful," I whispered.

"It sure is." He sipped his wine.

I wondered if he was looking at the view or at me, like that moment in the car on our way there, but after his comment in our room, I decided he was looking at the view. I kept my gaze below the deck and noticed a dog wandering around the vineyard; it must belong to the winery.

"Are you a dog or a cat person?" I asked Michael as I touched the glass to my lips and took a sip of my Rosé, sending an immediate warmth down my body. *Interesting.* Usually, Rosé didn't affect me that quickly.

"Dog—definitely. You?" he said, bouncing the question back.

"Both."

"Both?" he asked, surprised, as if having both cats and dogs was against the rules.

"You seem surprised. Don't you think a person can be both a dog and a cat person?"

"Well, I've never had a cat, so I guess…" he shrugged. "I just think you either like cats or you like dogs."

"Well, I used to think that as well. Growing up, we had dogs, and I never liked cats. Then, while in college, I became involved with an animal sanctuary that finds homes for abandoned animals. One day, a black kitten was dropped off while I was volunteering. The poor thing stayed at the sanctuary for months, ignored by adopters. I grew fond of him. He was very affectionate for a cat. Usually, they have attitudes; at least that's what I hear people say, but not Nelson. Before I knew it, I was buying cat food and a bed. Nelson slept on my bed."

"*Nelson.* You named your cat *Nelson*?" he asked with a slight chuckle.

"Yeah, what's wrong with Nelson?

"Nothing, it just sounds like a person's name." He grinned.

"I didn't think anything was wrong with it. I thought it was endearing," I said, then took another sip. "I had a friend in college who named a turtle, Gary." After I said it, I chuckled. Even I thought Gary was an odd name—funny, but weird—for a turtle. We both started laughing.

"Wait, did you say he sleeps in your bed?"

I smiled faintly. "Yes, but in a smaller cat bed."

"Gotcha," he smirked. "Where is Nelson now?"

"He's with my sister in Arizona."

"So, tell me about your sister," he said, toying with his empty glass.

"Hang on," I said as I finished what was left in my glass, positioned my hand holding the empty glass under the sunlight, and snapped a quick photo of it with the vineyard in the background.

"Okay, where were we?" I asked when I was done.

He smiled. "Your sister."

I told him that we were three years apart, that people thought we were twins—though she looked more like our dad and I, our mom—and that she was getting married next year, and that we were very close. A sudden lump in my throat formed, wondering if I'd make it to her wedding.

"You must miss your family."

"Very much." I forced a smile, holding the tears that were ready to fall any minute.

He placed a soft and gentle hand on my shoulder and I flinched a little. "Don't worry; it won't be long, and you'll see them again. *That* I promise," he said with conviction in his voice as he stared at me, his eyes glistening.

I relaxed and a sudden, unexplainable feeling took over me. My eyes rested on the curves of his slightly plump lips. I started to lean in. He didn't take his eyes off me. I could almost feel him anticipating my approach, but I had to remind myself that Michael was there to protect me. I *was* a *job*. That was it. I pulled back.

Chapter Thirty-Two

JIM

PRESENT

*D*id she really think she could leave me just like that? That she could keep running? I would find her. She couldn't hide from me; I would find her *again*. Jenna didn't realize how good I was for her. How good... *No... Great.* I was simply outstanding, and no woman would ever leave me just like that. Gosh, if she only knew that I had only married her because of her looks. Well, I did like her, loved her even, but I simply married her because she made me look good. She would realize one day how much she loved me. I just had to prove to her that she had made a mistake and that she needed me.

I walked back to the office after dodging the dark sedan that had been following me for nearly a week. I didn't know who he was, only that he watched my house and trailed me everywhere—to work, even to the airport. I needed a diversion. Whatever they were after, they weren't getting it. So, I decided to leave California for a while. Cabo. That's what I'd tell my secretary. She booked the flight and hotel, and I told her I'd be away for conferences. That was the plan.

I took an Uber to the airport, knowing that whoever was watching me would be following. So, I talked the driver's ears off, discussing Cabo and all the conferences I'd be attending, as well as how I would be overseas for weeks, even months. Just in case the idiots following me were cops, the driver could give them the information I had planted, even though he wasn't very interested in my story.

I got out of the car and walked into the airport, pushing my luggage. I glanced back, and sure enough, the guy was there. He was a few feet behind me, but I ignored him. Walking straight to the counter, I made small talk with the attendant, making her laugh before taking an empty seat near the jetway. The man was a few rows behind me. *Did this guy really think he could outsmart me?* A grin plastered on my face, making the lady across from me stare like I was going crazy. Maybe I was. Jenna had that effect on me, and now that she was gone, it just drove me mad.

The announcement came on for my flight, and I immediately stood. Being a *one-million miler* had its perks for sure; you got to board before the rest of the passengers. I wouldn't have it any other way. Once I was in my seat, I waited a few minutes, making sure I gave whoever was following me ample time to leave. I got up, pulled out my carry-on from the open bin above me, and started the drama.

"Are you kidding me! Now? Okay, I'll try to be there." I blabbered frantically on the phone as I made my way through the aisle, making my voice as loud as possible so the attendants would hear me. Finally, one of them turned to me as she closed the overhead bin before my row. "Is everything okay, sir?" she asked.

I dropped the phone to my chest, as if I were trying not to let whoever I was talking to hear me. "Um. Yeah. Um. My wife is unexpectedly giving birth. She's only seven months along. They're rushing her to the hospital now. I need to get off the plane," I said with panic in my voice.

The lady motioned for assistance from another flight attendant, a supervisor, I assumed, but I was already near the exit when the other attendant caught up. After a few minutes of dramatic explanation of how my wife needed me, that she was carrying our firstborn, and how she wasn't due to deliver yet, yada, yada, yada, I was walking down the jetway on my way out, rolling my bag, bumping into others who were boarding the aircraft. I stopped just right before the entrance and scanned the waiting area. The guy was gone. I rushed out of there.

A few hours later, I was back in Fallbrook, unpacking some of my belongings in the small Airbnb I had rented a few days ago under a different name. I opened a small box full of Jenna's photos and other information I needed to find her and started pinning them to the brown board I'd brought. I listed her family and all her friends' information, where they lived, their contact numbers, and where they worked. I also noted her friends' friends and their information. After I was done pinning everything, I stared at what looked like an evidence board from a police station, used to investigate a crime. Well, it was my case board. A case of finding a stubborn runaway who thought she would be better without me. Ha! I admired the board.

I'd contacted her sister again a few weeks ago, but she was quick to dismiss anything I said. She and I had never gotten along from the start. I tried to call their parents, but they wouldn't answer any of my texts or calls. I suspected Jenna was staying with them. Jenna was predictable; she'd run back to her mommy the first chance she got. So, first on the list was to visit my precious *in-laws*.

***

I arrived in San Diego after a few hours of an enjoyable ride in my brand-new, black, sleek Range Rover and stood in front of the red wooden door where my in-laws lived. I rang the doorbell and waited. Nothing. Knocked and still nothing. I stared at the ring camera in front of me and wondered if Jenna was inside watching me. Heat saturated the back of my neck, and I wanted to pound on the door and yell for Jenna to open the stupid door, but I took a deep breath and decided against it. Instead, I walked across the street where I had parked my car and waited for someone to come out of the stupid red door.

Eventually, I glanced at my phone and realized I had been sitting there, watching the door for almost an hour, and nothing had happened—no one had come out. I was just about to leave when a neighbor stepped out of her gate and walked across the street with her miniature schnauzer. I instantly got out of my car and stretched. As the woman passed, I gave her the most innocent smile I could muster, hoping she wouldn't think I was some creep. She smiled back. *Great!*

"What a cute puppy," I said as she approached where I stood

"Thanks," she replied. The puppy sat and scratched its ear.

"How old is he?" I asked. I needed to gain her trust before asking any other questions about the people who lived next to her.

"*She's* five months," she said as she tried to tug on the leash, getting ready to walk away.

"Sorry, *she's* beautiful. Well, have a good walk," I said, dismissing her quickly, so I didn't come on too obviously that I was snooping around. I pretended to open my car door, then promptly turned around again before she could go farther. "I'm sorry," I called out. "I was in town for a conference and thought I'd stop by and surprise my wife and her parents—The Rivers?" I smiled, looking for a response. Any response. None came. She gave me a blank stare. She almost looked like she didn't want to talk to me. I had to take a deep breath to hide my irritation, but I forced another smile instead.

"I head back home tomorrow. That's their house, right?" I pointed at the wrong one on purpose. "I've never been here," I quickly added.

She studied me, wrinkling her forehead, then asked. "What did you say your name was?"

Dang it! "Sorry, I'm Jenna Rivers—" I started to say, then quickly rephrased. "Jenna Miller's husband. I'm Dr. James Miller."

Her eyes lit up then. "Oh, you're Jenna's husband. I haven't seen Jenna in ages. How is she?"

Even though I didn't feel like having a friendly chat with the woman, I sucked it up.

"She's doing great, busy with her gallery," I lied.

"Wait, did you say you're stopping to see Jenna and her parents? Jenna is here?" she asked, confusion evident in her reaction.

I had to think fast. "Yes, she came in a couple of days ago—" I started to say, and was going to come up with some other lies, but then she interrupted.

"I've been out of town for two weeks and just got back. I'll have to stop by later and say hello to Jenna," she said excitedly, tugging on her dog as it tried to pull her.

The timing couldn't have been more perfect.

"Anyway, the Rivers live next to me. That house with the red door," she added, pointing at the house where I was standing just an hour ago. I immediately thought about me standing in front of the Rivers' home. What if she had seen me standing at the door next to her house earlier? She would have said something. I waited. She didn't say anything else.

I gave a faint laugh. "Ah, my wife and her directions."

She snickered.

"You'd think she'd tell me about the red door. Hard to miss that one," I said, rolling my eyes.

The woman smiled before tugging on her dog's leash again.

I said thanks to her, and she walked away with her dog.

I got in my car and drove off, heading back to Fallbrook, but I looked in the rearview mirror before I could go far.

The woman and her dog stood on the sidewalk, watching me drive away as if suddenly realizing something. Whatever it was that she realized, I didn't care. All I cared about was finding Jenna and knowing that she wasn't at her parents' home irritated the hell out of me.

Chapter Thirty-Three
MICHAEL
PRESENT

I could have sworn she was studying my lips and had leaned in to... *What? Kiss me?* But then, she pulled back. *Why was I disappointed?* I had told myself that I was going to keep my distance, but it was more complicated than I thought. A kiss would only make my job harder than it was. Yet, as we drove the pebbled driveway out of the winery, I kept wondering how her lips would have tasted.

Kate and I spent the day exploring several of Green Ridge's neighboring towns, stopping at several wineries. We stopped at Front Royal as we originally planned on our way back. It was almost four in the afternoon when we arrived. Something caught Kate's eye in one of the quaint stores we passed by, and she asked if we could go in. The store was filled with souvenirs, from magnets and coffee cups to shirts, hats, socks, and other novelty items. I glanced at the right wall, where I found Kate staring at what caught her attention. On the wall were assorted metal prints of landscape photography.

I watched her as she studied the photos above, and I could swear I heard her sigh. She was smiling, but I could tell she missed taking photographs like the ones on the wall. A man who looked to be in his forties, smiling, approached her, and I immediately rushed beside her in protective mode. Kate looked at me, and I gave her a boyish smile. She understood.

They began discussing the framed prints on the wall. He was apparently the photographer and the owner of the place. They discussed travel, recommended photo spots, and mentioned an *f-stop.* It was followed by what sounded like camera settings, so I assumed it had something to do with photography.

Kate was in her element, that was for sure. She was confident and passionate, excited to talk about photography. She seemed to glow as she spoke about it, which made her even more attractive. I found my eyes darting down to her waistline again. I wouldn't have chosen the fitted mismatched print dress layered under an oddly textured slouchy sweater she wore today, but it was much better than the other ones she'd worn since I'd met her. The dress looked good on her. Perhaps it was because it was a little fitted at the waistline, accentuating her figure. The dress fell past her knees, where it met her black knee-high Doc Martens boots. Her fiery red hair almost touched her shoulders, and I watched her tuck a few strands behind her ear as she continued to study the images on the wall. She was beautiful, and I wondered just what Jenna's style was really like.

She gestured for me to come, and I did. "This is Ron. He and his wife own the place, and he's also the one who took all those beautiful photos," she said eagerly, pointing at the wall above us. "Aren't they beautiful?"

I nodded and smiled, though I wanted to say, "*I'm sure yours are better.*" I wasn't sure why I would say that when I hadn't seen any of her works. Kate snatched up a leftover Christmas ornament shaped like the Front Royal Plaza from a display rack, and after paying for it, we said our thanks and goodbyes and headed to the coffee shop down the road. As we sat inside, sipping iced teas, I watched Kate fiddle with the ornament.

"Ron took this photo and had someone make it into an ornament. Isn't that neat?" she said, the setting sunlight hitting the side of her face, making her red hair glow.

"That's pretty cool," I said, sipping from a straw. "You miss taking photos, don't you?"

She gave me a faint smile and lowered her head slightly as she wrapped the ornament back in white tissue paper before placing it in the paper bag.

"Yes. Taking photos was not just a job for me, you know. It was therapy, an outlet for me when I'm feeling anxious or sad or whenever I miss my family. It was a way for me to keep my mind occupied," she explained.

Something inside me understood how she felt. My work had been my outlet since Zoey died. I couldn't imagine not having an outlet like that; it would probably drive me crazy. "I can understand," was all I could say.

My phone vibrated in my jeans pocket. I quickly pulled it out and glanced at the number. It was Derrick.

"I'm sorry, I have to take this," I said as I stood and walked towards the other corner of the café, still close enough to see and reach Kate if something were to happen. "Derrick, what do you have for me?"

"Bad news, I'm afraid," Derrick said over the phone. From the music and traffic noises in the background, I assumed he was on the road following Jim.

"What? What bad news?" My voice must have been loud enough to startle Kate because she glanced up from whatever she was looking at on her phone.

I adjusted my tone, not wanting to worry her. "What do you mean, bad news? What kind?" I asked, my voice lower as I smiled at Kate.

She smiled back and returned to her phone.

"We lost him, man. He supposedly went out on vacation with his new gal—"

"Wait. Vacation? Where?"

"Cabo. We followed him as far as we could, but there was nothing we could do. Even Sergeant Stevens at Sac PD told us there was nothing we could do. He wasn't breaking any laws, but *man*, that guy is one arrogant prick. He knew we were tailing him, and he just gave us a wicked grin."

Derrick's encounter with Jim made my jaw clench; it hurt. The guy thought he was invincible. "Are we sure he got on that plane?"

"Yes, Sergeant Stevens and I checked the manifest. It wasn't easy," Derrick said.

"Did you call his office and find out how long he'd be gone?" I smiled again at Kate.

"Yes, the secretary couldn't tell us for sure. She said he had conferences to attend after, but couldn't tell us anything else."

"*Couldn't* or *wouldn't*? Ah, never mind," I huffed. If Kate were standing next to me, she would have seen the veins popping out of my neck from trying not to react to Derrick's news.

I paced in the small area I was in. "Let me know as soon as you find out something new. One of these days, this guy will make a mistake."

I ended the call and walked back to our table while I regained my composure. "Are you ready to walk around some more? Get dinner?" I asked, hoping Kate wouldn't sense the tension I was feeling from the call.

"Everything okay?" she asked, anyway.

I really should work on my poker face. Zoey once told me I could never gamble because my face always gave away my hand. *Bologna,* I wouldn't have lasted in the Marines' special ops if that were true. Then again, I probably couldn't hide my feelings from people I cared about. Perhaps that was the case, remembering what my mother had always told me as a kid. *You couldn't lie to me if you wanted to, son. Your face gives it away.*

"Yes, work was just checking on us," I lied. Well, I tried anyway. I didn't think she could read my face. *Or could she?* I guess it didn't matter, since after this job, we would go our separate ways.

I waited for her to question me more, as my mother used to, but Kate stood up and dropped her phone in her purse. "How about we walk around some more?" she said before heading to the door, dropping our cups in the trash bin on the way out.

The sun was dipping, and a slight breeze kicked in; it wasn't strong, but it was enough to make Kate cross and rub her arms. "Let me get my jacket from the car," I offered, but she shook her head.

"No, I'm okay. Once we're inside somewhere, I'm sure I'll be fine. Thank you, though," she said as she patted my shoulder.

"Are you sure?" I asked, trying to ignore the goosebumps tingling down my arms from her touch. I'd gone soft, that was for sure.

She nodded. We walked a few steps, and in the corner was a blue wall with multicolored letters spelling Front Royal vertically. Kate snapped a photo of it and tried to run towards the wall, but I grabbed her hand before she could.

Startled, she protested. "Hey!"

I let go of her hand. "I'm sorry, I didn't mean to do that. Gosh!" I said, raking my fingers through my hair. "Please don't run away from me like that," I explained, my voice gentle.

She knitted her brows together. "I was just going to take photos by the mural and was actually going to ask you if you would join me," she said, staring at me. "Are you okay?"

"Yes, it's just that... Supposedly, Jim went to Cabo, but I'm not buying it."

"And you think he could be here?" she asked, her eyes darting nervously.

"I doubt it, but just in case, please stay close to me."

She nodded. "Okay. I promise."

I let out a big huff and smiled. "Okay, let's go take that picture." And just as I was about to take a step, she grabbed my hand without a word and walked toward the mural.

We tried different poses, including some funny ones, and even took a couple of selfies with the new phone I had provided her. To my surprise, I actually had fun. We wandered around for a while, taking in the charm of Front Royal. I had to admit, Oliver and Hannah were right—it was a neat little town. After crossing to the other side of the street, we spent a few minutes in the park. The surrounding trees had burst into colors, their leaves in soft shades of green, pink, and yellow; spring was settling in. Kate's phone was ready, and suddenly, she was crouching on the ground.

"What are you doing?" I asked as I watched her point her phone in different directions.

"I'm taking photos of the tree from different angles, capturing different foregrounds and backgrounds," she said, working her camera phone, not even looking at me.

I nodded like I knew what she was talking about.

"Look," she said, showing me the images on the phone I had given her.

They were stunning. She had transformed a simple red maple tree into something worthy of a gallery wall. The way she angled the shot showcased the tree's branches perfectly, and the full crown looked stunning. The trunk in front tied it all together. *I knew her photos were better than those at the store we visited earlier.*

"You really know what you're doing. They're very, very good. If I took that photo, trust me, it wouldn't look like that," I snickered.

We sat on the bench near the pavilion and spent a few minutes admiring the surroundings. The multicolored sign *LOVE* was visible from where we sat. She snapped a photo of that, too, then turned to me and paused.

"What?" I asked, wondering what she was looking at.

"Don't move."

I squirmed.

"No. No. Don't move. Just like that," she said, smiling before taking a photo of me.

"Okay...What was that about?"

"The sun was hitting your face at just the right angle. Sorry, I had to. I hope you don't mind. I can delete it if—"

"No. I don't mind," I said softly, surprising myself.

The almost angelic smile on her face made me want her to take more photos of me. I couldn't believe photography made her smile that way. Suddenly, a lump formed in my throat as I remembered what she told me earlier—*I just lost interest.* She didn't have to say, but I knew it was after she lost her baby. My heart ached for her.

We sat in silence for a few more minutes, then decided to keep walking to find a place to eat. There was an old cinema on our left as we walked on the sidewalk, dodging other passersby going the other direction. My nose caught a wafting smell of something delicious in the air, and as we got closer, we realized it was coming from a Thai restaurant.

"Do you like Thai food?" I asked.

"*Do I?*" she said, her eyes widening in excitement. "Hannah and I used to have Thai food delivered to the clinic at least once a week," she added, her tone full of excitement like a little kid who just spotted the ice cream truck in the neighborhood. "There was this place down the block with the best Pad Thai—so garlicky, so perfect."

"Table for two, please," I said as we walked into the restaurant, hoping the food was as good as the one Kate had had with Hannah. I didn't want her to be disappointed.

Chicken Penang was my favorite, so I had that, and Kate ordered the Pad Thai, of course.

"So, what's your favorite subject to photograph?" I asked, lifting a forkful of Penang to my mouth.

"Flowers, mostly. I like landscapes, too, but mostly flowers and botanicals," she replied, twisting the Pad Thai noodles with her fork. "Oh, and bugs," she said before taking a bite.

"Bugs? You take photos of bugs?"

She smiled. "As a hobby. I like seeing the details on tiny bugs. I'll show you some cool ones I took."

"Later, after we're finished eating," I replied.

"Are you afraid of bugs?" she asked before taking a sip of her Thai tea.

"Depends," I replied. "I don't like spiders."

Her eyes lit up. "Ooh, I have some cool spider photos. Different types," she announced excitedly.

"Okay, Okay. Settle down. I don't wanna have nightmares later."

She reached for my hand, and my body reacted right away, sending goosebumps all over. "Don't worry, I'll protect you," she said before squeezing my hand.

Oh, for the love of God!

Chapter Thirty-Four

JIM

PRESENT

I didn't want to be too far from Temecula, just in case Jenna ever came back. I doubted it—it had been a couple of years of searching and waiting for her, on and off, chasing down every lead. The PI I hired found her a couple of times before she disappeared again. But who knew? Maybe she'd finally knock some sense into that tiny brain of hers and come home.

The two-bedroom home I rented in Fallbrook was tucked away from the city, situated on a hill, and its neighbors were miles away. Oddly enough, no one knew who I was; I wasn't used to it, because in my town, I couldn't move around without anyone recognizing me—who wouldn't? I'd done a great job in the community, but I needed it to be this way for now. Whoever it was following me probably thought I was now enjoying my time in Cabo, sipping a salted margarita under a tiki bar. If they only knew. No one could outsmart me.

The property owner must have enjoyed plants because this place was covered with them, from various cacti to several colorful flowers, to some plants with vines I didn't recognize, not that I would. I'm no botanist, then again. I should get to know all these plants, just because I love knowledge and knowledge loves me. Several trees of various sizes and a gazebo in the middle of all this vegetation, overlooking the city. I sat on the concrete bench, gazing at the mountain and valleys, an ice-cold beer in my hand.

The place was beautiful. Jenna would've loved it. I loved Jenna. Surely, she knew that. Why did she have to be so stubborn? I swirled the last of the beer in the bottle, staring at nothing as the breeze brushed my skin, wondering how I was going to find Jenna. It shouldn't be this hard. She wasn't that smart—how had it become so difficult to track her down? The nurse she'd befriended was no help. Threatening her job hadn't worked, but she did seem genuinely clueless about Jenna's whereabouts.

I returned to the house and studied all the information I had pinned on the board. I glanced at the list of people I needed to see. I stiffened at the last name, remembering the night that had started it all. *Jason Adler.*

Perhaps it would've been easier to just file for divorce; no woman was worth this much of my time. But the thought sent my stomach spiraling to the ground, and then I snapped out of it, out of my outrageousness. *No, I will not let you go, Jenna. I won't let you win.* I stopped in the hallway and glanced at my reflection in the mirror. No woman had ever said no to Dr. Jim Miller. *What were you thinking, Jenna? You had it all.*

I walked to the kitchen, fetched another cold beer from the refrigerator, and, as I passed the mirror again, grinned, watching my reflection. *You will come back to me, Jenna. No one else can have you. I will find you even if it's the last thing I do.*

Chapter Thirty-Five

KATE

PRESENT

We got in late, and though the day had been fun, I was exhausted. I went to the bathroom to get ready for bed, and as I opened the door, I didn't realize Michael was standing right outside. I bumped into him, stumbling straight into his muscular arms, my face landing squarely against his well-defined, bare chest. I froze, savoring the unexpected closeness, oblivious that my face was still pressed against him. My brain must have short-circuited or something.

He held on to me, steadying me with surprising gentleness. Slowly, I stepped back, taking with me a lingering trace of citrus and something else I couldn't quite place, but whatever it was, it made my knees buckle. I expected him to step aside, but he just stood there, staring at me with those mesmerizing, dark brown eyes. I stared back, frozen, waiting for what would happen next.

Suddenly, the room felt warm, and I could feel the tension between us. He bit his lower lip, making me want to lean in and just have a little nibble, but I held my ground. I wasn't going to be the first one to make the move. It felt like time had passed, and he finally stepped aside and apologized as he put his shirt on and climbed into his bed.

It would be a lie if I said I wasn't disappointed.

"Do you always wear kids' pajamas to bed?" he asked as he lay on his bed, gazing at the ceiling as if nothing had happened, but I heard humor in his voice.

"Kids' pajamas? Just because they're pink and have a unicorn, doesn't make them kids' PJs... and yeah, I wear them when I'm with company," I mumbled, as I stared at the lines our lamp reflected on the ceiling.

I heard him chuckle.

"What's your favorite color?" he asked instead.

"Blue. You?"

"Not green, red, yellow?... Huh, Surprising," he said, with a soft chuckle. "Mine is blue, too," he added.

"Just because I wear a lot of multi-colored clothes nowadays doesn't mean they're my favorite colors," I said, turning my body to face him, but he didn't move. "Blue, huh? Something we have in common," I added.

"About your clothes—" he started to say.

"*Again?*" I asked, my voice rising a slight octave.

He quickly sat up. "No, no, listen. I know you're trying to wear clothes Jim won't recognize you in, but don't be offended. I think the loud colors and random patterns might attract more attention, that's all," he explained as his gaze softened, weighing every word.

I stared into space. "You know, that makes a lot of sense." He was right—Jim was very observant. If something caught his attention, he'd notice it and recognize me. Perhaps that's how he'd found me in the first place. I made a mental note to make some wardrobe adjustments.

"Anyway, I also have a little sister; another thing we have in common," he provided, snapping me away from my thoughts of Jim and my clothes.

"I'm sorry?"

"I said, I also have a sister. Something we have in common."

"Oh? What's her name?" I asked, shifting under the blanket and turning back to face the ceiling.

"Haley. She's way younger than me. She's twenty-one and finishing college in Hawaii."

"Hawaii? Why Hawaii? I mean, it's a gorgeous island, but what made her choose Hawaii?" I asked.

"Friends," he replied as he let out a big yawn.

"Interesting. When was the last time you saw each other?"

Suddenly, there was an eerie silence as I waited for the answer.

"Zoey's funeral," he said flatly.

I was right. I immediately regretted asking the question. "I'm sorry."

"She's been back several times since then, but I've been busy." He paused, and then I heard a loud sigh. "I should make plans to see her soon," he added, then wriggled under his blanket and took a deep breath, like he was suddenly uncomfortable. I decided to end our question-and-answer portion for the night. "Good night, Michael."

"Good night, Z," he whispered.

I whipped around so fast to face him, I swear I pulled a neck muscle. I was about to ask him to repeat what he just said, but

I heard his soft breathing, and I knew he had fallen asleep just as he called me his wife's name.

✳✳✳

A loud roaring thunder jolted me up. Not that I had fallen asleep. How could I? After Michael called me, *Zoey?* There was no way I could sleep. Rumble. Lightning. Another loud boom followed. I sat up, pulling the blanket over me as if it would protect me from the anxiety I was feeling. Another bright light flashed, and that's when I saw him. Jim stood right in front of me. My heart skipped a beat; it raced and spasmed.

The room was dark. "Michael," I called out. "Michael," I called out again. Another lightning burst, and I readied myself, fixing my eyes where I last saw Jim. He wasn't there. Where was he? Was he next to me? Was he there to kill me? I trembled.

I wanted to reach out and turn on the light next to me, but my body froze. "Michael," I called out again. *Where the heck was Michael?!* I pulled my legs up, wrapping my arms tightly around them, and started rocking. "Michael," I whispered. Just as another thunderclap roared, a flash of lightning vividly revealed Jim, staring at me and slowly moving toward me.

There was nothing else I could do but scream as loud as I could, just as another shattering boom shook the whole house. "MICHAEL!"

"I'm here. I'm here," Michael said as I tried to push him away. "It's me. Jenna, it's me, Michael," he said in his frantic but comforting voice.

I opened my eyes, and there he was. There was Michael.

"It's okay. Shh... It's okay."

I looked around; the lamp was now illuminating the room, and there was no one there, except Michael and me, and there was no storm. The room was calm, quiet, and still.

"It's all a dream. You're safe." He squeezed me in his arms.

I sobbed on his chest. "Jim was here. It felt so real," I whispered.

He gently rocked me. "I'm here. It was all a bad dream. You're safe."

I lay in bed for hours before finally falling back asleep next to Michael. When I told him that he could sleep in his own bed, he wouldn't hear any of it. I couldn't stop thinking about the nightmare—and the fact that he had called me by his wife's name.

A noise woke me, and a sliver of sunlight pierced through the curtain. I glanced next to the space next to me; it was empty. When had he left? Where had he gone? My heart thumped violently as I remembered Jim's face illuminated by the lightning the night before. *It was all a dream.* I reminded myself. I sat up quickly, about to get out of bed, when I heard the door click shut, and Michael was standing there holding a box.

"Well, good morning sunshine," he greeted as he walked past me and set the box at the foot of his bed.

"You were here. You never left?" I asked, my voice cracking.

"I never left," he said, smiling. "Sorry if I woke you."

"But," I looked at the door.

"Sally dropped something at the door. So, how are you feeling?" he asked, warmth shining in his eyes.

"Better." I smiled and decided not to ask what it was that Sally supposedly dropped. If he wanted to tell me, he would have.

"Good. Now get your butt up and get ready."

"What?!"

"I meant... get your butt up and get ready," he said, grinning.

I threw a pillow at him, but he was quick to catch it.

"Why are you still in bed? We're finally driving to Shenandoah Park today," he asked, placing the pillow back on the foot of my bed.

"I wanted to stay in bed a bit longer." What I really wanted to say was: *Did you know you called me your wife's name last night?* Now the question was, why did that even bother me? It wasn't like we were together, but for some reason, it felt that way. My heart tightened at the thought. Then, as if things couldn't get any worse, I had a nightmare about Jim. *What's up with these exes sneaking up on us?* I wanted to say.

"Well, get your butt up, lady, and get ready," he said before rummaging through his suitcase and pulling out a blue sweatshirt.

I wiggled out of my blanket, fixed my bed, and was about to head to the bathroom when he softly grabbed my hand. When I turned around, he quickly let go like a kid touching a hot stove.

"I'm sorry. Damn it! I need—"

I shook my head. "It's okay, you didn't startle me." And it was the truth. His touch felt natural, my nerves staying calm in a way they never did with anyone else—especially not with Jim.

"Good. Anyway, I promise I'll try to be more careful."

I smiled before entering the bathroom to get ready.

A few minutes later, I was in my dark denim jeans and a black-and-white flannel shirt. I stepped into my boots, bending over as I tied the laces. I could feel his eyes on me, and I quickly stood straight. He quickly averted his eyes from me. I grinned. It wasn't a dramatic change of wardrobe because that's all I had—still, he noticed.

"Bring a jacket or sweatshirt, it's a bit chilly today," he said casually, like I hadn't just caught him checking me out.

"In late March?"

"I checked the weather app earlier, and it said it would be cloudy with a slight breeze. The high is sixty-four degrees, and the low is thirty-seven. I thought you might get cold," he said, grabbing a jacket from the chair next to his bed.

I pulled my long, multicolored cardigan from the drawer, then quickly folded it back and returned it. Instead, I grabbed a jean jacket and slipped it on. I glanced at the tall mirror in the corner closest to Michael's bed. *I look good.* The whole fashion façade was getting old. I couldn't wait to dress like myself again. I glanced at Michael sitting on his bed and caught him eyeing me. I pretended not to see.

"I'm ready."

"Hold on," he called out. "I have something for you," he added as he placed the medium brown box he had carried in earlier on the foot of my bed.

I looked at him with my furrowed brows. "What's this?"

His eyes glistened as he watched me walk back toward my bed. "Just a little something to help you with our trip today."

I gave him a side eye and grinned in anticipation like a little kid on Christmas day as I touched the box.

"What is this?" I asked again.

"It's a surprise. Open it," he smiled like a little boy. His eyes twinkled.

I sat on the edge of my bed and pulled at the tape on the box—it was already halfway open. I reached inside and instantly recognized the white box in my hand. Taking a deep breath, I turned to face him, trying hard not to let the tears in my eyes fall. "Michael," I said softly. "I couldn't believe you did this."

He rose from his bed and sat next to me. "It's supposed to make you happy, not cry," he teased. "Did I get it right?"

"Oh, you got it, right, all right," I replied as I lifted the tab to open the white box containing the new Sony a7 IV bundled with a lens kit.

"I wasn't sure what lens to get, so I asked, and they said 28-70 mm should be good for the park. They had a bundle, so I went for it. They told me about ISO and f something and all that, but I didn't know what they were talking about. I just hope I got the right thing."

I removed the lens from the box and attached it to the camera, my hands shaking. I've gotten so many surprise gifts from Jim, but there was just something special about this gift.

"Oh, I hope you don't mind, I had to open it to charge the battery. There's also an extra battery in the box, charged and ready to go. The sales guy told Derrick to make sure I had an extra battery—"

Leaving all my inhibitions aside, I threw my hands around his neck, almost knocking him onto the bed. I held him tight, and he returned the embrace. Being in his arms felt right—my head resting on his chest, his chin gently pressing against my head. Everything about it felt natural, like it was meant to be.

"I wasn't trying to make you cry," he said softly through my hair.

"I know. You just don't know how much this means to me," I explained as I slowly pulled away.

"Oh, I think I do," he said, wiping the tear that had finally escaped my eye.

"Thank you. Thank you *so* much," I told him as I glanced at the camera in my hand, still not believing what this man had just done. He just made it more impossible not to be attracted to him. He even charged the batteries for crying out loud! Who wouldn't be attracted to him?

"Are you ready?" he asked.

"Not yet," I answered while adjusting the settings on my new camera, then turned the lens toward the most beautiful subject I'd ever seen. His stunning face deserved to be the first photo captured with the gift he'd given me.

Click.

"Now, I am."

Chapter Thirty-Six

MICHAEL

PRESENT

After a couple of hours on the road, we entered Shenandoah Park. Observing Kate in her element was like watching Picasso paint his masterpiece; she was fluid, seamless, and magnificent. I watched her step onto a rock, then crouch behind another. She moved from one spot to the next, sometimes only a few inches apart. One moment, she chased the light; the next, she hid from it. Whatever she was doing, she moved with grace, pausing to steady her hand, then pressing the shutter.

Suddenly, Jim Miller came to mind. I couldn't blame him for not wanting to let go of Kate; she was... rare, but for Pete's sake, the man was stupid—blind. There I was, only a couple of weeks with her, and she'd already carved her way into my thoughts.

We hopped back in the car, and not even a few minutes later, there was another lookout point.

"We don't need to stop at each point..." She paused and looked out the window.

I smiled and parked. "Isn't that what we're here for?"

"Thank you!" she replied as she stepped out of the passenger side, pulling the camera strap over her head.

Kate took a few shots of the Valley in front of us before walking to the side to study the area across the street.

"What are you doing? The lookout is that way," I said, pointing to the view behind us. One man, wearing an Indiana Jones-style hat, stood on a rock with a tripod, snapping several shots of the magnificent view. He looked like a professional photographer, like Kate, but Kate was on the other side, looking at the street. I was confused.

Kate smiled. "I already got a few on that side," she said giddily, not removing her eye from the camera's viewfinder.

Click. Click. Click.

She finally glanced up and walked towards me. "Sometimes, we miss gems because we only look at what's in front of us. That's why I always make it a point to be intentional so that I don't miss any. Come." She grabbed my hand, and we walked to where she had stood taking photos minutes ago. "Look that way, what do you see?"

"The road," I replied, unsure of what *she* was looking at and whether there were any *gems*; I didn't see any.

"What else?"

I looked around, but there was only one gem I saw, and she was standing next to me. All I could think about was her beautiful face.

"Well?" she asked, waiting for me to reveal the gem I had found.

I couldn't very well tell her what I was thinking without sounding cheesy, so I parted with my thoughts and tried harder. "A tree with colorful leaves, and a boulder?" My reply came out as a question.

I waited for her approval like a nervous kid in class. I heard a few clicks from her shutter, then she beamed.

"Exactly! Look," she exclaimed as she turned the camera's viewfinder for me to see.

I'll be damned. The images were incredible, perfectly composed—even *I*, not a photographer, could see that. A boulder in the foreground, a winding road leading to the massive red maple tree surrounded by smaller trees with bright yellow and golden leaves.

"Kate, these are amazing! I would not have thought to look that way."

"Thank you." She smiled and curtsied as if to say, *'Thank you, my job is done,'* and then clicked the camera's button a few more times.

I watched her take a few more photos, and I found myself searching for subjects the way Kate's eyes would see them. It wasn't easy. I wasn't as creative as Kate was. After a few more clicks, we were back in our vehicle.

"Penny for your thoughts?" she asked as we drove away.

She must have noticed me deep in thought. I was just thinking of how talented the woman next to me was. A hidden *gem* that Jim had missed for sure. I kept that to myself. I kept my gaze on the road. "Was just thinking of the photos you took."

"And?" she asked excitedly.

I couldn't tell her that the photos made me think of us—the boulder was me, led into this beautiful red maple tree—Her. Yeah, cheesy, I knew it was, that's why I didn't share it with her. It wasn't me; I'd never enjoyed interpreting art before, not even when Zoey had dragged me into galleries where we would view abstract paintings from local artists in Sacramento, and she would ask me what my thoughts were about each painting. To me, they looked like kids' scribbles or paint splatters, but for some reason, now I was seeing what Zoey had been seeing. I was *feeling* what the artists were trying to convey, as Zoey would say.

A sudden, gentle breeze brushed my face, and I glanced at Kate, who was still waiting for an answer.

I wondered if I was going crazy. I swear I felt a familiar touch—Zoey's touch. She used to brush the back of her hand against my face when she knew I was contemplating something important; it was her way of calming me down. *Was I missing Zoey, or was I feeling guilty for thinking of Kate?*

"Are you okay?" Kate's voice spun me back to reality.

I nodded.

"So, you said you were thinking about the photos, care to share?"

Oh, yeah, the photo. I had forgotten. "I was just thinking how amazing photographers' minds work. Like everyone else at the last lookout, I wouldn't have thought of aiming my camera in the opposite direction, as you did. That image is stunning," I said, trying to move past what I felt was Zoey's presence. I didn't want Kate to think the person responsible for her safety had lost his mind.

"Just wait till I'm finished with the edits," she said casually, giving me a slight grin before looking out of the window.

We stopped at a few more spots, including a wooded area where Kate found a path with the sun shining through. She clicked and clicked that camera like there was no tomorrow, pointing to the right, to the left, crouching down, and aiming it up and down. She was fascinating to watch.

After a few hours, we decided to turn around and head back to Green Ridge.

"We have a couple of hours before dinner. I think I'd like to rest for a while," Kate said as we entered our room.

"Of course. I'll step out for a bit and make a call."

"You don't have to," she said, shaking her head. "I just need a quick fifteen-minute nap."

"I know, I'll just be out in the foyer. I'll be back in fifteen," I said as I closed the door behind me. I walked the hallway toward the open foyer, where I could see anyone who would pass through. By this time, I knew the faces of all the guests in the manor, plus all the workers.

I glanced over the big bay window, and outside was an expansive yard leading to a beautiful lake. Next to the lake were two massive trees with vibrant yellow and orange leaves. It had been a little cooler and breezy lately, and I watched while a few of the leaves fell on the ground. Just as I was about to call Derrick, a silhouette of a woman outside caught my attention. My heart thudded. I placed my phone back in my pocket, blinked, leaned closer to the window, and searched for the woman. When my eyes met hers, she smiled and waved. *It couldn't be.*

I moved to the other window across the room and looked, and there she was in a white sleeveless dress that flowed all the way down to her ankles. It was one of my favorite dresses she'd owned. It was the dress she wore on our first date. Zoey stood under the maple tree next to a black wrought-iron bench. I shook my head and shut my eyes to regain focus and perhaps shake out the hallucination that had suddenly crept up on me, but when I opened my eyes, she was still there, sitting on the bench. She stood gracefully and started walking toward the woods. She paused, looked over her shoulder, and smiled as she vanished like a puff of smoke.

My heart dropped to my stomach. This couldn't be happening. Was this what Haley meant about not grieving properly? I'd told her everyone grieves differently, but she'd been adamant that I see someone before my mind started playing tricks on me. That's what it was. My grief, I concluded, and made a mental note to see my grief counselor once I was finished with my job. My phone vibrated, and though I wanted to forget what I had just seen, I couldn't, and I answered the phone, still in a trance.

"Hello," I said, not even looking at who was calling, my mind still reeling.

"Mikey, just dropped Kate's stuff at your cousin's house like you asked. The wife took care of them."

Derrick. It was Derrick. The mention of Kate's name shook me out of my trance. "Sorry, Derrick, you said something about Kate?" I asked, as I refocused. He repeated what he'd said.

"That's awesome, man, thank you."

"How's the babysitting job?" Derrick asked.

I paused. I had initially thought this was going to be a babysitting gig, but it turned out to be... *what? Fun?* It *was* fun.

"You still there?" Derrick's voice jolted me out of my thoughts.

"It's work. You know how that is."

"You sure, man? I heard Virginia is for lovers." Derrick chuckled over the phone.

"Man, *LOVE* signs everywhere." I gave a faint laugh.

"Told you. With that beautiful woman and in the "love" state? I bet it's romantic."

His comment took me aback. *How did he know Kate was beautiful?* Then it hit me, of course, he'd know. After all, he was the best PI I had worked with.

"I'm here for work. That's all."

"I know, just saying, it's been a while. I think it's time for you to—"

"Derrick, let's not go there today," I said, still trying to breathe from 'seeing' Zoey.

"All right, all right. Anyway, I called to tell you, I got eyes on Miller. He's renting a BNB outside Temecula."

"Really? Interesting. I wonder why."

"I would guess that he is trying to throw us off the scent," Derrick said, which made sense. "I'm keeping a close eye on him."

"Great. Keep me posted."

We ended the call, and I decided to go downstairs before returning to the room. Kate was already up and ready to go when I got back. I contemplated telling her what I saw, but decided against it. Instead, I handed her a Styrofoam cup.

"Here, I got this downstairs for you. It's hot tea. I thought you might enjoy one after your nap."

She gave me a suspicious look and then took a sip. "Oh, my gosh, you put chocolate in this," she said, her eyes sparkling with excitement.

"Yeah, Sally had some. Not *Dove*, but it's supposed to be better, she said. She told me she uses it for her pastries. I tried it, I hope you don't mind. I see why you like it; it's not bad."

Absentmindedly, I rubbed my fingers, still stinging from the burn I got pouring the boiling water into the cup.

"See, I told you. Thank you, Michael; this is so thoughtful of you," she said, smiling. Then, suddenly, her smile vanished. "What happened?" She placed the cup on the table and gently grabbed my hand.

"It's nothing. Just me being clumsy."

She looked at me, then, shaking her head, went through her purse, pulled out a small tube, and applied the ointment to my red fingers.

"You carry an antibiotic ointment in your purse?"

"Be prepared. That's my mantra," she said, then kissed my hand gently. It was like electricity. It shot through me, making my heart race, but I pretended like it didn't faze me. "I was on the phone with Derrick. He dropped your things at Hannah's and Ol's."

"Really? Thank you," she said timidly before hugging me.

This woman will be the death of me. I took a deep breath before turning around. "I'll just take a quick shower if that's okay," I said before walking to the bathroom.

I let the hot water fall on my tensed body as I stood still, allowing the water to drain all the tension that had built up from... *what? What was it exactly? No, not a what, but a who? Was it really Zoey I saw? Why now? After three years, why now? Then there was Kate. The kiss. The hug.* I was in huge trouble—that's what exactly.

Chapter Thirty-Seven

KATE

PRESENT

Something was bothering Michael; I could sense it. Did he find out more about Jim, but did not want to tell me? Or could it be that he was thinking of Zoey? A sudden knot formed in my stomach. Why was it bothering me so much?

The shower finally shut off; it felt like he'd been there forever. We had to be at Sally's for dinner in less than thirty minutes. The door opened, and my jaw dropped. He had nothing but a towel wrapped around the bottom part of his muscular, shimmering body. My eyes darted inches above the towel, and all I could see was the V-shaped part of his lower abdomen. Michael's hair was tousled, dripping as he rushed to pick up the clothes he had left on the bed.

"I'm so sorry, I forgot my change of clothes," he said, not looking at me, and ran back to the bathroom.

"It's okay," I yelled out, not sure why I felt I had to do that, but I did as I watched the ink on his back. I was pretty sure it was of an American Eagle and some words underneath it.

He stepped out of the bathroom, his hair already dry, and it was neatly tied back in a bun. He sat on the edge of the bed and put on his shoes. I could smell his cologne from where I sat, and it was sending electric pulses throughout my body. *What is going on with me?* Could it be the fact that we were sharing a room in the *love state*, or perhaps because it had been a minute since I was with a man? *Nonsense.* I snapped out of it, stood, and grabbed my purse.

"Ready?" I asked.

"Yup, let's go."

The dinner at Sally's was great. She was a lovely lady, and her daughter, Nichole, was just as sweet. We stayed for a couple of hours and had a couple of glasses of wine after dinner while we sat in Sally's living room and chatted the night away.

After dinner, Michael and I decided to open one of the bottles of wine we bought from the wineries and walked to the lake. The night was chilly, the moon was crescent, and the sky was filled with celebrating bright stars. Now I knew what Hannah was talking about; this place made you feel things. We sat on the bench in silence, sipping our wine. I glanced at Michael, and though he was next to me, his mind was elsewhere; it had been all night. I watched him study the wooded area in front of us.

"Dinner was good, wasn't it?" I said, breaking the silence and attempting to bring him back to earth.

He took a deep, loud breath. "Yes, Sally is a great cook. I would've eaten more if my stomach wasn't about to explode," he replied with a soft chuckle.

"The apple pie with ice cream on top—yum." I rubbed my stomach.

More awkward silence.

"Kate," he called out softly without a slight glance toward me.

I turned to him, "Yes?"

"Do you believe in ghosts?"

What in the world? Of everything he could come up with to talk about, he asked if I believed in ghosts. *Unsure how to take that.* I kept the thought to myself.

Suddenly, a slight breeze drifted through the trees, the leaves rustled overhead, and I could feel the subtle scent of the flowers surrounding us. *What timing!*

"Uhm, I'm not sure. I would say, no?" I said, but I also pondered the idea.

"Was that a question or a statement?"

"Uhm, I'd say no because I've never encountered one before. Why do you ask?"

"Oh, nothing, just curious," he said, crossing his hands behind his head, leaning back on the back of the bench, and stretching his legs before crossing one over the other.

"C'mon, there's got to be a reason why you asked such an odd question," I prodded.

"You'll think I'm crazy."

"Try me," I encouraged as I watched a few ripples dance across the glistening lake in front of us.

Michael took a deep breath and exhaled forcefully. "Sometimes I can feel..." He paused.

"Zoey?"

He rose abruptly and stood in front of me. "Crazy, right?"

"Not at all," I said, and it was the truth. I didn't think it was crazy. *Ghost?* I wasn't sure about that, but I did believe that when our loved ones pass, a part of them always remains with us, like my baby Savannah. "Perhaps I believe more in God sending his angels to watch over us, but I also know that grief can manifest in odd ways," I said, though my thoughts drifted back to my daughter. The thought made my heart tighten, and I brushed them away. I knew there were things only God could explain, I reminded myself.

I stood and grabbed his hand. "You'll always feel Zoey's presence around you because she lives in your heart," I said, trying to appease him, and it was the truth.

"I know, but lately, I feel different, like she's right here. *Real*," he said, looking distantly as he stood and paced in front of the lake.

My heart ached, suddenly feeling exactly what Michael was feeling. I missed my baby girl. I knew it was crazy; she was only four months in my womb, but we were connected, and our hearts beat together. There were times while I slept that it was almost as if I could still feel her heart beating with mine. She was real—*very real*.

Michael turned to face me; our faces were just inches apart. I could suddenly feel heat penetrating my body. Another breeze swept across my arm, gentle and calm, almost urging me to get closer, lean in, and *what? Kiss him?* I watched him stare into my eyes as if contemplating the same thing. Before I could move away, his warm lips covered mine. Electricity surged through my body. I'd never felt that way before, not even when I was with Jim. This was different. Just when I closed my eyes to savor the moment, he pulled away.

"We can't. I'm sorry. I shouldn't have done that," he whispered as he distanced himself from me as if just realizing I had some kind of contagious disease. "I can't fall for you, and Kate, you can't fall for me. I'm not going to..."

What just happened? As soon as I was able to take a breath, my head swirled, not sure whether it was from the mind-blowing kiss that just happened or from the shock of him pulling away so fast and telling me he can't fall for me. I stepped back, unsure whether to walk away, but his raspy voice stopped me.

"Kate," he called out as he approached me again.

"You don't have to explain anything," I managed to say, though my voice cracked. "It's this dang place. Hannah warned me about it," I gave a faint laugh. *Fake, faint laugh.*

"That's funny. Ol warned me too. You're right. This place makes you do stupid things."

Stupid? That's what he thought of it? Stupid?

"Yeah, it does. Stupid things." I cleared my throat and rubbed my arms to warm myself. "It's getting chilly, and it's already late. I think I should head back. I'm getting a little tired, too," I announced as I walked away. I didn't hear a reply, but I heard his footsteps behind me.

"Kate, listen. I didn't mean—"

"It's okay, Michael. I understand. You have a job to do, and we can't compromise that. I understand," I replied, not looking back because if I did, he would see the tears rolling down my face.

"I need to focus, you know. Your safety comes first. That's what's important. If something happens to you, I wouldn't be able to forgive myself." He paused, then sighed. "Maybe when..."

I knew what he was about to say, so I had to cut him off. I didn't want to have false expectations. Who knew where he would be and how he would feel after *this job*? The word started to have a different meaning; I loathed it. *I was just a job,* and what happened earlier was nothing but a *stupid mistake.*

We got into our beds that night, and neither of us spoke for a while. *Was our 'before-bedtime talk over'?* Gosh, I didn't want things to be different between us. He was right, he had a job to do, and I was making things difficult for him with my feelings. *I had feelings for him.* It wasn't a surprise, but the revelation still hit me like a ton of bricks. I curled underneath the blanket. *I had feelings for him.* What was I supposed to do with that now? I sighed.

"Are you okay?" he asked, his voice muffled.

Wow, bionic ears. I didn't think I sighed very loudly. "Yeah, *are you*?" I asked, trying to ease the awkwardness. "You sound kind of funny."

He chuckled. "I'm under the blanket. Can't you see?"

I sat up to check what he was doing, and as I watched, he popped his head out, pouting. *The plump lips. The puppy eyes. He wasn't making things easy for me, that's for sure.*

"Why?" I asked flatly.

"Cause you're mad at me," he replied, sounding like a little boy in trouble.

My heart melted at his attempt to apologize. "Get outta there. I'm not mad at you, silly," I said, lying back down.

"You sure?" he asked, peeking through the blanket.

"Yes. C'mon, get outta there."

"Your turn," he said as he slid out of his comforter and propped himself up.

I picked up my phone and checked the time. It was past one in the morning, but I wasn't complaining. I'd enjoyed these 'before bedtime talks' we had been having.

"Your favorite time of our day today."

"Everything," he answered quickly.

"If you can only pick one."

Silence.

We both stared at the ceiling, and after what felt like forever, he finally spoke. "Lots to choose from..." He paused again, then let out a deep breath. "I'd say, watching you take photos. It was quite fascinating."

The response caught me off guard. My heart quickened even though I decided to distance my heart from him.

"A place you'd like to visit."

"Guam," I replied.

"Guam? Why Guam?"

"Hannah spoke about it a lot, and I looked it up. It seems like a beautiful place to visit. Tropical."

"I've been there. It is beautiful," he said, as he lay down.

I rolled to my side to face him. "You have? Tell me about it."

He faced me. "Yeah, just for a week. I was stationed in Okinawa, and we had some work there. It's small, but there's a lot to see. Friendly people, rich history, white sand beaches, beautiful hiking spots, and the food—amazing. You know, a lot of people I know don't even realize where Guam is. They think it's just some remote island. But it has major restaurants, elegant hotels, gorgeous golf courses, and high-end shopping boutiques. I'm telling you, it's beautiful. You'd like it there."

"Wow, I didn't know that. Hannah told me, if we go, we'd have to go to the Philippines, too, to make the travel worth it."

"Yeah, it is a pretty long flight, but the Philippines is another beautiful country to visit."

"You sound like you've traveled a lot."

"Well, my job took me to a lot of places," he said, then let out a big yawn. "Sorry."

"You'd better get some sleep. It's late. Good night, Michael," I said as I lay down and pulled my blanket over me.

"All right. You, too. Good night, Kate. Sleep tight."

Chapter Thirty-Eight

JIM

PRESENT

I stepped into the Airbnb after meeting with the private investigator I'd hired to find Jenna. He handed me an envelope thick with photos. Jenna was with a man—and I didn't like the way he looked at her. They seemed way too friendly, too comfortable. Who the hell was this guy? He didn't fit Jenna's type; there was no way he was a boyfriend. The idea of Jenna dating again made my blood boil. We were still married, for Pete's sake. But what the hell were they doing all the way out in Virginia? It was time to find out, but I needed a plan.

"Do these things have to be displayed around here? It's ruining my mood," my 'girlfriend' complained as she passed by the board that had all of Jenna's information pinned on it.

"Sweetheart, I need this, *remember?* I need to find Jenna so I can get her to sign the divorce papers so that we can move on," I lied.

Deanna rolled her eyes. Yup, I was dating Deanna. After Jenna had disappeared, I had visited Deanna at the gallery. Of course, then, I had told her that Jenna had been away with her mom, recovering.

At first, she wanted nothing to do with me, as if I couldn't tell that she was merely playing hard to get, that she'd missed me. It didn't take long; she started flirting with me again. No one could resist my charm; she should have known that.

Right away, I noticed the difference in her outfit. She wore at least three-inch stilettos, clicking and clacking as she sashayed around the gallery in her black princess-style dress cinched at the waist with a white belt, just like what Jenna wore—it wasn't how I remembered her. From what I remember, Deanna was always in her animal-print outfits, which were a bit too tight or a bit too loose. She wasn't even close to Jenna's level of elegance, but it was obvious what Deanna was doing. Jenna could make any outfit look beautiful—effortless and graceful. Heck, she was elegant even in her sweats. Deanna couldn't pull it off.

Ann rushed to my side, asking when Jenna would be back. Deanna intercepted and asked Ann to fetch something from the back room. Ann rolled her eyes and walked back to her desk instead. Now, Ann was simple. She was in her pink floral blouse, beige slacks, and matching flats. She looked natural, had no make-up, had hair in a ponytail, and was tall, even with her flats. She was probably around five-eight; however, she was not my type.

"Jim, I *mean* Dr. Miller. What brought you in?" Deanna asked, smiling, revealing a few wrinkles on her forehead and crow's feet around her round eyes—poor gal, she used to be cute. The perfume she wore almost knocked me off my feet, and not in a good way. This lady must have doused herself with cheap perfume before coming to work. I turned around and took in some much-needed air, blowing it out with force. She glanced at Ann, as if to make sure she didn't hear us.

"Are you okay?" Deanna asked, creasing her forehead, which revealed more wrinkles on her fully made-up face.

"Oh, I'm okay. I just got lightheaded. Must have been a migraine coming on," I said, and I wasn't lying.

She led me to a beige couch where clients often sat while they waited for the art they'd purchase or to talk to the artist, who was my wife.

"Would you like a drink? Wine, coffee, champagne? Oh, you have a headache, let me get you some water," she offered, then turned to yell for Ann to do the job, before sitting next to me. I smiled at Ann, and she did get me the water while Deanna watched her.

There was no way Jenna would've just neglected her gallery. I was certain she'd reached out to them—she had to have. She loved her gallery. I didn't know why; I thought it was a waste of time, but she loved it. "So, how have you ladies been?" I asked nonchalantly as Ann handed me a bottle of Evian.

"We're good. How have you been? How's Jenna?" Ann asked, and I could see Deanna curling her lip from the corner of my eye.

"She's doing okay. Recovering," I replied.

"Oh, we miss *dear* Jenna," Deanna chimed in.

"Has she not called you?" I asked, hoping not to be too obvious.

"She did once. But that was a while back. We tried to call her cell, but she hasn't been picking up. I'm worried about her," Ann said.

I nodded. "Yeah, she just needs some time," I said.

"Well, just let her know to take her time. The gallery is in good hands," Ann said as she threw a look at Deanna, who just pursed her lips.

As I stood, a couple of new art images across the room caught my eye. "Was Jenna showcasing a new artist before she..."

Ann rolled her eyes, about to answer me, but Deanna slipped her arm through mine and rushed me to the wall where the images hung, clicking her heels and swaying her hips on purpose. I cringed.

"These are mine," Deanna proudly announced, then described each one. Despite my disagreement about Jenna being an artist and owning an art gallery, as I last checked, this place was called Jenna Miller's Art Gallery. I wouldn't think Jenna would've allowed any other artists' work to be displayed unless it was an exhibit she was showcasing.

"I didn't know you..." I glanced around for Ann. She was back behind the counter a few feet away from us. "Took photography. Was Jenna okay with this?" I asked.

Deanna grinned. "Just a hobby. Temporary, you know, until..." she gave me a smile that hinted at something she wasn't saying aloud.

"She said Jenna said it was okay," Ann chimed incredulously as she approached.

It was Deanna's turn to roll her eyes, huff, then look over her shoulder. "She did. She even encouraged it."

"If you say so." Ann walked away, shrugging.

Deanna had always craved being the center of attention. The way she copied Jenna's assertiveness at work and even her clothing styles, I could assert now that she struggled with a personality disorder. I guess I had never noticed it before. She once told me she had always been very competitive, even as a child. Deanna was one insecure woman who suffered from what I called HPD, or Histrionic Personality Disorder, and even though I didn't want anything to do with her anymore, she was my gateway to Jenna, so I did what I had to do.

Deanna pushed the board to the side as she sashayed toward the kitchen in my white shirt that came past her knees; it was too long for her short stature. She was a lot shorter than Jenna, a little pudgy, but Deanna was cute; she'd always been just cute. She grabbed a wine glass from the cupboard and a bottle of Merlot from the rack and poured herself one. She swirled the glass, brought the glass to her nose, and sniffed the aroma as if she were a wine connoisseur. I rolled my eyes.

"It's ten thirty in the morning," I said.

"What? It's brunch, would you like a glass?" she asked, still swirling the liquid in her glass, playing with it. "So, have you found out anything new about Jenna and where she could be?" she asked as she sat, extending and crossing her legs on a chair.

I ignored her and walked toward the window in the living room. Outside, the man who had been lurking around was back. This time, he was behind the bushes with his long-lens camera, like the ones photographers used at sports events.

"Get some clothes on, will you?" I demanded over my shoulder before I rushed outside to confront the man.

"Hey, what do you think you're doing? This is private property," I yelled as I hurried down the paved driveway, barefoot. The man took more photos, aiming at me before turning around, quickening his steps, and getting into his parked car a few feet down the road. I recognized the car immediately. It was the vehicle that had been following me a week ago. *How did this idiot find me?*

"Who was that?" Deanna asked as I stood there, trying to make out the license plate, but it was already too far away.

Damn!

I shrugged, not wanting more questions. I was pretty sure the guy was an investigator of some sort. I needed to find out why they were following me. Was it regarding Jenna, or had my past finally caught up with me?

Chapter Thirty-Nine
MICHAEL
PRESENT

I decided to take a walk while Jenna had coffee with Sally and Nichole at the library. The last few days had been very interesting, to put it mildly. My relationship with Kate had become complicated. Well, at least in my mind, it had. My feelings—that was what changed; no matter how I fought against it, I couldn't help but be attracted to Kate. All the little things she did, things she said, the way she moved, the way she smiled, everything was just so damn distracting. I was in trouble; I knew it. Everything shifted. Kate was not a job anymore. Kate was someone I cared about, and I would do anything to protect her from her lunatic husband.

The sun had started to set, and a cool breeze drifted through the air. The sky was streaked with shades of orange and pink, casting a warm glow over the lake. I immediately wished Kate were next to me, then a sudden knot tightened in my stomach, realizing this would all be over soon. We had been in Green Ridge for over a week, and the older couple we had met early on, and a few other guests, had already left. Neither Kate nor I had asked if a room had opened at Serenity Manor. I wouldn't question it, but part of me felt like I should. I decided I would talk to her about our accommodation later.

I kept thinking of the night we kissed. Her soft lips on mine were all I could think about, and the sweet scent of her hair wafting in the evening air as she welcomed my lips, parting hers and matching my tongue's rhythm while she wrapped her soft arms around my neck was absolutely intoxicating. I knew I wouldn't be able to get enough of her, but something in me needed to be logical, so I had pulled away. Why did I pull away? Calling our kiss a mistake was a pure lie, because it wasn't in fact, calling it a mistake took all I had not to protest my own words. But what was I supposed to do? I had to be her protector first. Could I keep her safe and kiss her soft lips again?

My phone rang, and I immediately answered on the first ring. I knew it would be Derrick. I walked toward the lake and saw Kate standing by the window. She smiled and waved at me, and my knees almost gave out. I waved back as I listened to Derrick on the other line. I finished my call as I saw Kate approaching. She had her hair pinned up and no makeup what-soever. I'd never seen her more beautiful. Just as she got close, a few hair strands fell on her face. I wanted to brush them back, even slip those gigantic tortoise-shell glasses off her nose, just to see her eyes clearly, but I resisted.

Suddenly, a cold breeze brushed against my arms, and that same sensation I'd felt days ago at the back of my neck returned. *Zoey.* I searched the surroundings, particularly the spot where I thought I saw her standing before. I must be going crazy. *Grieving can manifest in odd ways.* Kate had told me.

"Taking a walk without me?" Kate asked as she stood next to me.

I wrenched the thoughts away, but I couldn't speak. I stood there mesmerized by Kate in her light denim pants and white shirt. Yes, she was wearing blue denim jeans and a white T-shirt, not the usual disguise she always wore. I wondered why. I studied her. She probably thought I was being rude, but God, she looked beautiful—simple but beautiful. I felt a gentle brush on my cheek that shook me away from staring at her.

"Sorry?" I said, touching my face gently.

She smirked and shook her head slowly.

"Never mind. Was that Derrick on the phone? Any news? Can we go home now?"

Her last question made me wonder if she was getting tired of being with me. I wouldn't blame her. I had been pushing her away. Though it had felt like a vacation, she was still running and hiding from her dangerous husband. She probably couldn't wait to get back to normal, whatever that was.

"Yes, he sent some photos, but I have not checked them yet. He did tell me yesterday that Jim had been back in California."

"Well, can we check them?"

I turned my phone on and checked the images that Derrick had sent. They were random photos of Jim, some in a car, coming out of a car, and some were inside a house. I showed them to Kate.

"That's Jim, but that's not our house," she said, thinking out loud as she swiped through the photos.

My phone vibrated. "I think Derrick sent more."

"Let me see first," I said, wanting to ensure no upsetting photos were sent.

She handed the phone back. I stared at Jim, who was with a woman inside a car, in a few different restaurants, and inside the house where Derrick had taken the last few photos. It must be the new girlfriend Gayle was talking about, but then again, this didn't look like the model she described. I showed them to Kate.

She was silent as she studied the photos, but I could tell something had shifted within her. Was she jealous? I hope not, because whoever that woman was, she was not very attractive. Most of all, it was because that meant she still had feelings for her husband. I found the idea unsettling. I waited till she spoke.

"I can't believe it," she said, frowning.

"What?" I asked almost too eagerly.

She handed me the phone. "The woman in those photos is Deanna. She works for me at the gallery. Looks like she's dating Jim, now." She knitted her brows as if thinking hard.

"Are you okay?"

Kate sat on the black wrought-iron chair, and I sat next to her. "Yeah, I'm okay," she said, facing me, still frowning.

"Are you upset that they're dating?" I asked bluntly, bracing for her answer.

"Of course not, but..." She shook her head as if in disbelief.

"But?" *Lady, you're killing me. Say something like, no, it doesn't bother me. No, I couldn't care less... something. Something in my favor. Hello, weren't you the one who said she can't fall for you?*

"I know Jim. It's either he's using Deanna to get to me, or he really *is* dating her; either way, I need to warn Deanna," she announced, concern plastered on her face.

"Kate—"

"*Michael*, if something happens to Deanna, even though she was a pain in the you-know-what, I still wouldn't be able to forgive myself," she said, her eyes pleading.

I placed a hand over hers. "Yes, yes. I understand. Let's think about this, okay? Everything will be fine. I promise you."

"Thank you," she said softly.

We sat there, enjoying the sunset. The lake in front of us glistened as the leaves rustled slightly on the ground.

Kate shook her head as if thinking of something she disapproved.

"Yes?" I asked.

"I just remembered what Ann had told me."

"What's that?" I stared at the lake, then looked at her, wishing we were there under different circumstances.

She smiled, and my heart skipped a beat. Her smile had that effect on me.

"Actually, it was a warning," she gave a faint laugh as if remembering their fun conversation. "She told me that Deanna had a crush on Jim. She told me several times. She said, 'You better be careful, I feel like the moment you blink, Deanna will take over your spot, especially with Jim. I see how she looks at him.' I ignored it, knowing that they knew each other before Jim and I did. Gosh, was I oblivious?"

"That's right, you did say she introduced him to you."

"Something like that. It was in passing. I didn't even ask how they knew each other, and honestly, it never came up. But now, looking back, Ann was right."

"I guess she was." My back snapped straight. "Sorry, I didn't mean it like that," I said, regretting my tone.

"No, you're right, she was. I just didn't see it."

***

Later in the night, the weather turned, and the sky became dark and ominous, so we stayed in after dinner. It was a good thing we got back to the manor before the torrential rain started. We decided to stay at the cozy bar downstairs and grabbed a couple of drinks. I walked toward the table by the corner next to the window, and Kate halted, her wine in her hand.

"Why don't we sit over here?" Kate asked as she stood in front of the floral couch and set her glass on the center table.

"Sure," I said, sitting beside her, sensing her uneasiness.

"Are you okay?" I asked.

She nodded as she pressed the glass to her lips and took a sip of her Pinot Grigio. "Just not a fan of bad weather, that's all."

"It'll pass." I comforted her. She was probably still uneasy after the nightmare she'd had about Jim during the last storm.

We spent about an hour, and the storm came rumbling in. Kate flinched each time the lightning struck outside the window.

She took a deep breath and exhaled forcefully, then stood. "Would you mind if we continued our conversation in our room?"

"Yeah, no problem," I replied, sensing her growing uneasiness.

As we walked upstairs, another thunderclap came, followed by a bright light from the lightning. Kate jumped, instinctively linked her arm through mine, and held it tightly.

I held her close as we walked to our room, rubbing her arm to soothe her. "It's okay; we're almost there." I opened the door without letting her go and led her into the room. "Here, sit on your bed." She held on to my hand tightly. "I'm just going to shut the curtains, so the light doesn't penetrate," I reassured her, and she hesitantly let go of my hand.

Another searing bolt lit up the night, and she shut her eyes tightly.

"I'm sorry, I'm astraphobic, fear of thunder and lightning," she explained, scooting up on the bed. She sat down, pulled her legs in, and wrapped the blanket around herself like a scared little kid, only her head sticking out. "Had it since I was a kid."

Now it all made sense. She'd told me about her nightmare the other night; no wonder she was so frightened. "No need to apologize. I'm sorry... that must be terrible for you. It won't hurt you, though."

I could feel her trembling as I sat at the end of her bed, so I moved closer and rested a hand on her covered knee. "What can I do to help?"

"You're doing it already. Just keep talking and please stay next to me," she breathed.

My heart melted as I watched her. I scooted next to her and held her until she fell asleep.

Chapter Forty
KATE
PRESENT

I woke up sometime at dawn, and Michael was still sitting beside me, propped up, holding my hand. Something stirred deeply within me for this man. He never left my side. I tilted my head slowly to the right to get a better sight of him, making sure I didn't startle him in case he was asleep. His eyes were closed, and I took the opportunity to study his face. He must have let his hair down before he fell asleep; a few strands were on his face, and I noticed his five o'clock shadow. He looked peaceful despite sleeping upright in an awkward position. I wouldn't have been able to. My eyes landed on his lips, his rosy, heart-shaped lips. That's when I remembered them pressing on my forehead before drifting to sleep. I smiled.

I felt him caress my hand with his thumb. "You, okay, Kate?" he asked in a whisper. The way his raspy voice said my name made my whole body tingle.

"You're awake," I whispered as I positioned my head back on the pillow.

"Uh huh. Go back to sleep. The storm has passed," he said, not moving. I couldn't see if his eyes were open. He knew I was awake, but he still hadn't let go of my hand.

"Uhm, you should get some sleep, too," I mumbled.

"I have."

"Uhm... it couldn't be comfortable sleeping sitting up. Why don't you lie down?" My heart skipped a beat as I asked.

He didn't answer. Instead, he let go of my hand and wiggled himself to lie down next to me. "I didn't mean..."

"Do you want me to move to my bed?" he asked, not moving.

"I didn't say that," I replied, my heart now racing a hundred miles an hour.

"Good. Now close your eyes; you're safe," he said before switching off the lamp. Then he reached over, pulling me close to him. "Good night."

"Good night," I whispered back as I comfortably nestled into his arm with a massive smile on my face.

Michael's presence next to me felt safe. I felt safe. I hadn't slept like that for... years. Perhaps there had always been something off with my time with Jim, even in the beginning. I never felt safe in his arms like I had been in Michael's. Perhaps that should've been a warning, I've always had a good intuition about people and situations, but sometimes my trusting heart went against it.

I woke up the next morning, and Michael was still asleep. I could feel his breath on my neck as I lay there with my back pressed against him, with his heavy, but soothing arm over me. Michael had shut the curtains the night before so that I didn't see the lightning when it struck, but there was a sliver of light reflecting from the window through the mirror. I could tell the sun had just started to rise. I didn't want to move. I could stay in Michael's safe embrace forever, but he moved and lifted his arm away from me.

"I love you," his whisper was barely audible.

WHAT? I tensed, about to turn around, but something told me I shouldn't.

"I will always love you, **Z**," he whispered.

I tensed some more. There I was feeling good in this man's arms, but his heart was with someone else. Of course. What was I expecting? I shifted a little not to make it too obvious that I heard his undying declaration of love to his late wife. Was he feeling guilty? Was that the reason he was dreaming of Zoey? A psychology background can sometimes be a curse, making you read too much into things. I often wondered why that background didn't make me question Jim's personality before I married, because looking back now, it was as clear as a sunny day. The warnings were all over the place, but I didn't listen, I ignored it. I guess whoever said love is blind was right. I was totally blind.

As I attempted to rise from the bed, I shook the thought away, but his arm caught me. I slowly lifted his arm off my waistline and got up. I headed to the bathroom and sat on the toilet, contemplating my feelings. *Am I really attracted to him? Are you crazy? Yeah, you are. Ugh. But Zoey... How am I supposed to compete with her? I bet she was wonderful.* I shook my head as I stood up. *Snap out of it, Jenna. What is wrong with you?* I washed my face and brushed my teeth. I glanced up, caught my reflection in the mirror, and saw a different woman staring back at me. *This isn't you, Jenna. You can't keep setting your feelings aside like they don't matter. You matter.* That's when I realized it, the confident, strong, fearless woman I used to be had faded. It was like my red-dyed hair, once bright, now washed out and forgotten. Even the mismatched outfits I wore felt like they had slowly erased the true me. All because of Jim, and the thought of competing with a dead woman just made it all worse. I was tired of running. I needed to face him. I needed to get my life back. I needed to put myself first.

I got out of my PJs, stepped into the shower, and when I was done, I slipped into a white sweatshirt I bought from the boutique we'd stopped in during our walk downtown, and got into a pair of light blue skinny jeans. I dabbed a little moisturizer on my face before applying tinted BB cream, added a slight blush on my cheeks, and put a tinted pinkish/reddish gloss on my lips. I couldn't dye my hair back yet. I wanted to have it done right this time, so I pulled it all up in a bun before stepping out of the bathroom.

Michael was up; his eyes fixed on me. He studied me from head to toe and then returned to his seat.

"Wow," he said. That was it, nothing else.

Wait till you see me back to my original hair. I grinned like a woman with a devious mission.

I decided not to mention what I had heard earlier as we sat together and ate breakfast, as if we hadn't just fallen asleep, cuddling. I had to remind myself that he was just trying to ease my fears, that was all. He'd probably do it for someone else if he had to. After breakfast, we drove around to hit the wineries we hadn't been to and had lunch. As I got in our SUV, I froze. A chill ran down my spine. Someone was watching me. I spun around, but no one was there. Several cars were parked in the parking lot, but no one was around, yet I couldn't shake the feeling that someone was watching me. I could feel that piercing glare I got to know so well. I glanced and skimmed the surroundings. No one.

"Are you okay?" Michael asked, knitting his brows. He'd gotten good at sensing when I felt off—scared.

"Yeah, just thought someone was watching us," I explained.

He immediately scanned the area, walking back and forth and checking around the cars, his hand on his holster. "No one's here but us, oh, and Sally. There by the window."

Of course, all I had felt were Sally's eyes. I waved as she smiled and waved back.

"I guess that storm has me paranoid today," I said, now in the car, enjoying the morning ride. The sun was out, but it was still cloudy.

"I could make a quick call to Derrick to make sure he still has eyes on Jim," Michael offered.

"What exactly are we waiting for now? When can we go home?" I asked, and as my words came out, I noticed a little shift in Michael's demeanor.

"I'm sure you're getting tired of—" he said.

"Tired? Of this beautiful place? Not at all. I just want to know when I can return to normal, you know?" I said, assuming he thought I wanted to go home.

"Well, your husband is careful and has not attempted to contact you, but he will, and when he does, we will be there to get him. It's just a matter of time."

For some reason, they couldn't touch Jim yet, something about probable cause. I knew they were waiting for him to make some impulsive mistake, but it had been a couple of weeks, and it hadn't happened yet. I knew Jim; he was careful about everything. But I needed to do the right thing and warn Deanna. Whether Michael would agree, I wasn't sure, and I didn't care either way. I had to warn Deanna about Jim.

I contemplated making the call without letting Michael know, but I decided against it.

"Are you sure you want to do this? What if Jim answers? What would you do?" Michael asked casually, studying the area as we walked into Old Town Vineyards, one winery in Rappahannock County. Just like the other vineyards we'd been to, this place exuded nostalgia, where time slowed down, with people's faces painted with smiles of satisfaction and relaxation. Perhaps they were just drunk from the wine. Whatever the case, the place was beautiful, and the people were happy.

We found an empty picnic table with an umbrella outside, next to a tree. We both placed our wine glasses on the wooden table while waiting for the food we had ordered to arrive and continued our conversation.

"I'll deal with it," I said, finding a new sense of courage. Perhaps it was because Michael was with me. "But Jim is dangerous, and I will not forgive myself if something happens to Deanna because I didn't warn her," I said adamantly. I was no wine connoisseur, but I absentmindedly swirled the drink in my hand, releasing a mixture of fruity and spicy aroma as my lips met the rim of the wineglass. "Wow, this is good," I added as I took another sip.

I was more of a white wine, Rosé kind of woman, but I would occasionally step out of my comfort zone and try new things. Well, red wine wasn't new to me; I just avoided it because it gave me migraines, but we were in a place where vineyards surrounded us, so I had to try something else.

"Okay, I understand where you're coming from. You can call her."

"Michael, I wasn't asking for permission. I just needed you to know," I said in a soft tone, careful not to sound condescending. I knew he wasn't trying to control me, unlike Jim; he was just being cautious.

He nodded and took a sip of his Cabernet. Our food finally arrived, and we enjoyed lunch under the shade of the tree. A gentle breeze drifted through the air, the sun shone softly, and grapevines that were nestled at the foothills of the Blue Ridge Mountains surrounded us. It was picturesque. Suddenly, the thought of all this ending made my heart ache. Michael was a great guy, and though I knew he was there to protect me per Oliver's request, I knew Michael cared. I fiddled with the fries on my plate, thinking of how quickly I had gotten attached to the man in front of me. I felt him staring, and heat washed over my face when I saw his glistening brown eyes—they looked amber in the sun.

"What?" I asked sheepishly.

"What's on your mind?"

I glanced at our romantic surroundings before answering. "I will miss this," I said softly.

I expected him to follow my gaze, looking around the area, but he only bit his lip, stared into my eyes, and said, "Me, too."

Chapter Forty-One
KATE
PRESENT

We drove around before heading back to the Manor. We were supposed to have another dinner at Sally's house. She wanted us to meet her son, Dillon, who, according to her, was in town for a visit. After a few hours, we were back near the Manor, and as we were pulling in, I noticed a dark blue car parked outside the entrance. I couldn't tell if anyone was inside; the windows were tinted. I looked at Michael, but he didn't seem bothered by it much.

When we got to our room, I called Deanna. The phone rang a few times, and I was about to hang up or leave a voicemail; I hadn't decided. But then I heard Deanna's voice on the line.

"Hello?" There was a question and uncertainty in her tone, like she wasn't expecting me to call.

"Deanna, it's K... Jenna."

"Jenna..." She paused, and I heard footsteps, like she was pacing to get some privacy, but I didn't know. Then she got back on the line. "Oh my God, Jenna! How are you, dear? Where *are* you? Are *you* okay?" Her pitch was three times higher than what I was used to.

Dear? When did she start calling me that? "I'm okay," I said, smiling as if she could see me. "How are you?"

She blabbered for a while, telling me about Ann, how she'd been slacking off at the gallery, that she had to step up, and so on. She never once mentioned Jim, so I had to bring him up.

"Deanna, I heard about you and Jim—" I said.

"Oh, Jenna, honey, it just happened. We're familiar, you know?"

Familiar? I thought they were acquaintances. She'd never even talked to me about him, nor had Jim. *Familiar?*

"You know how Jim Miller can be. He's very sweet, and he told me that whatever you had was over. You guys are over, right? In fact, he's been looking for you. He wants a formal divorce," she rattled on, and her last statement flabbergasted me. *He wants a divorce? I filed for divorce, but he wouldn't sign it!* I wanted to yell. My blood boiled. Oh yeah, this time she called me *'honey'. Dear... Now, honey?* Something was off; Could it be guilt? Guilty for dating Jim without telling me?

I took a deep breath before responding. "Deanna, listen to me. I don't know what Jim told you, but he isn't the man you think he is, you need—"

"Hey, wait a minute!" Her voice rose an octave higher, if that was even possible. "You walked out on him, Jenna. You can't be saying things like that about Jim. Of course, I know Jim—"

"Deanna, listen—"

"No, Jenna, you listen! You hurt Jim, and now he's finally moved on, and I know you didn't expect it to be with me, but what can you do? Not everything is about you, you know. I know it sucks that he finally wants a divorce from you and wants to marry me, but that's just how it's going to be. Stop making him the villain," she snapped over the phone.

My concern for Deanna vanished, replaced by irritation. Suddenly, my head started to throb, and I could feel my blood pressure rising. *I walked out on him?* I guess that was right in a sense, but I had a reason for doing so. Jim had made it sound like I just walked out for no reason, like I had cheated and run away or something. Typical Jim. He was always so good at making people believe certain things, even without saying anything. And now he wants to marry Deanna?

"Deanna—" I started to say again, but she kept on interrupting, and honestly, her yelling wasn't sitting well with me anymore, so I let it go.

"Okay, Deanna. Can you at least do me a small favor?"

"What?!"

"Please be careful," I said, my tone soft, and I meant it.

"Whatever!" And just like that, she hung up.

I pressed a hand to my forehead and sat at the edge of the bed just as Michael opened the door to our room. He immediately read the frustration etched on my face.

"Everything okay?" he asked, a slight panic in his voice as he sat beside me.

"Sort of," I replied, shutting my eyes in frustration.

He shot up quickly and stood in front of me. *"Sort of? What does that mean? Was Jim there? Did he talk to you?"* There was almost an edge in his voice.

"No, no, nothing like that. I didn't talk to Jim. I don't know if he was even there, and if he was, I didn't care."

"Kate—"

"Deanna won't listen. She yelled at me. She said I walked out on Jim, and that I don't have the right to talk badly about him just because I was jealous or something like that," I interrupted, not wanting to hear him tell me I was being reckless.

Michael blew a heavy breath and sat back down next to me. "I'll have to call Derrick later and see if he has any updates about Jim. We can't be too careful," he said, his voice gradually losing some of its edge.

"Thank you. I'm sorry. I just needed to protect Deanna," I said, leaning my head on his shoulder. "I hope you understand."

"Well, you tried, kid. That's all you can do. And yes, I understand," he muttered as he placed his hand on top of mine.

I rose from the bed quickly, and Michael flinched. "Oh, and guess what else?" I said, raising my voice. "Jim is looking for me so he can ask for 'divorce'." I threw a heavy air quote. "So he can marry Deanna. Can you believe that?!" I finished acidly, rolling my eyes.

I would've missed the question flickering across Michael's face if I hadn't glanced back at him while pacing the small room. I stopped, facing him. "Am I wrong to be frustrated?"

"Of course not. You were trying to help," he explained, looking up at me. "It's okay, Kate. Remember, Jim probably used his charisma on her to get to you, or if this whole relationship is true, I'm sure he told her a bunch of lies, starting with who he is," Michael reminded me as he gently grabbed my hand and pulled me to sit beside him. Suddenly, I was aware of his hand on mine, and I felt a surge of electricity that immediately made me forget my frustration, causing me to look into his concerned eyes. What happened next took me by surprise. Michael planted a kiss on my forehead.

He backed away just as quickly as his lips touched my forehead. "I'm sorry, that was a habit," he announced regretfully—embarrassed.

"It's okay. I appreciate it, and honestly, I needed it," I said, smiling slightly.

"We have to be at Sally's soon. I think it'll be good for you to be around people, but let me jump in the shower and rinse off quickly, if that's okay," he said before slipping his shirt over his head. I guess he now felt comfortable doing that in front of me. Well, it wasn't like he was taking the rest of his clothes off.

"Hey," I called out softly.

He pivoted. "Yeah?"

"What are the words on your back?" I asked. I'd been meaning to ask him about it. I'd seen it before, but it was only a glance when he changed his shirt when we first arrived, and the writing was small.

He stepped closer, and the warm trace of his skin, mingled with the fading edge of this morning's cologne, sent my senses reeling. "Oh, here," he said, bending slightly so I could read what was written on his back.

"*Semper Fi,*" I read aloud, fighting the urge to trace the words with my fingers.

"It's short for Semper Fidelis, which means always faithful. Marine Corps' motto," he said.

He stood straight, smiled, and headed for the bathroom, leaving me with my head still reeling from being inches away from his bare skin.

Chapter Forty-Two

KATE

PRESENT

The night was bright, illuminated by a half-moon surrounded by twinkling stars, and, if my astrophotography lessons were correct, a few planets as well. I was sure Venus was one of them, just down to the moon's left. We said goodbye to Sally's family, and when we stepped out of the door, the hair on my neck perked up again as I felt eyes on me. I spun my head, looking to see if someone was around. No one. Yet, someone was watching me, watching us, but I couldn't find him anywhere. I decided not to tell Michael, but he was on to me.

He pulled me in closer. "You're okay. I'm right here."

We walked back to the manor after our dinner at Sally's. She had prepared pasta with her well-simmered, well-seasoned marinara sauce—her exact words. It was apparently her son's favorite. After dinner, we had her famous baked apple pie with vanilla ice cream. Her kids had joked, "It's to die for." Michael and I enjoyed it. It was to die for.

I was laughing at something Michael had said as we were heading upstairs. Suddenly, I heard someone call me. "Ms. Rivers," The lady from the front desk stopped me. I turned around to face her; a smile was still plastered on my face from my conversation with Michael.

"Ms. Jenna, this was dropped off for you earlier," she said, smiling, handing me a bouquet.

Michael rushed down from the steps and pulled me in closer. "Are those eleven roses?" he asked rhetorically as he held on to my hand tightly and scanned the lobby. I, on the other hand, remained speechless at the sound of my real name being called, my heart dropping to the floor as I stared, *no, glared* at what I once thought was a beautiful bouquet of white roses. Over the last couple of years, they quickly changed into something that sent me into a spiral of fear and dread. Only one person would have sent me that exact arrangement—Jim.

"When were they delivered? Did you see who delivered them?" Michael asked the lady, who took a few steps back as Michael questioned her.

"I'm sorry, I didn't get a good look at the guy," she said, shrugging her shoulders.

"Was he young, old, tall, short? Anything you remember?" Michael continued to interrogate the poor young lady. "I know the place has a couple of cameras. Can we check them?"

Sally must have heard the commotion because she rushed right next to me as she passed us by from the kitchen area. "Everything alright, Margaret?" she asked, looking at her staff, still holding the flowers. "Those are beautiful."

"I didn't mean to upset anyone, but this was delivered earlier," Margaret told Sally, frowning.

"What happened?" Sally asked. I could tell she was worried that Margaret had done something wrong.

"I don't know." She shrugged. Confused. "The kid who delivered them said it was for Mrs. Miller, but I said no one was staying here by that name. Then the kid pointed at her." She looked in my direction. "Gosh, I didn't think anything of it. I was helping another couple check out. I'm sorry. I hope I didn't do anything wrong," she said, her voice cracking.

"I'll take that, thank you." I gently grabbed the flowers from Margaret's hand. "This doesn't look like it came from a shop," I said.

"Note?" Michael asked.

I shook my head.

How did he find me? Anger was quick to brew inside me—not at Jim, but at Michael. *Wasn't he supposed to be protecting me?* How did this happen?

Sally tilted her head slightly to one side. "Did Margaret do something wrong?"

We never told Sally the whole story, and I didn't think Michael would tell her now. My shoulders slumped. Poor Margaret, she was just doing her job. "I'm sorry. It's a long story." I said, facing Sally. "No, she did nothing wrong. We'll explain later."

Glancing at Michael, I waited for him to say something, but he was quiet, his face red.

"I'm sorry, it's not your fault," I said, lightly touching Margaret's shoulder. She gave me a faint smile as she started to walk away.

"If you remember anything..." Michael finally said.

She turned, nodded, then continued to walk away.

When Michael asked to see the cameras, Sally led us down the hallway to her office. "That's Isaiah. His family just moved into the neighborhood not too long ago," Sally said as we stared at a young teenage boy in shorts, a white shirt, and a baseball cap, holding the bouquet, walking towards the front desk.

"Do you know where he lives? I want to ask him some questions," Michael asked.

"I'll do you one better. I'll bring him in; he's outside talking to my son, Dillon."

We followed Sally towards their house, and outside were Dillon, Nichole, and Isaiah.

"Isaiah, this is Mr. Michael. He'd like to ask you about the flowers you delivered to the house earlier," Sally said.

"Hello, sir," the teen said, then smiled, his bright blue eyes suddenly sparkling with excitement as he looked toward Dillon. "I was just telling Dillon that it was the easiest fifty bucks I've ever made. Flowers didn't even cost that much."

"You purchased the flowers yourself?" Michael asked.

"Oh, no, sir. I know, because I bought red ones for my mom's birthday a few weeks ago. A man asked me to deliver it to Mrs. Jenna..." he paused, trying to think of my last name. Then, like a light bulb suddenly turning on, he remembered. "*Miller*. That's right, Jenna Miller. But the lady at the manor said no one by that name stayed there, so I pointed at you," he explained, looking at me.

"How did you know I was... Jenna Miller?" I asked in a low voice, as my heart tightened.

"The man showed me your photo," Isaiah said.

"Do you still have that photo?" Michael asked, his eyes narrowed, each word sharp, but he was also holding back, trying not to scare the boy.

He shook his head. "No, sir. He kept it."

"What did this man look like?" Michael asked.

Isaiah wrinkled his forehead as if trying to recall. "He was in his car, he had a baseball cap on, and had sunglasses, so I really couldn't tell. I was just excited about the fifty bucks," he said. Then his face softened. "Wait, did I do something wrong? Did I get someone hurt? Oh man, did I?" He shoved a hand in his pocket and pulled out a fifty-dollar bill. "Here, you can have it back."

"No, man, you did nothing wrong. Tell you what. I'll trade you for another fifty," Michael said as he took out his wallet, grabbed another bill, and handed it to the kid. "Thank you for your time."

But before the kid could walk away, Michael called out. "Wait, what kind and color was the car, and did you see the license plate number?"

"Blue," he said, then shook his head.

***

"How did he find me, Michael?" I asked softly, but I was sure he could sense my fear and disappointment.

"Kate, we don't..."

"Michael, who else would it be? It's Jim. He found me! Again!" I said, knowing what he was about to say. *Lies.* Lies so he could make me feel at ease. That's the last thing I needed from him. What I needed was his protection and for Jim to stop stalking me. I needed my life back. That's what I needed. Not lies!

I stared straight into his eyes. "I do, Michael. I know it was him," I said flatly, then I stepped outside to get some air. A soft breeze brushed against my skin; suddenly, I could feel eyes on me, and my skin crawled, my heart thudding. I stood frozen, scanning my surroundings.

"Get inside," Michael said sharply, one hand resting on his holster.

I froze. In front of me was the parking area just behind the round, sculpted bush. I could see the parked cars and a couple just getting out of their vehicle. To my right was the gated swimming pool with a few outdoor chaise lounges between two lighted poles. Two ladies were chatting the night away, dipping their feet in the water, and sipping wine. I spun my head to check the vast lawn on my left. I studied the pebbled pathway between the massive trees, but no one was there. The manicured lawn was huge, and my eyes couldn't scan fast enough, but I swore I saw someone sitting on the wooden tree swing, far from where I stood. I wasn't sure; it was almost a silhouette, so I rubbed my eyes and took another look. No one was there, but I still couldn't shake off the feeling that someone was watching me. *Still.*

His voice softened but was firm. "Kate, *please* get inside and stay with Sally. I'll look around."

I let out a deep breath I didn't realize I was holding in and nodded as I turned around and walked inside the house.

Michael came back after what felt like an eternity. He looked calm, but I could see that he was frustrated.

"Everything is good," he announced as he came closer.

"Are you sure?" I asked coldly, nauseated from the sight of eleven white roses.

"Let's go back upstairs. I'll make a few calls and find out how Jim figured out where we are." He gently grabbed my arm, but I instinctively brushed it off. I was exhausted. I didn't want to talk, mostly because I didn't want to say anything I would regret later. I was mad at Jim, but angrier at Michael for letting this happen. I just wanted it all to end.

"C'mon." He offered his hand, and I stared at it. I wanted to confront him, blame him, but I knew he'd been in touch with Derrick several times a day. He had been doing his job; maybe it was my fault for distracting him with my feelings. I looked back toward the swing and checked one more time. No one was there.

Chapter Forty-Three
MICHAEL

PRESENT

The night dragged on, and sleep eluded me. Kate barely spoke to me when we got back to the room. I knew she was scared, and for good reason—I failed her. I let my feelings cloud my judgment. Now I could sense she'd lost trust in me.

But Derrick had eyes on Jim back in California. So, who the hell was the man with the flowers? It wouldn't be beneath sick, twisted Jim to hire someone and just mess with Kate's head. I needed to refocus. Earlier, I'd spoken to Sheriff Darrin Rodgers and asked him to keep an eye out for a blue sedan. Not much to go on, but in a small town like Green Ridge, an outsider with a blue sedan would stand out. Hopefully.

Now back to basics—to the facts. I needed to dig, to question, to trace every detail the moment we arrived. Someone knew Kate was here. Someone wanted her afraid. If that someone wasn't Jim, I needed to find out who.

Jim had been careful. I'd dug into Jim's past before we came to Virginia, but I went deeper last night. I couldn't sleep anyhow, so I figured I might as well try to find something—anything about this infamous Jim Miller. But I couldn't find anything new, just records of his college years onward, clean, immaculate, almost too perfect. Whoever he was before no longer existed.

This morning, Kate started talking to me again; thank God, but I could feel something had changed. After breakfast, she asked to go to a beauty salon downtown, the one that Sally had recommended. I didn't ask. Not that she would have told me anyway, but I didn't ask. I just stayed outside the salon and waited. I did notice the shift in her wardrobe. She wore black leggings, a black top, white sneakers, and that long beige cardigan we'd picked up the other day. *Was she starting to revert to her old style?* Though she wasn't in a sheath dress and three-inch stilettos, like in the photos she'd shown me, I liked it. This was simple, clean, and collected.

At the salon, several women and men had come in and out while I waited by the car, and for a second, I almost didn't recognize Kate when she finally stepped out. She didn't just look different, she moved differently; held herself different-ly—she even glowed. She was a whole other woman. Her hair was straightened, making it appear longer than she had ever styled, dyed back to its original dark brown. It shimmered under the sunlight as she walked toward the car where I stood, leaning with my right foot on the bumper. She wasn't Kate any longer; she was full-on Jenna again. She was gorgeous.

She smiled as she approached the car. "Well?"

I wanted to say something, but the words escaped me. I was mesmerized by her natural beauty. She wasn't wearing too much makeup this time. I assumed she applied a slight blush to her cheeks and dabbed a shimmering tinted gloss on her lips.

I trembled, fighting so hard not to kiss her. Her brown eyes sparkled in the sunlight, and my heart fluttered like a butterfly.

Her smile faded. "You don't like it," she said softly, touching her newly styled hair.

Her frown jolted me back to my senses. "You look gorgeous, Kate," I said, releasing a squeaky voice.

She gave a faint laugh. "Jenna. Jenna Rivers," she announced and extended a hand for me to shake as if introducing herself to me for the first time.

I cleared my throat and repeated it. "You're gorgeous, Jenna."

"Thank you. I was afraid there for a second, thinking you didn't like it. I was going to go back in there and ask the hairdresser to dye it back to red," she teased before reaching for the car door handle. I jumped quickly and opened the door for her instead.

"Why, thank you, sir." She grinned before claiming the passenger seat.

I got into the driver's seat but didn't start the car. Instead, I looked at her beautiful face, happy that she was bantering with me again. "You look beautiful with red hair, but I think this is you," I said, staring into her sparkling eyes like a star-struck fanatic.

"Thank you. This *is* me," she smiled. "Now, I don't have to go back and dye it red."

"Thank God!"

"I knew it!" she said, pointing a finger at me with her eyes glaring as if she had just caught me in a big lie.

We started laughing. Seemed like we were back to normal. *I hope.* Then she held my hand and stared into my eyes.

"Michael, I can't run anymore. I'm tired of hiding. I'm tired of being a pushover and not putting myself first..." she paused, and I wondered if my failure had caused her to feel this way.

"Jenna—" I started to say, but she squeezed my hand.

"Please," she whispered, asking to let her finish.

I drew in a deep breath and let it out slowly, bracing myself as she continued.

"This is me. This is Jenna. Confident, strong, tenacious. Somewhere along the way, I got lost. I fell in love, got blinded, and everything changed. Especially when I lost my baby, I thought my heart would never beat again. Then you came..."

She stared at me, her eyes glistening, almost penetrating my soul, and my heart dropped all the way south. I could hardly breathe.

"And my heart woke up, but I realized I can't compare to the memory of Zoey you're still holding onto. That's on me, too. I had been putting my feelings aside for a long time; I'd run, I'd hidden, I even reinvented myself, for what? So that Jim could win? So that I would always live in fear? No, I can't do that anymore. I won't. I need to come first. Not second to fear. Not second to Zoey."

My heart clenched. I hadn't realized I had made her feel like she was second to Zoey. "How..." I started to say, but words escaped me. I stared ahead, eyes fixed on nothing as everything in me went still.

"You whisper her name in your sleep. You even called me by her name once. Michael... please don't get me wrong. I like you, and I think you like me, too," she paused, waiting like she needed me to confirm it and say something. Anything. But I stayed frozen.

Almost defeated, she lowered her gaze and spoke softly. "But you were right all along. You were right to pull away from me. I had blamed you for letting your guards down and letting Jim find me, but it was all my fault; it wasn't yours. I got too comfortable too soon. Ol told me to trust you, and I did, but I also dropped all my defenses. I seem to do that, you know?" she said, trying to make me understand. "Now, I need to come first, and I know that with Zoey still—"

I couldn't take it any longer. My heart was threatening to burst out of my chest. And in one swift motion, I claimed her lips. At first, she protested, then kissed me back. Warm. Soft. Welcoming. For a moment, I almost wanted to cry.

When we finally came up for air, I stared straight into her eyes, tilted her chin up, and wiped a tear that had fallen on her beautiful face. "You'll always be number one to me, Jenna. I'm sorry I made you feel otherwise. You're right, I like you, too. I tried not to, but you make it so damn hard." I paused. "But Zoey will always be a part of me. I'll always love her, *miss* her. But it's time for me to move on, and I hope you let me move on with you after we take care of your problem," I said, nervous at what her reply would be.

Jenna's eyes glistened as she cupped my face with both hands. "Zoey will never be forgotten. She'll always be a part of you." She pressed her palm to my chest. "But maybe someday, I'll take up more room there."

I kissed her again, like there was no tomorrow, and when I opened my eyes, across the street, I noticed a blue sedan. The windows were tinted. I didn't want to alarm Jenna, so I started the car and pulled out of the parking spot.

"Blue Sedan across the street," I said casually. "Don't turn around, in case it's the same car. Let's see if it follows."

Jenna kept her eyes on the road, but I could tell she was anxious. I held her hand. "You're safe, I promise."

"I trust you," she said.

Chapter Forty-Four
MICHAEL
PRESENT

*T*he blue sedan followed us, but after a few turns, it must have sensed I was on to him. After a while, it took a different turn. It looked like a man driving, but I couldn't make out the face. Baseball cap and sunglasses, just as Isaiah had described. So, there was no mistaking it; it was the man who delivered the flowers for Jenna. I did get the license plate, which turned out to be a rental under some random name Jenna wasn't familiar with. I did some research, and nothing came up.

That afternoon, Jenna and I decided to stay at Serenity Manor. "Do you want to take a walk? The sunset looks so beautiful. We won't have many of these when we get back to Sacramento," Jenna said as we sat by the pool sipping wine.

There was no stopping her from going back to California, so I agreed, but the stipulation was that we had to be joined at the hip, and she agreed.

"Sure, in a bit?" I replied. After our encounter with the blue sedan this morning, I had a strong feeling that it would be hanging around the manor today, so I wanted to check. "Why don't you go inside? I just need to get something from the car, and then we can go for that walk," I said, gently placing my hand on her back, leading her inside.

Sally was by the door. I had told her about our encounter that morning, and she called Sheriff Rodgers immediately.

"Come, dear. I have a fresh-baked apple croissant. It's still warm," she said, softly pulling Jenna's hand and escorting her inside. I mouthed the words "thank you," and Sally nodded.

I didn't want to alert the driver in case he was indeed outside, so I tucked myself behind a wide and tall tree trunk just inside the gate where I could peer from without being seen. I was right, the car was parked just off the road, low behind a patch of trees, barely visible to someone who wasn't looking.

I snapped a few photos with my phone, then made my move. Keeping low, I slowly crept forward, hoping I wouldn't be noticed. I got close, and just as I was about to confront the driver's side, it peeled off. But not before I caught a glimpse of a second person inside. *Damn it.*

I pulled the phone from my pocket and called Derrick.

"Hey there! Was just about to call you," Derrick said.

"Dude, are you sure you have eyes on Jim Miller?"

There was a sudden alertness in Derrick's voice. He sounded thrown. "Yeah, in fact, I was about to send you some photos I took earlier. Why? What's going on?"

I huffed. "Jenna—*Kate* received some flowers from Jim the other night, and today we noticed a blue car following us."

"License plate?" Derrick asked, his tone sharp.

"Yeah, it's a rental under some random name. I already checked; nothing came up."

"Huh, is it by chance under Mark O'Brien?"

"No. Who's Mark O'Brien?" I asked, even though I knew the answer.

"Our infamous Dr. Jim Miller. Get this... Apparently, this Mark kid was ambitious. Wanted to be rich and started hanging out with a bunch of rich kids from a nearby private school. Told them he was traveling from Europe and started partying with them. What a dope! Anyway, one kid found out and exposed him. They shunned him and, from the sound of it, bullied him, too. Guess the kid had a breakdown. After his mother passed, just after he turned eighteen, he left with his girlfriend, and they never saw him again."

"How did you find out all of this? And who's they?"

"Thanks to Jenna," he said.

"What?"

"Well, when we dropped her stuff off at your cousin's house, I noticed a high school yearbook in one box. It nagged at me, so I went back and checked it out. One photo stood out. The name was erased, but it was screaming young Jim Miller to me, so I sent the photo to the school, and spoke to the principal, and voila!" Derrick explained enthusiastically.

"Great job, Derrick. But if you have eyes on Jim—*Mark*, then I'm assuming he'd hired someone to scare Jenna," I said as I started walking back toward the gate. "Oh, there was a second person in the car, but I didn't get a good look."

"This guy is good, Michael, so it wouldn't surprise me if he hired some people. Don't worry, we'll get to the bottom of this and will update you."

I thanked Derrick and walked into the house to find Jenna. I decided to keep the news to myself for now. Jenna, Sally, and Nichole were in the kitchen, gathered around the counter in front of a few apple pies. The scent wafted in the air, almost making me want to have a bite, but I was too preoccupied with what had just happened.

Straightening myself, I kept my voice neutral. "Just got off the phone with Derrick."

She straightened her shoulders, suddenly alert. So were Sally and Nichole, all their eyes on me. "Please tell me he didn't lose sight of Jim."

"No, Jim's still in California. Derrick just sent me photos from this morning. Here." I said as I started to show her.

"I don't want to see them," she said flatly. "So, the man in the blue car?" Jenna asked, frowning slightly.

"Jim probably sent him to scare you."

She rolled her eyes.

"Typical psycho," she said matter-of-factly. Then, she came closer with a plate of pie and a fork in her hand and smiled. "Have a bite." She fed me a piece of warm apple pie with ice cream on top.

"It's to die for," I said, winking as I opened my mouth.

"Right?" Sally replied, and Nichole rolled her eyes.

"Are we still going for a walk?" Jenna asked.

"Of course. Are you ready?" I replied.

"Let's go before it gets dark. I love the sunsets here, so visibly glowing and radiating," she said.

We took a sunset stroll inside the compound, holding hands and walking along the pebbled path. It felt natural.

I kicked a pebble to the side; there was no sense in keeping the truth from her. "The blue car was outside the gate. I had tried to confront the driver, but he saw me and peeled off before I could."

"Did you see the face?"

I shook my head. "He had a baseball cap and sunglasses on. But there was another person inside," I said as we passed by the horses.

"Who do you think it was? You said Derrick still had eyes on Jim." Jenna halted to face me, her hand tensed.

"It could be anybody. He could be a friend—partner of the man your husband hired to scare you," I replied, squeezing her hand, trying to ease her concern. She relaxed, and we continued walking. For a while, we walked in silence.

"I'm ready to face him, Michael," Jenna announced out of nowhere.

I halted, and she did the same, still holding my hand. "Jenna, are you sure?" I asked. My voice is low. I wanted to support her in her decision, but I was also hesitant about having her around Jim.

She nodded. "I'm not afraid anymore, especially knowing you'll be with me. You will protect me, right, Michael? My protector?" She grinned.

The question hit something deep inside me because it was the same question Zoey had asked me once long ago. We stood on a paved stone pathway, the sun was behind her, facing me. I squinted a bit, staring into her golden eyes, then my gaze dropped to her lips. She stood in front of me, waiting for my answer, with her dark brown hair flowing in the slight breeze that had suddenly appeared. I tucked a strand behind her ear, still getting used to the real Jenna. She smiled. Blood rushed through my body, and I instantly covered her mouth with mine.

She slowly welcomed my hot, longing lips. We stood under the sunset, cool air on our skin, and I could hear the rustling of the leaves surrounding us. Our lips locked together while the sun set behind us. Before I knew it, the darkness seeped through. Though it had only been a few minutes, it felt like forever, and I didn't want it to stop. We looked at each other, and I was sure her eyes mimicked my ignited passion.

"Mark O'Brien, have you heard the name?" I asked, my voice wavering.

Jenna repeated the name and shook her head. "Is he the man I married?"

"Yes."

Chapter Forty-Five

MICHAEL

PRESENT

Michael, I heard Zoey whisper into the air as she stood in the garden outside the manor in her white, ruffled, long-sleeved maxi dress. Her dark blue eyes sparkled under the sunset, and her long blonde hair flowed and danced with the soft breeze. She was angelic.

Zoey placed a flower on the wooden bench next to the garden and approached closer. She lifted my hands and put them on her heart, as if asking me to feel her heartbeat.

"Z," I cried.

Zoey smiled a smile I'd never seen before, almost like she glowed; it was beautiful. Zoey pointed up, and suddenly, a soft breeze followed, and I could practically feel something touch my heart. I couldn't explain it.

"Oh, Z—" My heart spasmed.

She picked more flowers but avoided the white roses. When she came back to where I stood, she held the flowers in her hand. The sun was fading fast. A soft breeze stirred the leaves in the trees, making Zoey's dress float in the air.

She handed me the bouquet and smiled, her eyes twinkling under the sun setting behind her. Zoey placed a hand on my heart. *Promise you'll love again.* The words seemed to echo in the air.

"I promise," I whispered, though she was already fading away.

"I will always love you, Z."

Zoey looked over her shoulder, smiled, and then vanished with the sunset.

Chapter Forty-Six

JENNA

PRESENT

I lay in bed, thinking about how we only had two more nights in Green Ridge, and I wasn't sure whether it was the company or the place itself that made me want to stay longer. I knew for sure that I'd be coming back; whether it'd be with Michael, I wasn't sure, but I hoped so. Either way, I knew I'd be back. We had kissed again, and this time it lasted longer than the first. Gosh, the look in his eyes after he pulled back was intoxicating

The last time I checked my phone was almost midnight. The thoughts of how I would face Jim—*Mark O'Brien* occupied my brain, and I couldn't sleep. I also couldn't believe that he had moved on with Deanna, of all people. Why Deanna? She wasn't even his type. She was one of those social climbers, trying hard to look expensive but couldn't. Still, I felt I needed to protect her from Jim, but how? She sounded like she was under his spell. Jim was good at that; heck, he got me. He got me good.

I wondered what his real story was. What made him change his name? Was he running from someone, the police, the government? *Was he an escaped convict? God, I've seen movies about escapees; they never end well.* I pulled the blanket tighter around me, trembling—*embezzler, or maybe worse.* My thoughts scattered everywhere.

Michael suddenly moaned, making me sit straight on my bed to check on him. He was talking in his sleep. At first, he was just moaning and groaning, then there it was again.

"Z," he called out like he was trying to stop her.

I wondered what they were talking about. I sat there and listened, and for a moment, I felt like I was invading their privacy. Suddenly, *I* felt guilty, but what was I supposed to do? Leave the room in the middle of the night so he could have a private conversation with his dead wife in his dream? So, I listened.

"I will always love you, Z," he continued.

The words stung a bit, and suddenly my heart tightened, questioning whether I could really move forward with him. Still, I listened.

"Goodbye, Z."

Goodbye?! Was he finally saying goodbye to Zoey? He couldn't be. What was I thinking? It was a dream, for crying out loud. He rolled to his side, and that was the end of their conversation, at least out loud. My mind wandered. What if he was kissing her in his dream? Of course, he kissed her in his dream; she was his wife. *Snap out of it, Jenna!* I huffed and plopped my body back down on the bed.

"Are you okay?" *Great, I woke him up.* I wasn't sorry; I could use the company while my brain worked overtime, tossing between the thoughts of Michael dreaming about Zoey and Jim dating Deanna. And of course, his bedroom voice sent electricity down my spine on top of the butterflies doing acrobatics in my stomach.

"I'm sorry; did I wake you up?" I asked.

"No, I was half asleep," he mumbled through his yawn.

Liar. I kept that to myself. What was I supposed to say? *Ah, no, you were not. I heard you talking to your wife while I sat here watching you and getting jealous. Wait, did I just say jealous? No, I wasn't jealous... Eh, a little.*

"Go back to sleep," I said.

"Are you okay?" he repeated in his raspy voice, which sent more chills down my body. It took all my strength not to toss my blanket to the side, climb out of bed, and climb into his.

"Yes, I'm okay," I lied. I wanted to tell him that things wouldn't work out between us.

Suddenly, a bright light flashed through the window, and not long after, a deafening blast erupted. My heart thudded. Michael was quick to his feet, tossing the blanket aside and pulling the room-darkening curtain over the sheer one.

I hated that I feared storms; it made me look weak. Whatever happened to me as a child really did a number on my psyche. Throughout the years, I learned to manage the fear; I only got anxiety over it whenever I wasn't in the comfort of my home, but this one caught me by surprise. I didn't know a storm was coming. I did my breathing exercises and tried to calm my nerves as I pulled the blanket and comforter over me, as if to shield me from the storm.

"Scoot a bit, will you?" he said as he climbed onto the empty side of my bed.

"Uhm," was all I muttered, apparently out loud.

"I'm your protector, remember? Here to protect you from the big, bad storm," he teased, not even glancing my way as he settled beside me in his white shirt and multicolored flannel pajamas. *Multicolored.* The ones I had once used to disguise myself. The ones he said were totally unflattering—the ones I wouldn't be caught dead in under normal circumstances. Yet, my brain short-circuited, and I found them hot—really hot. *Where in the world did he get that?*

I knew he was joking, trying to keep my mind off the storm as the thunder roared even louder in the background. Michael sat back up and walked into the bathroom. When he came back, he handed me a pair of earplugs.

"C'mon, scoot over," he demanded again playfully as if I had moved from where I was before he went to the bathroom. For a moment, I had forgotten about the torrential rain outside, looking at the earplugs in my hand, surprised at his thoughtfulness. During the years I was married to Jim, he never once offered me earplugs or comforted me through the storm.

"I'd wear those before another... you know." He gestured toward the window.

There went my heart again, thudding, but not from the thunderstorm roaring in the background, but from the man now lying next to me, comforting me, protecting me.

"Thank you," I whispered as I adjusted the earplugs inside my ears.

"You're welcome; now lie down and try to get some sleep."

Yet, even as I lay next to Michael, my eyes fixed on the ceiling, it was not Jim or Deanna who occupied my thoughts this time. It was the man beside me. I took a deep breath, slowly let it out, and rolled to face his back. I could smell his masculinity, and it sent my senses into overdrive. I heard him breathing. It wasn't a snore, but I knew he was asleep; it was soft breaths in and out. Suddenly, he rolled to his side to face me, just as another bolt of lightning struck; a sliver of light shone through the corner of the window, enough for me to see his eyes open. Despite being dark, I knew we were staring into each other's eyes in silence as if having a mutual feeling of anticipation and passion. I could feel the heat emanating. I could feel the heat grow stronger between us, a connection I'd never felt before.

I felt him move, and suddenly, his warm lips touched mine, lips that were burning, waiting since the last time we'd kissed. I welcomed him by parting them slightly, but his hunger over-powered my attempt to be demure. He claimed my lips with such passion, and I returned the favor. He was a good kiss-er—no, great kisser. He kissed me like I'd never been kissed be-fore. Our rhythm was seamless, every movement, every breath, in tune.

Michael rolled over on top of me without breaking the kiss. My body reacted, sending heat all over, pulling me to oblivion. He drew back so we could both sip some much-needed air and then moved to my chin, kissing it softly. I tilted my head slightly, giving him access to my anticipating neck, and when his hot, wet lips touched it, I let out a soft moan that sent him flying back to my lips, claiming them with much sweet aggression. I forgot everything; I forgot where I was. All I knew was that I was with this man. I was with Michael, and we were both where we wanted to be, completely surrendered, completely gone.

Before I even realized, the storm was over, and I was still nuzzled under Michael's comforting embrace, wearing his white shirt. I felt safe.

"Get some sleep, Babe. We have a few more hours before the sun starts to shine," he said as he kissed the top of my head, and I fell asleep, feeling high from him calling me *Babe*. Oh, and of course, the kiss.

The following day, I woke up lying next to this hunk of a man; his eyes were still closed, his hair loose, with a few strands falling across his face. I studied his strong, well-chiseled jaw before landing my gaze on the lips that had covered mine just hours before. That's when everything started flooding back. Suddenly, the butterflies in my stomach awoke and started doing somersaults. I fixed my eyes on his lips; they looked plump and satisfied, though not as satisfied as I would've liked them to be. So, I decided perhaps they needed a little more plumping. Then, as if on cue, he moaned, and before he could even move, I immediately kissed those savory lips.

"Morning, Babe," he said, smiling widely at my greeting.

Chapter Forty-Seven
DEANNA
PRESENT

S itting in the dark in my apartment, sipping a glass of wine, I thought about Jim—he was back, and I was happy, well, somewhat, because there was still something he was not telling me, and I needed to find out. I couldn't help but think about Jenna. She was the only one in the way of my happiness with Jim. I took another sip as I thought of her.

I heard she had graduated from college with honors—*big deal.* I didn't graduate and had to leave the university. Well, I couldn't very well stay after my scandal with Jim. On top of that, the murmurs around campus became unbearable. They made me feel like I had leprosy or something, gawking and murmuring whenever I passed by.

I cringed at the memory and swallowed what was left of my wine. I stood, grabbed the bottle from the tiny counter, and poured some more. I walked toward the window, drawn to the thin sliver of light sneaking in from the busy world outside. The apartment was almost painfully bare—just the couch the previous owner left behind, a bed, and a single dresser. It wasn't much, but with what I could afford, it was enough at least for now. I thought about Jim—the time we spent together as high school sweethearts in Minnesota. He was still my Mark then. We were happy, but we also had our own problems.

"Don't worry, Baby, I'll take care of you, I promise," he'd said as he sat next to me on the bleachers, brushing my tears away. He looked so young and innocent then in his ripped, denim jeans, white T-shirt, and baseball cap.

I looked out to the field, the sky was blue, the sun was hot, but I didn't care; I needed him, and he was there. "I don't understand. He hurts her, Mark, but she wouldn't leave him," I cried as I told him about my mom's useless boyfriend. My mom worked hard, but her boyfriend worked even harder to get the money she made.

"I know, baby. I don't get it either," Mark said, holding my hand.

"Let's run away. Just you and me," I said, facing him, waiting for him to say yes.

"You know I'll take care of you, but we've got no money right now. Where would we stay?"

"Take me to your house. I can't stay one more day in mine." I wiped my tears away.

"You know I got my own set of problems at home. I can't let you stay there; it wouldn't be safe.

Mark's dad was a drunk, and he beat the crap out of him with every move he made. I felt sorry for him, but Mark took it well. He'd always tell me he would get out of his situation soon, and I believed him.

"Baby, I hate it at my house. I hate it there so much," I said.

"I know, Baby, but your mom needs you. You should stay with her. Promise, I'll come back for you."

I shot up. "Come back for me? Where are you going?" My heart dropped at his announcement. He never told me he planned to leave.

"I don't know yet, but now that we're done with school, I need to get a job, but not just a job. Something that will make us rich, you know? And I've been thinking, the only way that'll happen is for me to get a job and go to college."

"College? How are you going to do that?"

"I'll figure it out."

Mark was good at figuring things out. That was the only way he and I survived our families, and Mark had ambitions, so I knew he would achieve whatever he planned.

"You know those rich kids I hung out with?"

Mark met a couple of kids from a nearby school for wealthy kids and hung out with them until they found out he wasn't one of them—a rich kid from Europe visiting a family in the area —and then they avoided him.

"Yeah, I don't like them," I said, laying my head on his shoulder, pursing my lips.

"Well, I'm going to be rich, and I will prove to those punks that I am better than them," he said, his eyes burning with intensity.

"How?" I asked, lifting my head, looking at him, trying to figure out what exactly he was planning.

He kissed the back of my hand. "I don't know yet, but I would have to go away for a while."

"Why?"

"Shh. Shh. Trust me, I'll be back for you, okay? Can you trust me? No questions."

No questions, those were his infamous words. Whenever I'd ask about something he was doing or going to do, it was always, *no questions*, so I nodded, then leaned in to kiss him.

A few months later, his mother passed away, and Mark left after the funeral.

"I will come back for you. I promise. No questions, just trust me," was the last thing he said.

After what felt like an eternity of not hearing from Mark, he was suddenly outside my house. He came back for me in a rented car, smelling good, dressed in jeans, a blue blazer, and white tennis shoes—he cleaned up good, looked expensive, too.

"Hi, Baby! I told you, I'd come back for you," he said, smiling, and kissed me like he'd never kissed me before.

I didn't know how he did it, but I knew then that he'd accomplished what he was after. A few days later, Mark and I flew to California. He helped me get into Sierra Vista University under a scholarship and got me a job with a professor. Mark told me he'd changed his name to Jim Miller and that we had to leave our past behind. I was glad to leave our past behind, finally, so I didn't ask. All I knew was that he was back. I was happy.

But when we got to California, he told me no one could ever know of our relationship, since he also worked for the university. I didn't question him. You never question Mark O'Brien. But also, because he promised that after I graduated, we would get married and move to another country. Not sure where, but that didn't happen—obviously.

One day, I had made the mistake of seducing him while the professor I worked for was away, we got caught, and I was kicked out of the university. Mark told me to lie low, to stop hanging around him until the situation died down.

Months later, it had become harder and harder to get a hold of him, until one day, he just told me to get lost. *GET LOST!* I couldn't believe it. I was heartbroken. I had nowhere to go. I had no friends because Jim told me not to get close to anyone. Then I remembered one person: Jenna Rivers. I happened to follow her on Instagram one day (she never followed me back) and saw one of her posts. She looked so happy, smiling in her beautiful white sheath dress and black stilettos, holding giant scissors. It was the opening of her new art gallery in Temecula. That's when I decided to visit her, and what a coincidence, she was looking for a sales associate.

"When can you start?" she asked.

"Now. If you want me to," I said eagerly.

She had no idea who I was, and I didn't bother to enlighten her, considering my past. It was kind of embarrassing to go down memory lane about how you got kicked out of the university for messing around with a professor, even though he was technically my boyfriend. I just needed a job, and she gave me one. I enjoyed working there, learning photography and art from Jenna. She was talented—that, I could give her.

Months later, Jim walked into the gallery.

"Mark—I mean, Jim." Surprised to see him, I tried to hug him, but he pulled back.

"Deanna," he whispered under a smile, looking past me.

I looked back and saw Jenna watching us.

"Where have you been?" he asked in a sudden change of tone.

"Well, after you—"

"I've been calling and looking for you. I've missed you," he said, still in a whisper, and barely touching my hand.

Happy to see him, I ignored it. "Really?"

"Yes... but, you know, our arrangement back at Sierra V? We still have to do that... for a bit longer."

"But why?"

"I'm close. Really close to getting what I want, and after that, we can be together. Can you give me that? Just a little bit longer, Baby," he said, then gave me the smile I'd missed so much.

I looked at him, searching his eyes, and I knew he still loved me. I nodded.

"Your boss... she's looking at us," he said.

"I'll take care of it."

I didn't know why, but when it came to Mark, my logic seemed to disappear. He *had* been there for me back home and had always stood up for me in high school. I had also waited so long, and now he was back. But then, I blinked, and before I knew it, Jim and Jenna were dating. Heartbroken and betrayed, I confronted Mark.

"Baby, trust me, you know I'd come back to you. I have a plan. You trust me, don't you?" Mark said one day while lying on the couch in my apartment, resting his head on my lap.

"But, now you're going to marry her? What about me? Us? Our plan?" I asked, tears coming down my face.

"Come on, I came back to you before, didn't I? Our plan is still in motion, Baby. Trust me"

"Yeah, but you left me," I said, stroking his hair.

"I didn't leave you, Baby, you knew that. You know I had to leave... for us," he said, then sat up and kissed me on the cheek. "Trust me, this is for us—"

"But—" I started to say.

"No *buts*, remember? Remember high school? When you were bullied, who was there for you? When no one wanted to hang out with you, who was there for you? I took care of you, didn't I? No questions. You know, I'll come back," he said, kissed me on the forehead, then walked toward the door, paused, then looked back. "Maybe you don't trust me. Just tell me, then I won't bother you anymore," he said, hurt.

I ran to him. "No, no. Of course, I trust you. I trust you, Mark," I said, hugging him from behind.

He turned around, kissed me on the forehead, and smiled. "Good girl."

Mark had that hold on me. I knew he was coming back; he always did.

I kept my mouth shut, supporting Dr. Jim Miller even after he'd married her, because soon, after he got what he wanted from Jenna, he would divorce her, and I would become his wife. I pretended not to know him, watching him visit Jenna at the gallery, go out to dinner with them; it was excruciating, but it was all for *us, the plan.* I went along with his plan for months, watching the happy married couple, my heart breaking every time I saw him with her, until something shifted in their marriage. I knew then that Mark was coming back to me soon.

Suddenly, I'd noticed something different about Jenna—she wasn't as happy as she was when they first got married. Of course, she wasn't. Her husband didn't love her. He loved me.

One day, I followed her and saw her coming out of the gate of their beautiful, expensive Mediterranean-style home with a few ladies I didn't recognize. Jenna had large bags with her, acting all skittish and in a hurry. She hugged the lady in scrubs before getting into a car I had not seen before. Jenna didn't own a beat-up Toyota Corolla. Something was up.

Jim had told Ann that Jenna was staying at her parents' home in San Diego after her recent mugging. Something wasn't adding up. Jenna was up to something, so I followed her, and thank goodness she didn't drive far. She drove to Moreno Valley, about 45 minutes from Temecula, but for what? I watched her go inside an apartment, and that was it; I hadn't seen her since.

After going down memory lane, I decided who needs a glass? I drank the wine straight from the bottle and headed to bed.

***

One day, while at Jim's house, his laptop caught the corner of my eye, and I jumped down instinctively from the stool I was sitting on in the kitchen. *Password protected*, go figure. My heart raced as I felt the excitement of figuring out Jim's password. I typed his birthday, my birthday, and his middle name, only to be met with disappointment. Finally, I typed Jenna's birthday, and I was in. *Typical.* My blood boiled at the thought that he hadn't changed his password from Jenna's information to mine. Several folders popped in front of me, but I was only interested in one, Jenna's. I clicked it open and perused several pieces of information that didn't interest me until I came across one labeled *Receipts.* I clicked it open.

There were several receipts from jewelry stores, boutiques, and flower shops. One receipt had intrigued me. It was an order for a bouquet of eleven white roses. Why eleven? Why not make it a complete dozen? *Odd.* I closed the folder and noticed that his browser was still open. I clicked it open, and it took me to his emails. I smiled and gladly perused them until I came across one in his recent sent folder; it was to Jenna, and I read:

My sweet Jenna,

The last few months without you have been hell. I miss you so much. I miss us. Please forgive me, and please, let's talk. Give me another chance. I promise I've changed. I've even sought help from a colleague so I could become a better man, a better husband for you. Please, sweetheart, give us another chance. I love you, and I always will.

Your regretful husband,

Jim

My blood boiled, my eyes twitched, and my nerves screamed for murder. Jim had never intended to divorce Jenna; he was trying to reconcile with her. I clicked off the browser, closed the folders, and slammed the computer shut. Jim was mine. *Mark* was mine. Jenna never appreciated him. I had waited so long. I had to do something. I had to show Mark that I was the one he should be with, just like old times. Jenna had to be eliminated for him to see that.

I knew Jim had hired a P.I. again to find Jenna, so I looked up the number, called him, and asked for an update. Jim's PI told me he'd found Jenna in Sacramento, working at a veterinary clinic under the name Kate. I told him I'd pass the message to Jim, and that he didn't have to call him because he was busy in a conference and didn't want to be bothered.

I had made several trips to Sacramento, and each time I was there, I ordered 11 white roses and had them delivered to Jenna's work. I meant *Kate* or whatever. If she were really running away from Jim, I needed her to know that he had found her, to make her squirm. Eleven white roses—very unusual, so there was no doubt in my mind that she would've thought it was from Jim.

I had watched her go in and out of her apartment and the veterinary clinic where she worked. At one point, I watched her throw away the bouquet I had sent her—*ungrateful witch!* I'd seen her glance around several times before getting into her vehicle, as if she knew someone was watching her, exactly how I wanted her to feel. I wanted her to feel fright, paranoia, fear. I'd made several hang-up calls a day. I'd made little noises on the line, just enough for her to hear my breath, and she would quickly hang up. I had sensed her fear over the phone, and I knew I had gotten to her.

I called again a few days later, just to put more fear in her. But an unfamiliar voice answered. I hung up. A few hours later, I tried again, and the same woman picked up. My pulse kicked up. Something was off, and I needed to know what. I drove to Sacramento and did what I'd done before: watched for her outside the clinic. But she never showed. She was gone.

Chapter Forty-Eight

DEANNA

PRESENT

Jenna called a few days ago and dared to warn me against Jim. Ha! As if I didn't know. She just didn't want Jim and me to be happy. That's why she even made up stories about him. But that was Jenna, never satisfied with what she had. She had the gallery, and she had Jim, and yet, she was ungrateful. She didn't even thank me for introducing them. *Selfish witch! But who cares? I have Jim back. I have Mark back.* Just like we'd always planned.

I spent the night at the Airbnb Jim had rented in Fallbrook, and the next day I walked barefoot to the kitchen in Jim's shirt to get a glass of wine, passing by the nook where he had the board filled with Jenna's information. It looked like one of those things from an obsessed stalker you saw on TV, like Law & Order, but it didn't bother me. Mine probably looked similar, but instead of a board, mine was on a notebook.

I'm trying to track her to get divorced, finally, he'd told me one day, *Ha! Like I didn't know!* I still didn't care because I would be Mrs. Jim Miller sooner or later. I glanced around the coastal-themed house Jim rented. It had white walls with pops of ocean-inspired colors: sea-foam green, beige, and light blue. The living room looked like the beach had thrown up in it, with various sizes of seashells and starfish as the main decor. Papers were scattered on the dining table next to a large bowl of sand with shells and stars. I rummaged through the papers. Nothing pertained to where Jenna was, and then a brown envelope caught my eye. I opened it, and there were photos of a red-headed woman. A few images had a man next to her. I wondered if this was the man she left Jim for; they sure looked chummy.

A business card fell as I tried to put the photos back in the envelope. *Ralph Iriarte—Private Investigator,* I read silently. *Of course.* I returned the card, walked toward the kitchen, opened a bottle of Merlot, and sat on the stool in the nook area, staring at Jim's board and formulating my plans.

It wasn't hard to convince Ralph Iriarte to go along with my plan. I wore a low-cut leopard-print blouse that barely supported my tatas, tight black leggings, and black stilettos to our first meeting. Ralph's mouth drooled in anticipation as I approached the corner booth of the hole in the wall downtown where we agreed to meet. He was hesitant at first, but after I handed him an envelope with a thousand dollars and promised to go out on a date with him, the sleazeball believed me and gave me all the information I wanted.

The next day, without telling Jim, I was on a flight to Virginia with sleazeball.

We followed Jenna to an Airbnb called Serenity Manor in Green Ridge, Virginia. I wore my dark denim jeans, a black long-sleeve shirt, and a baseball cap, tucking all my hair in so I would look more like a man and slipping on a pair of dark aviators. If I didn't know any better, I would say I was one good-looking guy.

As we sat in the car waiting for them to show up, I wondered if she had really run away from Jim because of what he supposedly had done to her, or if she had run away to save face; after all, she was the one who'd left Jim. She broke his heart. I shook the thought away; it wasn't important. What was important was for her to understand that there was no reconciling with Jim. Jim was mine. She took him from me.

I watched Jenna and her man come and go from the manor, and suddenly I had the brightest idea. I picked up a dozen white roses from a nearby store and tossed one out. I wasn't sure how to get them to her, but luckily, I saw a teenage boy outside the gate, and he didn't hesitate to deliver the flowers.

A few days later, we followed Jenna and her man to a salon downtown. I studied him as he waited for her by his car. Yeah, he was good-looking, but was he a doctor? Did he have money? Whoever he was, all he probably had were good looks, unlike *my* Mark—*Jim.* I really needed to remember to call him by his new name; he hated it when I made mistakes. Anyway, he was *everything.* Someday, soon, I would become *Mrs. Jim Miller,* I reminded myself.

After munching on a few bags of Doritos while I sat in the car with the useless PI next to me, waiting for her to come out from the salon, Jenna finally emerged, her hair flattened straight and back to her natural dark brown color. I even caught a glimpse of sparkle in her eyes as she walked toward her man. Suddenly, there was a lump in my throat I couldn't get rid of. I forced a cough. *No, I wouldn't let her bother me,* I told myself. *I'm more beautiful than she could ever be, and*

Jim will be mine. I kept my eyes on her as she walked toward her man. I turned my attention to the man; I could tell he was in awe of her. He looked at her like no man had ever looked at me before. I swore I didn't see him blink as he watched her every step; they looked like cheesy characters in a romance movie. *Barf.* But watching them irritated the heck out of me, making my blood pressure rise, especially when he touched her hair, as if touching something so precious—so delicate. Aaaargh! I slammed both my hands on the steering wheel. *I hate you, Jenna Rivers!*

We followed them again the next day, this time to a vineyard a few miles out. I sat at the bar where I had a clear view of Jenna, and when she got up to head to the bathroom, I followed. Once she entered a stall, I slipped into the one beside it and stayed there until she came out.

I listened as Jenna chatted with another woman who came in after us. While washing her hands, she told her that she and her friend were leaving Virginia in a couple of days, heading back home. She said they'd miss Green Ridge and would definitely be back someday. *Blah, blah, blah.* Someone wiggled the knob of my stall, and I almost shrieked. I hadn't realized how tightly wound I was until that moment. "Occupied," I said, my voice unnaturally high. I just hoped Jenna wouldn't recognize it.

When I heard the door shut, I stepped out and darted for the exit, nearly knocking over an older woman on my way out. Jenna was going back home, which meant I had to book the first flight out the next day. Sleazeball and I needed to get back before she did.

Chapter Forty-Nine
JENNA
PRESENT

We arrived at Sacramento International Airport past eight in the evening and stepped out into drizzling weather. Oliver was already outside waiting for us. As I climbed into Oliver's black SUV, the sudden feeling of someone's eyes behind me returned. I froze and scanned the surroundings, feeling the drizzle on my head. Jim was around; I could feel it. My heart raced, especially knowing I could easily be recognized now that I had returned to my old self.

"Everything okay?" Michael asked as he held the back passenger door for me.

"I just..." I took a deep breath and slowly let it out. "I just feel like someone's watching me again, but I could be just overthinking, now that I'm back home," I said.

I knew Michael was way ahead of me as far as scanning the place for a threat, but he did it again, anyway. "Please get in," he said gently before closing the door. He surveyed the busy area before entering the passenger side. He turned around in his seat, reaching for my hand. "Everything is okay. You can relax." He caressed my hand to ease my worry. I could feel the grin forming on Oliver's face, but I ignored it; I didn't feel like entertaining his thoughts at the moment.

"Did you see anyone suspicious?" Oliver asked as he maneuvered the SUV out of the busy loading area.

"Not here. Not at this exact moment, but earlier I did," I replied.

Oliver's facial expression changed to worry. "What do you mean?"

"I've always felt a sudden panic whenever Jim is around; my vision gets blurry and my hearing gets muffled. I swear I felt the same thing last week in Green Ridge."

"Did you see him, Mikey?" Oliver asked as he focused his eyes on entering the interstate, but he also kept glancing at the side and rear mirrors, as if he was watching someone following us. I looked back and inspected, but I noticed nothing unusual.

"A suspicious car started showing up outside the manor a couple of times, but Derrick confirmed he still had eyes on Jim," Michael replied as he, too, studied the rearview and side mirrors.

I looked back again, but still didn't notice anything—just a bunch of cars speeding on the road at night, which was normal for the Sacramento interstate.

"So, who do you think it was?" Oliver asked, but not before I noticed him exchanging glances with Michael as they both looked at the rearview mirror at the same time.

"We think Jim may have hired someone to scare Jenna," Michael explained nonchalantly, trying not to bring any attention to whatever it was they'd noticed.

"Are we good? Is someone following us? I've seen you both check the rearview and side mirror a few times," I asked, my voice coming out in a high pitch I hadn't intended to use.

"Just making sure," Ol said as Michael reached for my hand again, and the grin on Ol's face was impossible to miss.

They continued talking like there was nothing to worry about, so I relaxed.

"So... any other interesting things happen while you were in the love state?" Oliver grinned as he asked the question.

Michael looked at me through the rearview mirror, and Oliver caught him.

"You know you two will have to tell Hannah and me all about it later, right? Over bourbon? I don't think I could take it without," Oliver said, glancing at the mirrors again. He wasn't just glancing for the sake of driving; he was glancing as if he were watching something or someone behind us.

"I don't know what you're talking about," Michael said as he smiled at me through the mirror.

"Like *that*? Really?" Oliver asked, as if offended.

I smiled.

Both men exchanged glances at each other, just when a sudden screech made my smile disappear into the night as our car swerved into the other lane, and my upper body was thrown sideways and back.

"Jerk!" Oliver yelled out as he settled our car back in our lane.

Michael was quick to unbuckle his seatbelt to check on me. "Are you okay?"

I rubbed my neck. "I think so. What was that?" I asked, still dazed.

"I noticed the car creeping in. I didn't think he would cut me off like that," Oliver said.

"I had been watching it, too. It followed us just as we got out of the airport," Michael said.

"Did you get the plate number?" Ol asked.

"Yes, it's a Cali license with a heart in the beginning and P—"

My head spun, and my heart dropped as I interrupted. "S-Y-C-H," I said, spelling the letters of Jim's Lexus custom license plate, my voice was low and tight. "I told you someone was watching me."

"We will get to the bottom of this. I promise," Michael said, anger evident in his heated voice.

"How did he know you were arriving tonight?" Oliver asked.

"Jim always has his ways," I replied, my voice cold and flat.

"Could he be the one in Green Ridge following you?" Ol asked as we finally pulled into the hotel's garage, where we had stayed before heading to Virginia.

"No, it wasn't him. Something is off," Michael answered. "I'm calling Derrick," Michael announced as we entered the hotel lobby, but his phone vibrated before he could dial the number. He answered and started pacing around the lobby.

"That doesn't make any sense. What car is he driving?" I heard Michael say over the phone.

I didn't wait for whatever was next in their conversation; whatever food was left in my stomach was coming up fast. I marched toward the lobby bathroom, placing a hand over my mouth.

"Where are you going?" Ol yelled out.

I squirmed and pointed at the bathroom sign a few feet from where they stood. Michael and Ol followed but stayed at the entrance. The bathroom had at least a dozen stalls, if not more. I chose the one in the center. I don't know why, but I never picked the first stalls.

I bent over the toilet as I felt the heave getting stronger. I heard footsteps coming in and out of the bathroom, people flushing, closing and opening doors, and finally, it was quiet. After I took care of business, I stepped out of the stall and glanced at myself in the golden-rimmed mirror. God, the color had left my face. I washed my hands and looked for the hand dryer near the door. I walked toward it, placed my hands under it, and let the loud swooshing air dry them. I felt a prick on my shoulder like a mosquito bite, and I instinctively brushed it off, but suddenly I could feel my legs giving out, and my vision getting blurry. I tried to stand straight, but my body went limp, and I went down. Someone caught me, and just before the blackness came over me, I smelled a familiar scent in the air.

Chapter Fifty

MICHAEL

PRESENT

I hung up the phone and searched for Jenna. When I didn't see her, I felt a surge of an unexplainable, ominous feeling in the pit of my stomach.

"What's taking Jenna so long?" I asked Ol who was standing in the hallway.

Ol just shrugged. My heart thudded; I could feel something was wrong. I rushed through the corridor and knocked on the door. "Anyone in there? Jenna?!" I called out. No response. "Ladies, this is an emergency. *Male* coming in," I announced as I pushed through the door. Oliver was behind me.

"Jenna, are you here?" I called out, the uneasiness in my stomach getting worse.

"Jenna," Oliver called out, knocking and pushing through each door.

"Excuse me, this is a ladies' bathroom. Get out!" an older woman's voice called from one of the stalls at the end.

"Sorry, ma'am. We're looking for our friend. I think she might be in trouble," Oliver explained as I knocked and pried open the rest of the stalls. There was no Jenna, and my heart sank deep. I could hardly breathe.

The lady finally emerged from the stall, headed to the sink, and frowned at us.

"You two should really not be in here," she said, looking me up and down, pointing her sparkly clutch at me, then at Oliver.

"Ma'am, was there anyone else here when you came in?" I asked.

She handed me her glittered purse. "Here, be a gentleman," she said as she turned on the faucet and washed her hands. "I don't like placing my expensive purse on public bathroom sinks, you never know what bacteria are on these things, you know. If you ask me, there should be a table next to the sink, not that far away," she babbled, pointing at the round wooden table in the corner a few feet away.

I could feel Oliver wanting to roll his eyes as I did.

"Ma'am, did you see anyone else here?" I asked flatly, hoping she would just answer the dang questions.

"You don't have to have an attitude with me, young man," she said, glaring her fake lashes at me. I usually didn't notice things like that, especially in this situation, but *dang,* her lashes could carry her up in the air like an eagle's wings.

"But yes, there were two ladies in here, one was drunk, and her friend was helping her walk, practically carrying her out. Young ladies these days just don't know when to quit," she said, rolling her eyes.

"I'll canvass the lobby," Oliver said before dashing out the door.

"What did the drunk lady—"

"They even almost knocked me over. The gall of those ladies didn't even apologize." She shook her head.

"What did the drunk lady look like?" I repeated, trying to keep the small amount of patience I had left.

The tiny, at least eighty-year-old woman gestured for her purse, and I quickly handed it back to her. "I think she wore a pair of pants and a black sweater. She had long brown hair in a ponytail," she said, knitting her brows as if trying to recall.

Jenna was wearing black leggings, a white blouse, and a brown blazer. Maybe it wasn't her. "Are you sure?" I asked.

"Young man, I may look old, but my noggin is still pretty sharp, of course, I'm sure."

I thanked the woman and started for the door when she spoke again.

"Wait! I got it mixed up. The friend helping the drunk lady wore black pants, a black sweater, and a baseball cap. The drunken lady, on the other hand..." She rolled her eyes again.

Lady, just get to it!

"She was also wearing black tights, a white shirt... I think, and a brown cardigan. That's right, a brown cardigan. She was the one with the long, brown hair in a ponytail. I remembered because it was dangling across her face while her friend helped her walk. If you ask me—"

This time, I didn't thank the lady; I rushed out the door. It *was* Jenna, *but who was the lady with her?*

As I rushed through the hallway next to Ol, I noticed the exit door I had seen on my way into the bathroom earlier. *Dammit!* I pushed it open, and it led me to another garage. "Jenna! Jenna!" I yelled, but all I heard in return were the echoes of my voice. Jenna was gone. I knew it. I could feel it.

The feeling when I realized I had lost Zoey came flooding back. I felt like I was drowning. I failed Zoey; now I was failing Jenna, too. *No, I won't let this happen again.* I pulled out my phone and called Detective Carl Willard. Our team had been working with him since the beginning, and he was a longtime friend of my father. Then I called Derrick and brought him up to speed. Before going back in, I glanced up, scanning for cameras. One sat close to the door. I rushed inside—but not before slamming my fist against the wall next to the entrance. Jenna was gone, and it was all my fault.

"What happened?" Ol asked as he glanced at my bleeding fist.

"Jenna's gone, that's what happened," I said, gritting my teeth.

"We'll find her, Mikey—"

"I think someone drugged her," I interrupted. "We need to see all the cameras. There's an exit door by the bathroom hallway leading to another garage. There's a camera there."

Ol was already summoning security.

"Who's in charge tonight?" I asked.

A tall man in his late thirties answered. "I am, sir."

"Good, I need some of your security to canvass the place," I said, trying to stay as calm as possible.

"And look for this lady," Oliver said as he started to scroll through his phone.

"No." I shook my head, taking my phone out of my pocket.

Oliver furrowed his brows.

"She doesn't have red hair anymore." I showed the security personnel a photo I had taken just before we left Green Ridge.

"This is the lady you are looking for. Go and let me know if you find any clues."

"Shouldn't we call the authorities?" the head security officer asked, a shorter, older man with salt-and-pepper hair.

"Done," I said.

*****

We were inside the security office studying the cameras for that night, between the time we arrived and the time Jenna went missing. We watched the monitors, and one of them showed us walking in, laughing. I saw myself on the phone and Jenna pointing to the bathroom, talking to Oliver. Many people were in the lobby, but I was looking for one person, Jim. We continued to rewind and fast-forward several tapes just as two detectives walked in: Detective Carl Willard, an older gentleman in his late fifties, and his partner, Detective Joe Stevens, a young guy in his mid-thirties.

"Mikey," Carl Willard shook my hand as both gentlemen approached. "Give it to me," he said.

I shook the younger Detective's hand before introducing them to Oliver and filling them in as we sifted through the monitors.

"Can you show us the camera on the east wing exit near the female bathroom?" Carl asked. One of the security guards fiddled with the monitors, fast-forwarding some. And there it was, Jenna, being dragged out of the hotel into the garage. The camera didn't show her face, but I knew it was her. The woman assisting her must have been aware of the cameras, as she was careful to avoid them. All we had was a woman about five foot three, wearing a dark baseball cap, a black shirt, and black pants. It could be anyone.

"Do any of you recognize this woman?" Detective Stevens asked.

Oliver turned his attention to me. I didn't recognize the woman, so I shook my head.

"Wait, wait, wait! Rewind that," I said to the security guard, who immediately pressed rewind. "Look at the car. Look familiar?" I asked, looking over my shoulder at Oliver.

"Yeah, isn't that the car that cut us off outside the airport? Jim's car?" Oliver said.

I nodded as I saw the man who exited the driver's side to help the woman shove Jenna into the car. He was a heavy-set young man.

"Is that Jim?" Oliver asked, with a shocked look, as if he couldn't believe what he was seeing.

I let out a faint smirk. "No, Jenna has more taste than that. That's not him."

"I was gonna say," Oliver huffed.

"Okay, tell us about this Jim guy," Carl said.

He's a psycho, let's start with that.

Chapter Fifty-One

JENNA

PRESENT

*M*y head throbbed, and my vision blurred. I tried to lift my hand to wipe my eyes, but my hands were tied behind my back. My legs were tied, too. I lay on a futon that reeked of urine and instantly wanted to gag, but my mouth was shut with tape. A light shone through a small square window in the top right corner of the room. I wiggled my body, but I was bound tightly; I felt like a fish wiggling on the shore, trying to get back into the water. Where was I? I tried to remember what had happened, and all I could remember was using the bathroom at the hotel with... Oliver and Michael. The thought of them made my heart race. *Where are they? Are they okay?*

Forcing myself to remember, I shut my eyes. I was with Oliver and Michael on the way to our hotel suite. I felt nauseous, so I rushed to the bathroom, and that's when I felt the prick on my shoulder; I remember it feeling like a mosquito bite, and I brushed it off, but after that, everything went hazy. Someone held me up, and at one point, I had tried to walk, but my legs failed me; I couldn't even feel them. The last thing

I remembered was being dragged toward a car and *voices*—I heard voices as someone shoved me into the back of the vehicle. Through the grogginess, I made out the silhouettes of two people in front of me; one was a woman, and her voice sounded naggingly familiar.

"Do you really want to do this?" the man had said.

"Are you kidding me? I've been dreaming of this for a long time," the female voice said in a high, piercing tone.

We hit a pothole, and that was it; everything went black.

Now, I was in what looked like an abandoned room, and all it had was this God-forsaken, stinky futon I was on and a rusted folding chair facing me. It reminded me of those suspense-thriller TV shows where someone was taken and held in an old house. My heart lurched. Could I be in an abandoned house in the middle of nowhere, and no one would hear me even if I could yell? I thought of Michael. I was sure he, Oliver, and the police were already searching for me. I prayed to God that they were and that they would find me... soon. Because if I didn't die at the hands of my kidnappers, I was certain the stench in the room would do the job.

There was a creaky sound from outside, like someone had opened a door, but it wasn't the door to where I was held. *Voices- Footsteps*—they were getting closer. It sounded like a man and a woman arguing, and then the door swung open. I shut my eyes, pretending to be unconscious. The footsteps were heavy, and I could feel the vibration from the thin, smelly futon beneath me.

"She's still out," the man said. I didn't recognize the voice.

There was a click-clacking of high heels on the wooden floor, and I wondered who would come to a place like this in heels. Then she opened her mouth, and there was no mistake, especially when I wafted the pungent scent that used to send me to the backroom of my gallery with a migraine and nausea; it was the same scent I had smelled before passing out in the bathroom. It was Deanna.

I opened my eyes, and her matching zebra leggings and tight shirt forced me to readjust my vision. The lines were everywhere, and it made my head spin. When I finally opened my eyes the second time, I aimed my sight at her face, avoiding the dizzying animal pattern on her clothes.

She looked rugged and old in the bright sunlight streaming in through the window, wrinkles visible on her forehead despite the huge dark sunglasses she wore, which she quickly took off before speaking. Her eyes burned like a flame as she stared at me.

I would've been afraid if she hadn't reminded me of the tiny primate Hannah had shown me from her mother's province in the Philippines. *What were they called? Ah, Tarsiers.* Deanna looked like a Tarsier that had stumbled upon a mascara tube and applied it all over its face.

"Well, good morning, sunshine," she greeted me with a grin venomous enough to kill an elephant.

I wiggled, muffled through the tape for her to let me go, but she just laughed. She laughed so hard, I swear I could see her uvula from where I lay. I squirmed some more as she knelt next to me. She made a disgusted face and waved a hand before her nose as if the smell was coming from me, repelling her. I rolled my eyes since that was pretty much all I could do to show her how angry I was.

Deanna gave me a devious smile before ripping the tape off my mouth, which sent me screaming bloody murder. I expected her to tell me to be quiet, but she simply stared at me, annoyed. I knew then that we *were* in the middle of nowhere. No one would hear me scream, but why tape my mouth in the first place? That got me wondering, and fear settled in my chest.

"What's the meaning of this, Deanna?" I asked when I finally had the chance to take some much-needed deep breaths. "Untie me," I commanded.

"Not yet," she said as she walked toward the rusty chair and sat, crossing her legs, then her arms.

I glanced at the young man beside her. He was probably in his late twenties or early thirties. He wasn't handsome, but he wasn't ugly either. His dirty blond hair was messy from running his hands through it constantly. He was on the heavy side, but there was something unexplainable in his eyes; it wasn't evil. It wasn't pity. I didn't know what it was... compassion? He looked nervous. I kept a mental note of it in case she left me alone with him later.

"Deanna, I don't understand."

She studied me, tapping her leopard-printed stilettos on the floor. "You know, Jim loved you," she finally said, uncrossing her legs, spreading them open, and leaning over, trying to get close to me. "Not sure why, but the bastard loved you. Well, until he realized what he was missing. See, Jim is in love with *me,* and *I with him,* but *YOU* had to step in the middle and make a mess."

"What are you talking about?" I asked, my breath coming in short, hard gasps.

She stood, approached closer, and stood over me. "That day at the gallery... Do you think I forgot? How you just swooped in, took over the sale with Jim, started flirting with him—and before we knew it, you two were *a thing*? He came for me, Jenna. He came back for me!"

Now I was really confused. *Came back for her?* "You asked me to help you, Deanna. You asked me to assist you, remember? If I had known you had liked Jim, I wouldn't have..." I took a deep, frustrated breath. It was the wrong thing to do; I gagged and almost vomited on myself. Instead, I swallowed the bitter bile in my mouth.

Deanna didn't utter a word, she only knitted her black-drawn eyebrows together and gave me a stare so full of venom like a snake in the jungle, ready to strike.

"Trust me, I wouldn't have dated Jim, had I known. Then, I would have dodged a bullet," I explained, rolling my eyes.

"Dodge a bullet?" She hissed, her nostrils widening like a volcano ready to erupt. "Ha! Jim was the one who dodged the bullet with you, Jenna! You are nothing but a trophy. An all-high and mighty artist, photographer, gallery owner, psychologist, WANNA be trophy! Do you think Jim was impressed by all that? No! He wasn't, was he? That's why he hits you."

My eyes widened.

"That's right, Jenna. I know. Do you think I bought your lies about your bruises?" She snickered. "But he wouldn't do that to me because he loves me; he always has," she said, grinning like a madwoman.

I had no idea where all these animosities came from. Deanna was so full of fury.

"I thought we were friends," I said in a disappointing tone.

"Friends?! You thought we were *friends*? Friends don't steal a *friend's* boyfriend, Jenna, or is it *Kate?*" Deanna asked in a screechy, high-pitched voice. She had a look I had never seen before. She looked hurt, angry, mad—mad as in lunatic mad. I had no clue at this point what she was blabbering about. I tried to rack my brain for some explanations.

"If you liked him, why didn't you say anything?" I asked.

She let out a big laugh. "Liked him? We were in love, Jenna."

"Deanna, I am so lost. Can you please just untie me, and we can talk about this?"

"You are one sleek lady, Jenna. Are you telling me you had no idea who I was when you hired me?" She paced around, shaking her head. She looked at me again, and hurt was drawn across her face this time. "Oh my gosh. You have not changed. You really didn't know who I was, did you? Until now, you still don't know who I am!" She huffed, then screamed. "Think, *Jenna Rivers.* Think back!" Her eyes welled up with tears.

Think back, Deanna said, so I did. Then I realized she was calling me by my maiden name and had called me Kate. That meant she knew me before I hired her, and she also learned about my secret life, but how and why? I thought back to high school. I didn't know why, but this type of drama only happened in high school. Still, I couldn't place her. I thought about my college friends, and *still* nothing. Deanna must have seen the blank expression on my face because she yanked my shirt, forcing me to sit up.

"Oh my God! Professor Donovan! I was Professor Donovan's former intern, *Dina*, as you called me, remember?" she said, her face inches away from mine. I could smell garlic on her breath, making it really hard to breathe.

Professor Donovan's intern? I tried to recall if I'd ever met her.

"You took everything from me," she said in a low voice.

I almost felt sorry for her. "Deanna, if you think I took the internship from you, you're wrong, I—"

"Shut up!" she screamed, making me flinch. "I didn't care about the stupid internship, you damn fool. You took Jim from me," she said, her eyes welling up with tears, but the fire never left.

"I took Jim from you. How?" I asked, confused.

She grinned.

I tried so hard to remember her. But I still couldn't place Deanna; it aggravated me.

"Deanna, I'm sorry, but there seems to be a misunderstanding. Please untie me, and we can try to sort this out," I begged and gave the man by the window a glance, hoping that after hearing our conversation, he would come to his senses, whoever he may be. For a moment, I thought he wanted to help, but he turned around and faced the window instead. My heart sank.

"Deanna, please," I begged some more. I wiggled my hands behind my back, trying to loosen the knot, the rope burning and digging into my skin, but I think it had loosened a bit, or I could have imagined it; either way, I kept prying on it. I wasn't going to give up without a fight.

Deanna was quiet, sitting on the chair with her head bowed. The only sound I heard was her ominous breathing. I continued to pull on the rope and glanced around the room to see if there was anything I could use as a weapon once I freed myself.

When she finally looked up, tears ran down her face. "You still don't remember me after all we've been through."

I felt defeated. I had no idea what she was talking about or who she was.

"I could have sworn you would've remembered me when I applied for the job at the gallery, but now I'm thankful you didn't, or else I wouldn't have had the chance to do this," she said, wiping the tears away from her mascara-streaked face, her finger trembling as she pointed at me. She continued, her voice soft as if she'd relaxed from her hysteria, yet her tone was still frigid as ice. My empathy vanished as quickly as her personality changed, and she suddenly screamed again, glaring at me.

"Maybe this will jog a memory in your tiny brain." Deanna started fiddling with her purse, pulling out a hair tie to tie her hair into a bun, then a pair of cat-eyeglasses, and putting them on. She started to look more familiar, but my memory still failed me.

"My hair was dark then, and I had braces," she said, almost in a whisper.

Short, dark hair, vibrant red lipstick, eccentric. That's when it hit me. Deanna Cruz. I had only heard the name once or twice after she'd left Professor Donovan's office. She was there when I first started working, and I vaguely remembered running into her in a coffee shop once or twice. I shut my eyes, trying to recall the woman. She had stringy hair pulled back into a ponytail, bangs framing her forehead, and wore glasses.

She was heavier, and a bit plump in the face, but no doubt... I opened my eyes... *It's Deanna.*

"I guess you never really had the brains to become a psychologist, huh? An artist? No wonder Jim—" She laughed.

"Did you and Jim know each other?" I asked my voice laced with irritation.

"For crying out loud, Jenna! How long will it take for that thick head of yours to figure out that Jim and I were together long before you and him..." She paused as if she didn't know what to say next.

"How? When?" I asked, curious. *Did this relationship really happen, or was she delusional?*

She looked at me with fiery eyes, then grinned. "Jim and I were high school sweethearts. Only, he wasn't Jim then. He was Mark—m*y* Mark O'Brien."

Deanna shook her head and started pacing. "We were so in love. He promised me the world, you know? But then, he got too ambitious—too good for himself. I knew what he was doing to you. He'd done it to me before, probably not as bad, but he did, but I was strong. Unlike you," she said as she paused and looked down at me. "Mark likes his women strong, but vulnerable and obedient. That's not you, Jenna. That's me."

"Deanna, I think you're confusing what being strong is. If Jim did to you what he'd done to me, then staying and taking it is not being strong. You're letting him—"

"Shut up!" Deanna cried. "Mark loves me. He came back for me then; he came back for now. We're getting married, you know?" She knelt in front of me. "He loves me, Jenna. He loves me."

My heart broke for Deanna. Jim had really done a number on her psyche. I wanted to reason with her and offer her guidance. She was a good person—a little confused, manipulated, but good. By all accounts, she was emotionally broken. She needed more than I could give. She needed therapy, and I needed to get out of there.

"Deanna. I'm sure Jim loves you, and I can tell you love him very much. You said you guys are going to get married. Now, you won't be able to do that if you're in prison. Well, you could, but you won't be together like you wanted," I said, trying to show her some logic to what she was doing.

For a moment, I thought I got through to her because she was still, quiet, got back on her feet, and approached me. I was ready for her to untie me when, suddenly, as fast as a lightning bolt, her palm met my face, and in an instant, blood trickled down my lips.

"So, Kate, did you enjoy the eleven roses I sent you at the clinic? How about the one I sent to your apartment? Oh, wait, wait, the best one was the one I sent you in Green Ridge," she said, grinning at me.

Suddenly, terror coiled in my belly. "Oh my God! It wasn't Jim watching me; it was you." I managed, my voice cracking like it was trying to escape my throat as I felt my strength drain away. She had been the one watching me at the clinic and my apartment. She was the one who was making the hang-up calls—the breathing. Then I thought about Jim outside my apartment. Suddenly, nothing made sense anymore, my vision blurred, and the room spun. There was no holding back any longer. I leaned over and vomited.

Chapter Fifty-Two

JIM

PRESENT

I paced around the living room with the phone in my hand, trying to call Deanna for the fourth time; it still went to voicemail. I turned off the TV and poured another shot of Macallan whiskey before heading to bed. Just as I was about to enter the bedroom, a loud knock and the police identifying themselves made me almost drop the glass I was holding.

"I'm coming," I yelled.

I slid the lock, opened the door, and three cops rushed in, followed by a few others. One handed me a paper, a warrant to search the house.

"What is this about?" I asked, bewildered.

"I'm Detective Bridget Fisher, and this is Detective Marcelo. Are you Jim Miller?"

"Yes. *Again*, what is this about?" I asked as I tried to read what was on the paper in my hand.

"We have a warrant to search your home, sir. Please step aside," Detective Fisher commanded as she walked past me into the living room and started looking around, opening cabinet doors, and going through papers in different drawers.

I couldn't help but notice how attractive Detective Fisher was. She could have been a model, especially with her shoulder-length blond hair, tight black jeans, and white shirt. With the boots she wore, she looked at least five foot ten.

"Warrant? For what?" I asked, my hands started to sweat.

"Do you know a Jenna Miller?" Detective Marcelo followed. He was a tall guy in plain clothes, looked to be in his forties, with dark hair and dark skin and a smug look on his face.

"Yes, she's..." I spun around as uniformed officers checked every crevice in my home. A few of them went straight to the garage, while one guy tossed everything in my kitchen drawer. He even opened my oven. *What the hell?* I followed a woman who went straight to my bedroom and watched her dump my underwear drawer with no facial expression. *Interesting.*

"*Sir*," Detective Fisher tried to get my attention back, her dark blue eyes glaring at me.

"Do you know a Jenna Miller?"

"Yes, she's my wife. Why? Did something happen to her?" I asked, as my heartbeat quickened.

"When was the last time you saw her?" she asked.

I furrowed my brows and shrugged. "I don't know. Almost two years ago," I replied, confused.

"Are you sure about that?" Marcelo asked.

I stared at him, lifted my chin, showing him that he didn't intimidate me. "Did something happen to my wife?"

"You call her your wife, yet you haven't seen her in a couple of years?" Fisher said, judgment in her tone. I wanted to erase that smirk off her face, but I kept my cool.

I took a deep breath and released it before answering. "She left me, *okay?* She left me for another man. Are you happy? Now, can you tell me if something has happened to her?"

Before they could respond, my head spun as I heard, *Clear! Clear!* Simultaneously, several uniformed police officers emerged from the garage behind. Another officer emerged from the back door. "The car isn't here."

"Where is she, Mr. Miller?" Detective Marcelo prodded; this time, his dark brown eyes pierced through mine.

"Where is who?" I snapped, refusing to be disrespected.

"Your *wife*, Jenna," Fisher yelled.

"As I said, I have not seen Jenna in two years. I have been looking for her, myself," I explained. It was the truth.

"Detectives," one of the officers called out from the kitchen. "You need to see this," he added.

I followed them to the nook where my board stood, and a few papers about Jenna were scattered around the table.

"This is interesting, Mr. Miller. Looks like you're stalking your wife, and by the looks of it, you even hired a PI to find her," Fisher said, her tone almost ready to convict as she held Jenna's photos in her hands.

"I told you. I have been looking for her, and yes, I hired a PI because I needed to get the divorce papers to her. He found her in an apartment in Moreno Valley a couple of years ago, but when I went there, she was nowhere to be found. I even waited outside her apartment for a few days, but she didn't come home," I explained, hoping the detectives would believe me. I needed to get them out of there soon, before the questioning led to my past.

Fisher leaned in. "Is that so? Tell you what, why don't we ride to the station? We have a few more questions," she said, her tone low but firm.

I cleared my throat. "Is that necessary? You can question me here. In fact, why don't you question the man she's with in the photos?" I said, putting both hands in my pajama pockets.

"It's better if you come to the station, Mr. Miller, unless you want us to arrest you now?" Fisher threatened.

I stepped back. "On what grounds? I did nothing wrong," I said.

"Kidnapping and assault," Detective Marcelo chimed in.

"What?! Kidnapping? Someone kidnapped Jenna? Who?" My heart thudded.

"That's why we're here, Mr. Miller. That's why you need to come with us, we're hoping you can shed some light," Fisher said calmly. She was trying to be civil, but I knew she was trying to manipulate me. She couldn't fool the master.

"Doctor," I corrected.

"Excuse me?" Fisher's head whipped around.

"It's Doctor Miller," I said.

She rolled her eyes. "All right, *Doctor*, you're coming with us."

"This is ridiculous. I had nothing to do with this. Why would I kidnap my own wife?"

"That's what we're trying to find out. So, how is it going to be, *Mister* Miller?" Marcelo asked with that stupid smug on his face, acting all tough just because he carried a gun.

Even though all they had was the board and photos from my PI, I was still nervous. What if they found out who I really was?

***

It was almost midnight, and I sat alone in the interrogation room. I knew what they were doing; they were trying to intimidate me. I stood and paced around the small square room. They had to come in soon. I needed to know what had happened to Jenna. The door swung open, and the two detectives walked in, looking ready to throw me into the cell.

They asked me about my whereabouts over the last two weeks, especially earlier in the night. They asked whether I'd flown recently. I told them about Cabo and that I had changed my mind because something unexpected had come up, which made them more suspicious.

"No, I have not been to Virginia or Sacramento. What would I do there?" I asked, annoyed.

"So, you're telling us you didn't know your wife was living in Sacramento? You didn't follow her to Green Ridge, Virginia, and you weren't at SMF last night?" Fisher asked, her voice sharp with authority.

"Sacramento? No. Green Ridge? I don't even know where that is."

"Like you didn't know. Didn't your PI tell you?" Fisher said, leaning back, one foot planted against the wall, looking effortlessly at ease, and for a minute, I focused on her authoritarian tone. I looked up at Detective Marcelo, who stood in front of me. Clearly, she was in charge. Tall, slender, sharp eyes—I found her sexy.

Marcelo banged on the table, making me flinch.

I blinked. "No, I only hired him once, and that's when I found out she was living in Moreno Valley," I explained.

Of course, they didn't believe me, but I was telling the truth.

"Who is Mark O'Brien?" Fisher sat on the chair across the table, staring me in the eyes.

I swallowed hard—*someone I wanted to forget from my past.* I wanted to say.

"Look at that, we got his attention," Marcelo said, sarcastically.

"Mr. Miller, you drive a white Lexus?" Fisher asked.

I nodded.

"Do you know where it is?" she asked.

"I loaned it to a friend," I replied, my stomach flipping suddenly.

"How convenient," Marcelo chimed in.

"And did your friend go to Sacramento, *Mark*?" Fisher asked.

"I don't know," I said, and it was the truth. I didn't know if Deanna had gone to Sacramento.

"Ha! So you admit *you are* Mark O'Brien," Marcelo announced, as if he'd just unraveled a big secret.

"It's not a crime to change someone's name," I said icily.

"It is if you stole someone's identity," Marcelo replied with a smirk.

Fisher pushed the chair back and stood. "We'll get back to that later. For now, I need to know where Jenna is."

Suddenly, I felt the heat in the room and started sweating. I wondered if it was me or if they had turned the heat to make suspects sweat. The thought of me as a suspect annoyed the heck out of me.

"I swear, I don't know," I said, pausing as I realized something that could help me.

"What?" Fisher asked, reading my face.

"I can find out, though," I said.

"How?" she asked.

I crossed my arms. "But you have to drop the false identity charges," I said.

Fisher stared at me before responding. "I can't promise that, but I'll talk to the DA. Will tell her you cooperated. Only if what you give us leads us to finding your wife."

"I can track the car," I said.

"No deal. GPS? We already tried. It was disabled. Nice try, *Mister Mark*," Marcelo said, sneering.

What a prick. I sneered back. "Not the device I installed."

I told them I had placed a tracking device on the car when Jenna was driving it. Of course, I omitted the last part, not wanting to add more charges against me.

"What's the name of this friend of yours?" Fisher asked.

I didn't know what Deanna was up to, but it was her or me at this point. I needed to give them what they wanted and work out a deal.

"Deanna. *Deanna Cruz*."

Chapter Fifty-Three
MICHAEL

PRESENT

I stood by the hotel window, staring at nothing. This was all my fault. This should never have happened on my watch. I took my eyes off Jenna for one minute, and she was gone. I felt a crushing pain in my chest, and I struggled to breathe. I tried to open a window to get more air, but none of the damn windows would open. *Get a hold of yourself, Michael. You need to find Jenna,* I reminded myself and took a few deep breaths.

My phone rang, and I immediately answered it.

"We got something," Derrick said over the phone. "Detective Willard spoke to the detectives in Temecula. They have Jim in custody," he added.

"And Jenna?" My heart tightened as I waited for Derrick to answer.

"Not with him, but we got a lead. Apparently, he loaned the Lexus to his girlfriend, Deanna Cruz."

"*Deanna,*" I said the name out loud. The same Deanna that Jenna had tried to warn about Jim. *Deanna has Jenna?* The thought pissed me off. "Did they find Deanna?"

"They found the Lexus, but they were gone. They may have changed cars," Derrick said.

I wanted to scream as I paced the room, feeling helpless. I should be out there looking for Jenna. Then I thought of something. "Hey, I'll call you back." I hung up without hearing Derrick's answer and searched for Jenna Miller's Gallery's number and called Ann.

Ann answered, and I explained to her who I was, what the situation was, and asked for her help. She gave me what I wanted—Deanna Cruz's number. After we hung up, I called Derrick back immediately. He picked up after one ring.

"Deanna Cruz. Track her phone." I provided the number Ann had given me.

"On it!"

I hung up, called Detective Carl Willard, and gave him the update.

***

After Derrick called me back with the information we needed, I called Carl back immediately, and within minutes I was on the road to Stockton.

Detective Willard and Stevens were already at the scene when I arrived. The address Derrick gave me led me to an abandoned school parking lot. Aside from the police cars, the lot was empty, except for a red Toyota Corolla parked in the corner. As I got out of my car, an officer rushed to me and told me to stay back, but Detective Willard motioned for him to let me through, knowing my military background. He knew I was trained for situations like this.

"Stay behind me," Detective Stevens commanded as he followed the senior detective into the building. It took all my willpower to tell him to go to hell, but I knew they were in charge, so I bit my tongue. I just needed to see Jenna safe.

The school's exterior didn't look neglected; a couple of lampposts were lit, and from where I stood, it still looked like it could function. But when we entered, the flashlight revealed a different story. Graffiti everywhere. Some I recognized as gang signs, some looked like they could pass for artistic murals, and some were just a bunch of profanities. The deeper we got into the school, the more vandalism appeared.

We strolled the hallway silently, listening to any noise that could give away where Jenna was being held without tipping the kidnappers off. We knew Deanna was there with a man, and the detectives discovered that it was the PI Jim had hired to find Jenna. But what was he doing with Deanna? I brushed the question aside and focused on finding Jenna.

We passed by several empty rooms; one had the light on. Shards of glass were scattered on the floor where the windows had been smashed, and pieces from broken chairs and tables were scattered around, with more graffiti covering the walls. We reached an area with two stairs, one leading up and one leading down. Detective Willard motioned for Detective Stevens to go up, and a couple of uniformed officers followed, while Detective Willard and I, followed by two other officers, headed downstairs. I heard voices before we even reached the bottom. I wanted to rush toward the voices and see if Jenna was okay, but I stayed behind Detective Willard, with my adrenaline pumping and my heart pounding, threatening to burst out of my chest. Carl motioned for us to halt as he slowly descended a few more steps. In front of us was an exit door, and to the left was another closed door.

I could hear the voices getting louder. I heard Jenna's voice; there was no mistake about it. My heart clenched. She sounded stressed, pleading to be let go, when suddenly, a devious laughter erupted, *Deanna.* We knew there were at least two of them inside besides Jenna. What we didn't know was whether they were armed. We had to assume they were, so we proceeded with care. Another laughter burst.

"Please don't!" Jenna shouted. Her voice cut through the room. I tightened the grip on my gun as I looked at Detective Willard, who was now in front of me, on the side of the door. I tilted my head to the side as if to ask, "What are we waiting for?"

Carl waved me off, signaling for patience, urging me to hold on, which I was barely doing.

"Stop, Deanna. I didn't sign up for this," the man cried, his voice trembling with fear.

"Don't be a coward!" Deanna shrieked. "Do it!"

That's when Detective Willard motioned for one officer to knock down the door, and we rushed inside, just as Deanna grabbed the gun from the man and pointed it in Jenna's direction. My instinct took over, and I dove to where Jenna was sitting, shielding her from the shot. For what felt like an eternity, I covered Jenna's body with mine, and we lay still. When I lifted myself from her, I felt the wetness on her body. Jenna's eyes were shut. *Oh God, there was blood.*

"Oh God, Jenna! No, no, no!" I wailed, my hands trembling as I checked her body frantically for the bullet wound. I worked quickly to untie her, her faint whisper reaching my ears, muffled and weak. I couldn't focus on anything but the blood—*so much blood*. I felt heaviness in my chest, fear wrapping around me like a suffocating fog. This couldn't be happening again. I couldn't lose her. I couldn't. Not like this. Not before I had a chance to tell her how I felt. Not yet. Not ever.

"Jenna, please hang on. I love you, God, I love you. Hang on, Babe," I tried to say as it became harder to breathe. As soon as she was freed, Jenna wrapped her arms around me—tightly. I could feel her heart beating as fast as mine.

"I'm here," I whispered, my pulse rising.

"I knew you would find me," she said in between rapid breaths, and my heart quickening at the sound of her soft angelic voice.

"Shh... Don't move. Hang on. I'm here, Babe." I kissed her lips, then pulled away gently, trying to find where the blood was coming from.

"I'm okay, Michael," she insisted, then quickly backed off. "*You're* bleeding," she whispered, her voice breaking with fear.

That's when I felt the searing pain in my left shoulder. My adrenaline was pumping from the fear of losing the woman I loved; I hadn't even felt the bullet hit me.

"You sure you're okay?" I asked, choking on each word, as I struggled to breathe. Just as the room started to blur, Jenna's angelic face was the last I saw before everything went black.

Chapter Fifty-Four

JENNA

PRESENT

*M*y mind was still reeling from the thought that it was Deanna all along, who had been stalking me and not Jim. Well, he did at first. The idea of Deanna and Jim or *Mark O'Brien*, as I later found out, were in cahoots, was mind-blowing. I still couldn't believe it. Jim went to jail for stealing someone's identity. I wanted to see him in prison, to stand in front of him and let him witness my strength and his own insignificance. Instead, I chose something harder: walking away, because he no longer deserved me. Of course, Deanna went to prison, too. So did the PI Ralph Iriarte, for accessory kidnapping.

On the brighter side, I got my baby girl's urn back. The feelings were indescribable. The only way I could describe them was that I was complete again.

Michael lay in the hospital because of me. I had watched him shield me with his body from a flying bullet. That's when I knew I would spend the rest of my life with this man. His hand felt cold as I held it, lying my head on the bed, sitting on the chair next to him. I glanced up with every little movement and noise he made to check if he was okay. This time, he squeezed my hand.

"Hey there," he said as he slowly opened his eyes.

I never imagined one could still look handsome after being shot, having surgery, just woken up, and in a hospital gown, but Michael did.

"Hey," I replied softly.

"You slept here?" he asked, furrowing his brows as he coughed, probably trying to adjust to the dryness of his throat.

"Of course. Nowhere I would rather be," I said, smiling back.

He winced as he reached for the bedside handset, then pushed it, trying to sit up.

"Let me help you," I said, propping a pillow behind him. "Are you okay? Do you need me to call the nurse?"

"I'm okay, babe," he whispered.

Babe. The word still sent a gentle warmth through me, pulling me back to the first time he'd called me that. I must have spaced out because he repeated it.

"Babe," he smiled. "Is that okay?" he asked, his dark brown eyes glistening, searching mine for approval, as if he needed it.

I nodded. "I like it," I said, feeling my cheeks warm.

"So." He swallowed. "Deanna and her accomplice are behind bars?" he asked as he reached for the glass on the table next to him.

"Yep," I replied, as I rushed to grab the pitcher, pour him a glass of water, and hand it to him.

Sensing the hesitancy in my voice, he frowned. "Everything okay?"

"I just feel bad for her. Jim or Mark manipulated her, too. He manipulated her since they were kids, and for what? Ambition? Money? She was a victim, too, you know? Now, she will be spending years behind bars," I replied.

"Jenna... she stalked, kidnapped, and tried to kill you," he said, convincing me that it was justice, and it *was*, but I still couldn't help but feel sorry for her. Deanna snapped because of how Jim treated her.

"Come here." He tugged at my hand. "This is exactly why I fell in love with you," he added, kissing the back of my hand.

He fell in love with me? My heart quickened, and my head spun in a good way.

"Is that why you took a bullet for me?" I asked, sitting on the bed next to him, running my fingers through his messy hair.

He smiled faintly and closed his eyes. "Yes," he murmured.

My chest seized for a moment, fingers pausing in his hair. "You could've died," I whispered.

"I'd do it again," he said, his voice gentle, and my eyes welled up with tears.

I leaned down, pressing my cheek onto his. The smell of antiseptic mixed with his warm, natural scent was surprisingly inviting. "*Babe*," I said.

"Uh-huh," he replied, not moving, but I could feel the smile on his face.

"Next time, no more bullets, okay? Just choose me."

He chuckled. "No promises. It's the protector in me."

Epilogue

I t was early September, and we decided to go back to Green Ridge with Oliver and Hannah. The following day after we landed, Michael insisted that I shut my eyes as we drove to an unknown destination. It was my birthday, but it was also nine in the morning. That meant it couldn't be a surprise party—not at nine in the morning. I guess it could have been brunch, but still.

"Don't you peek," he said. I could hear the smile in his voice.

"I'm not, but where are we going?" I asked, fidgeting in my seat, excited to find out what he had planned.

His phone rang through the car's speakers, the way it did via Bluetooth connection. He answered it.

"You guys close?" Oliver asked.

"You guys in on this, too?" I asked my eyes, still closed.

"Hey!" Michael protested.

"My eyes are closed, I promise," I wailed.

Oliver laughed. "You kids, hurry up."

"We're close, be ready," Michael replied, then hung up.

A few minutes later, the car stopped, and Michael got out, opened my door, and assisted me out, covering my eyes with his hands. He led me through what I assumed was the parking lot and into a building. As soon as he opened the door, I felt the cool air on my face, heard voices—*familiar* voices. Then everyone screamed, "Surprise!"

After my vision adjusted, my heart fluttered, and tears instantly welled up in my eyes as I saw my mom, my dad, and my sister Kayla. I ran into their wide-open arms, feeling the love I'd terribly missed. My heart was whole again.

I scanned my surroundings and couldn't believe what they had prepared for me, as if I were back in my own gallery in Temecula, with my work hanging on the walls, only we were standing inside a building in the middle of downtown Green Ridge, Virginia.

I couldn't believe it. My family was there, as were Ann, Gayle, her husband, nurse Mar, and her mom, Flor, and my two best friends, Hannah and Oliver. All these people were there *for me.*

"You all flew here for me?" I said, holding my tears back.

They all smiled and looked at Michael.

"Hey, I would love to take all the credit, but Hannah and Ol helped," he said, then winked at me. I had told him about how winks affected me. Since then, he winked whenever he got the chance. He was so adorable.

I glanced around the room again and studied the images on the wall. They were the photos I took while Michael, and I were there, now framed in various sizes and hanging on the wall under art lighting. I smiled at Ann, knowing she probably did all the work. She nodded and placed both hands on her chest as if to say, "You're welcome, and I'm so happy for you." We understood each other that way.

After saying hello and hugging everyone, I excused myself and pulled Michael to the narrow hallway toward the back of the room. I stared deeply into his eyes, tears slowly falling down my face. "I don't know what to say. A gallery in Green Ridge? This is amazing!" I said as he wiped my tears.

"I knew how much you enjoyed this town, so I thought you could open another gallery here, so there would be a reason for us to keep coming back," he explained. "And just say you love me, and we'll call it even." He winked. Again.

And just like that, I leaned in and kissed him. "I love you, Michael Leandro Rossi."

"I love you *more—Babe*."

Also by

J.J Marcell

The Green Ridge Series
Book 1 – The Promise

www.ingramcontent.com/pod-product-compliance
Lightning Source LLC
Chambersburg PA
CBHW051133130726
47988CB00005B/1823